Cat O' Nine Tails

PATRICIA LEEVER

OMNIFIC PUBLISHING
DALLAS

Omnific Publishing
P.O. Box 793871, Dallas, TX 75379
www.omnificpublishing.com

First Omnific eBook edition, August 2011
First Omnific trade paperback edition, August 2011

The characters and events in this book are fictitious.
Any similarity to real persons, living or dead,
is coincidental and not intended by the author.

Library of Congress Cataloguing-in-Publication Data

Leever, Patricia.
    Cat O' Nine Tails / Patricia Leever — 1st ed.
    ISBN 978-1-936305-86-5
    1. Historical — Fiction. 2. Pirates — Fiction.
    3. Romance — Fiction. 4. Rebellion — Fiction.
    I. Title

10 9 8 7 6 5 4 3 2 1

Cover Design by Micha Stone and Stephanie Swartz
Interior Book Design by Coreen Montagna

Printed in the United States of America

"It is never too late to be who you might have been." ~ George Eliot

To my family for supporting me through this journey,
I couldn't have done this without your love and support.

And to my Grandma Jean, who always knew I'd be a writer one day,
I miss you Grandma, and I did it!

Prologue

In a tavern just off the docks of the small port village of Oaksbridge, Orrin Walsh sipped his ale at a corner table. He paid no mind to the drunken strangers laughing and stumbling noisily around him; his attention was on his quarry, the bloated toad of a man across the room who belched and wiped the rum off his chin with the back of his dirty sleeve. Cormac Doyle, the once semi-respectable merchant and fisherman, had found that piracy was a far more lucrative business.

As Orrin watched, a large, hulking man ambled over and took the seat next to Cormac. A smaller figure passing by Orrin's table then stumbled on its own feet and landed in his lap.

"A thousand pardons, sir," a gruff female voice spoke from inside the darkness of a hooded cloak, her face completely hidden in the shadows. "For your troubles," she said as she pawed around in his lap with a creamy white hand.

Orrin shackled her wrist and swiftly pulled her away from his body. "Be on your way, woman," he mumbled. "I have no time for whoring."

"As you please," she said with a small curtsy and then made her way across the room.

Taking a good swallow from his drink, Orrin watched the woman approach his bounty. She whispered in Cormac's ear and twirled a lock of his greasy hair around her finger. As Orrin took another sip of ale, he started to feel strangely lightheaded. He tried to shake off the feeling, but that only seemed to make matters worse. Orrin blinked and held onto the table as the room started to sway around him.

Before he lost consciousness, Orrin saw the woman nod to the large gentleman sitting on the other side of Cormac, who paid for the rum and followed behind the pair as they left the tavern. As they passed his table, a lock of bright red hair fluttered out from under the woman's hood, and Orrin could make out her red lips curled into a smile.

The next morning, Orrin awoke in a strange bed in a room above the tavern with no recollection of how he'd gotten there. He'd only had half a cup of ale the previous night, and even a tankard of whiskey wouldn't have affected him like this. The only thing he could figure was that the damned hooded harlot must have tried to poison him. With a pounding head, he fumbled through his clothes and found he was less all his money and his father's brass compass. The strangest discovery was a scarlet lip print just above his right hip.

Orrin's vision was still slightly blurry as he staggered down the stairs and into the empty tavern. He shielded his eyes from the overly bright morning sun and saw the majority of the town gathered near the docks. As he made his way through the crowd, he stopped cold when he reached the landing.

Cormac Doyle's body was tied to a docking post, his throat sliced clean open. Cormac's blood soaked his shirt and trousers, dripping off his boots into a puddle beneath him.

Orrin listened to the harsh words of the people around him; clearly this was not a well-liked man. Mr. Doyle had cheated his former crew of honest workingmen out of their fair wages and fired anyone not willing to partake in his unlawful new venture. He'd blatantly kept company with whores and drank away any money he'd made, leaving his wife and son to beg for food on the street.

A rail-thin woman stepped cautiously up to the body. Her right eye was swollen closed, and her lip was bruised and split. True, it was a husband's right to make sure his wife obeyed his wishes by any means, but anyone who took to raising a hand to a woman was nothing more than a coward and poor excuse of a man in Orrin's opinion. It was becoming very clear that Cormac Doyle had gotten exactly what he'd deserved, and whoever had rid the world of his company was to be commended.

The woman squared her shoulders and spat onto the remains of her husband, cursing his soul. As she turned and picked up the hand of a small boy with a blackened eye, Orrin saw a coin purse hanging under her bodice. Stitched into the fabric in gold-colored thread was an elaborately scripted *A*.

"It can't be," Orrin said to himself as he watched the woman and boy head into market for probably the first time in a very long while.

"Ah, you're awake," the burly barkeep said, ambling out of the crowd. "I trust your sleep was well?"

"Yes, many thanks." Orrin raked his hand through his unkempt hair. "I do intend to pay you for your trouble…"

"No need." The barkeep patted the hefty purse hanging from his belt — Orrin's purse. "The lovely lass had her companion pay your debt in full before they left, and then some."

"I shall have to thank her for her generosity," Orrin said, the muscles in his jaw tightening as he clenched his teeth. "Tell me, where can I find her?"

"Last I saw, she was leaving with" — he turned to the macabre scene — "him."

"Did you see her face?"

"Aye." The large man sighed. "She was a vision indeed, that one. Truthfully, I would have let you stay free of charge if she'd asked."

"Did she give you a name?"

"No name, but I will never forget what she looked like…long red hair, white skin, lips ripe for kissing, amongst other things," the barkeep said with a wink and a nod, elbowing Orrin in the ribs. "Wait…you don't suppose she had anything to do with that, do you?" he asked, pointing to the scene of the murder.

"Yes, I do," Orrin hollered over his shoulder as he ran toward his ship. He skidded to a stop when a thought occurred to him. "One moment, where is Mr. Doyle's vessel?"

The barkeep looked around the docks and shrugged. "It's gone. It was moored right there last night." He pointed to an empty slip on the far dock.

Orrin's rage drowned out the sound of the barkeep, who prattled on. It had been her. He grumbled at the thought that he'd literally had that sea witch of a female pirate in his lap last night, for God's sake. Once again, she'd slipped right through his fingers. She'd not only stolen his prized possession, but also lifted the item right off of his person directly. And even though she'd clearly murdered Cormac Doyle in cold blood, it appeared as if she'd outright *purchased* his ship from his widow.

Nothing about this woman made any sense. She'd had ample opportunity to do away with him in any number of ways while he'd lain passed out and be rid of him, a pirate hunter, once and for all. But she hadn't.

What sort of pirate behaves in that manner?

Chapter One

Orrin stood on the deck of his ship, his arms crossed over his chest as he leaned back against the railing. The salty sea air bit at his skin, pulling strands of his hair free from the tie that bound it behind his neck and whipping the golden brown locks around his face. The sound of the water breaking against the hull lulled him into a near hypnotic state as the crisp fluttering of the sails rumbled down the mast and into his bones when the wind picked up, filling the massive pieces of canvas and making them billow out into the black night sky.

He often wandered the deck in the hours before dawn, when it was darkest. During this time, he frequently thought about that night in Oaksbridge and what he would do if he ever again ran across the she-pirate and her band.

As a legendary pirate hunter, Orrin scoured the seas with his younger brother Kale and their loyal crew aboard the brig *Iona*, bringing the devils to justice for the despicable deeds they had done. He knew all too well the horrible and heartless things of which pirates were capable. When he was a boy, Orrin and his family had lived in a small port town and seen their fair share of ominous ships dancing out in the waves over the years.

His father, Malcolm, had taken to the seas with Orrin and Kale as a transporter of various goods. Their vessel, the *Iona*, was fast and fierce and had garnered quite the reputation amongst marauders. They had been charged with transporting items of the highest value, for each member of the crew was an expert swordsman capable of removing a man's head with a single stroke and gutting him—blindfolded, no less. Needless to say, they'd been mostly left to pass through the waters as they pleased.

The men had been away at sea on such a voyage when their quiet little village was attacked by a particularly malicious band of pirates, one that showed no mercy to woman or child. The *Iona* had returned to its home port to find the entire village ravaged. Their beloved mother's throat had been slit in their very home and the bodies of all their sisters cast into the water like garbage after the filthy crew had had their way with their young, innocent bodies. No one had been spared. Not even babes in their cradles.

From that moment, Orrin, his father, and his brother had vowed to hunt down the beasts that had slaughtered their family like cattle and any other low-life scum that came across their path. The Walsh men and their crew had banded as bounty hunters, bringing pirate leaders back to the nearest port to be reckoned with by the law of the people, which at times could be as savage as the pirate's way.

One year into their quest, Malcolm had fallen ill and passed away, leaving his eldest son, Orrin, as captain of *Iona* and her crew, with Kale as his first mate.

Together, the Walsh brothers had pored over the ocean, bringing pirate after pirate to justice until they'd finally found the band that had taken their family from them. Descending on their rotting vessel like the black plague, Orrin, Kale, and their crew had meticulously dismantled the men, body from limb.

But even that savage revenge hadn't quelled the emptiness inside Orrin. Nothing seemed able to. Not even the warmth of a woman.

The ship had gained quite a reputation, capturing all its captain and crew set their word to.

All but one: a pirate that no man had been able to capture, the one that had plagued Orrin and laughed at him, disrupting his sleep night after night. The one pirate on the seven seas he hadn't managed to cross paths with since she'd slipped away in Oaksbridge two years ago. The she-pirate Aeron Lynch.

As fate would have it, Queen Winifred had sought out and commissioned the *Iona* and her crew to hunt down the thieving scoundrel. Aeron was rumored to have enraptured the Queen's lover, as she did every other man that came across her path. She was a most unusual pirate: she did not take what she wanted with a sword and threats of death but with a sway of her hips and a promise on her lips.

The bravest and strongest of men had fallen before her, relinquishing their riches to her willingly for just a brush of her lips across theirs or a smile to light up her eyes…eyes that were said to be neither blue nor green but variant shades of both and with the innate ability to see straight through to the very depths of a man's soul.

Orrin peered out into the night, deep in thought over the strange ways of this woman pirate he'd now been hired to find. He'd seen her handiwork in person and knew, firsthand, of what she was capable.

However, thinking about the commission, his stomach churned for an entirely different reason. There was something about Her Majesty herself that made the hackles rise on the back of his neck, something he couldn't explain. He tried to avoid royal hire whenever possible, but the lure of hunting *her*, Aeron Lynch, was far too great.

Orrin was so preoccupied with his own thoughts that he nearly leapt over the rail when Kale appeared behind him, wrapping his hand around his shoulder.

"Brother, you must sleep."

"I'll sleep when I'm dead," Orrin replied, his pensive gaze sweeping over the black, bottomless waters of the night.

Kale sighed and shook his head. "If you do not sleep while you can, your death will come sooner than you think."

"That is why I keep you at my back," Orrin said, curling his arm around his brother's neck and ruffling his dark hair.

Kale squirmed away from his older brother's grasp, and both men laughed like a pair of young boys. Kale settled back against the rail next to Orrin. "We will find that sea witch and whatever hole she's been hiding in for the last two years," he said, bringing some peace to his brother's brow. "It is what we do."

"Yes, it is what we do." Orrin nodded as he looked out into the moonlight shimmering on the ominous water. There, he spied a glow that was so faint it almost appeared as part of the moon's reflection on the ocean's surface.

Earlier in the day, Kale had spotted a plume of smoke on the horizon in that very spot, and together they'd decided it was best to wait until they had the cover of pre-dawn to investigate the source. Now, as the rest of the ship slept, Orrin, with Kale's help, slipped into a small dinghy and rowed alone toward the source of that light. Pulling the oars through the water, Orrin checked over his shoulder every couple of strokes to ensure he was on course, watching the trees that lined the shore come into focus the closer he got. After he beached, he hefted the small boat onto the sand and carefully covered it with fallen palm fronds, hiding it from view the best he could.

Orrin stalked through the jungle as the dawn broke over the island. He didn't need the crew to protect him from what he might find on the island; he was as fierce as a warrior. Orrin did not fear death—he welcomed it. He hoped that it would end the emptiness he felt in his soul.

The early morning sun washed over the thick veil of palm trees as Aeron rolled and stretched. Her long, auburn hair swept across the bed as she moved to sit up and smile at the sound of island creatures coming to life outside the window of her modest cottage.

This was her sanctuary, her hideaway, built by the men who served her and furnished by the men she conquered.

Her crew was large and fiercely loyal to her, willing to give their life to stay in her good graces, for they knew the ferociousness of her sword. It was not as well-known as her beguiling beauty, but it was just as lethal. She could render a man a eunuch with his own blade before he knew it was missing from its scabbard. Swordplay was, however, a skill rarely needed once she turned on her feminine wiles, and more often than not captives went willingly, hoping to be one of the select few to catch the eye of the seafaring beauty. Among those who traveled the high seas, Aeron's insatiable appetite for the company of men was common knowledge.

"Enter," she called as a swift knock pounded against her door.

The wooden door swung open, and an enthusiastic young man with blond hair entered.

"Captain, there is a ship off the horizon of the south shore," he said.

Aeron noticed that he tried desperately to avert his gaze from her barely covered body.

"Thank you, William. Tell the men to keep watch on the ship, and alert me if it comes into the shallows."

Young William bowed respectfully. "Aye, Captain. Anything else?"

"No, Will, you may go," Aeron said as she stood from the bed and reached toward the ceiling. Her thin chemise rode up her body as she stretched, exposing her calves before she moved about the small room to gather her bathing needs. While she was in motion, she felt the chemise drift to and fro, doing little to conceal her bare leg and the curve of her shapely hip.

William swallowed hard. "Aye, Ca-Captain," he stuttered, and scuttled out the door.

Aeron smiled to herself, then slipped out the back door of her cottage and down the winding path to her private lagoon hidden within the jungle.

As the sky brightened, Orrin moved on pure instinct through the lush green vegetation, deep into the heart of the island. He didn't know what he would find, but he traversed the undergrowth as if drawn by a siren song.

Then he heard it, a voice in the distance. A woman's voice.

Silently, he pushed through the trees and vines toward the angelic voice rising above the soft sounds of a waterfall. He deftly and silently moved the branches aside, revealing a glorious crystal blue lagoon at the bottom of a trickling waterfall.

The most beautiful creature he'd ever seen glided across the water, and Orrin blinked his eyes at the vision before him. He held his breath and drank in her beauty. Her hair swirled around her head like liquid fire, and slivers of sun peeking through the trees lit up bands of her flesh. Her porcelain skin practically glowed in the sunlight. Two perfectly shaped breasts crested the water just above the taut flesh of her milky belly. She looked like a dream, an aquatic goddess, and Orrin was almost surprised when he saw two delicately shaped legs kicking in the water instead of one sweeping mermaid fin. His body reacted instantly to the sight of her, tightening the muscles under his skin and pumping the blood through his veins.

The woman sighed in contentment as she slid through the water, and Orrin felt a white-hot jolt of desire shoot straight to his groin. He gritted his teeth and tried to calm himself as the most beguiling smile graced her full, ruby lips. His heart pounded in his chest as he watched her climb out onto the rocks beside the waterfall, her dripping wet hair hanging down her back and over the curve of her round buttocks. This was a sensation he hadn't felt in a number of years.

When she flipped her hair over her shoulder, however, she revealed dozens of thick, angry red scars across her back. Orrin clamped his hand over his mouth and turned away, squeezing his eyes shut. His stomach churned as an old memory flooded his senses.

Seven years ago, he had come into port a day early to find his wife, Helena, in their bed with another man.

Calmly, he had stepped from their home, only to retch just outside the door.

When the people of the village had heard of this, they had ripped her from the house and dragged her to the center of the village, where she would be persecuted as an adulteress and whipped in front of the entire town.

Orrin was well respected and loved by all in the tiny port village; never did he turn away a soul in need of food or shelter. So when he'd realized their plan, Orrin had run to the square, grabbing the wrist of the man with the whip just before the first crack was to be made across Helena's back. Although it was the law and his right as a husband to have Helena whipped for her actions, he refused. He couldn't bear that burden on his conscience.

He would also never forget the two thick scars that his sister — Iona, after whom his ship was named — had come home with when she'd returned from her brief stay on the mainland. Iona had refused to name the person who had wielded the instrument that marred her tender young flesh, but Orrin and his brother vowed to one day find that soulless beast and make him pay.

Orrin had further sworn he would never be the cause of marks of that nature on any woman's flesh, for any reason. Instead, he had chosen to place Helena on the next sailing ship — bound to where, it didn't matter.

As he had watched the ship pull away from the dock, Orrin had known on some level he should feel some sadness, but all he felt was relief. He'd never really loved Helena; it was no secret in the village that Helena partook in relations with many a gentleman passing through port, but her father had sworn those days were past when Orrin had married the girl as a favor, a marriage of convenience.

Orrin had looked into his wife's eyes as the vessel departed, and when he saw the same relief in them that he felt, he mouthed, "Thank you."

Coming back to the present and taking in a deep breath, Orrin turned back to the lagoon only to find his beautiful water goddess standing before him. Her eyes snapped in blue and green fury as her sword sat poised at his throat.

"See something inviting, do you?" the woman purred, crystal clear droplets of water shimmering along her naked flesh as she stood confidently before him. "Out, now."

Straightening to his full height, Orrin moved from behind the cover of vines and low-lying tree branches, his gaze traveling the entire length of her body.

Her eyes narrowed at him, and she pressed the tip of her blade to his throat after one step.

"Close your eyes," she spat, "lest I slit your throat this instant." Glancing down, she evidently noticed his obvious arousal and slid her blade down his body to the top of his trousers. "Or worse."

Clearing his throat, Orrin closed his eyes and stepped out into the open.

The woman swiftly rid him of his sword. "Sit," she commanded, "and keep your eyes closed, until I instruct you otherwise."

She plays at modesty when half the Queen's Navy claims to have borne witness to her wares. Orrin sat on the rocky ground, scoffing aloud at the ridiculousness. He felt her hand grip his face and the cold steel of what he imagined was a dagger against his cheek.

"*You* will not gaze upon *my* form as you see fit."

Chapter Two

Aeron dressed at her leisure and let the man sit on the cold, hard rock as she carefully looked at him. A warm breeze blew past the stranger, and her nostrils flared, inhaling his moist scent. It took her back to the dark tavern in Oaksbridge—this was the same pirate hunter, she was certain of it. She'd never forget the way his cool blue eyes focused on his target or his firm, commanding grip on her wrist. She'd never admit to another soul that she thought about that night two summers ago, and of him, often.

Perhaps it was seeing him in the light of day, but he looked better than she'd remembered. His golden brown hair was tied neatly with a black ribbon at the back of his neck. His lips pursed together, red and ripe, and curls of hair swirled across his chest beneath his shirt. Long, powerful legs were swathed in black fabric that clung nicely to every inch of him. The cuff of his boots stretched up over the top of his knee, and his strong hands rested in his lap. He truly was a beautiful creature.

Orrin Walsh. She knew his reputation as a pirate hunter, and if she wasn't on marks with him, she'd find herself in a cell on the mainland or, worse, swinging from the end of a rope. But he was far too decadent not to taste.

"You may open your eyes," she finally said as she tied her belt around her waist. She tucked his sword between her folds of fabric as she steadied herself and deftly pulled on her boots. She studied the eyes of the man before her, bluer than any other she had ever seen, she was sure—and she'd looked into the eyes of many men—but full of a sadness that made the pit of her stomach knot up around itself. "Stand and walk," she commanded with a flick of her sword as she tossed her chemise over her shoulder.

Orrin stood fluidly, gracefully, his eyes appearing to drink in every inch of her. Aeron was certain she wasn't clad like the women he was used to looking upon, but perhaps that was the novelty. No brightly colored skirts, no bits and baubles in her hair. Not even one hint of lace, only brown trousers that hugged the shape of her thigh like a second skin and a simple ivory shirt that silhouetted the outer curve of her breasts, its opening revealing her cleavage. She stood still, almost captivated as he silently appraised her body before she grew angry with herself for allowing it.

"Did you not get your fill when my clothes were off that you must now blatantly ogle me clothed?" she sneered, despite the heat she felt in her body at the way he took in her appearance. How many nights had she thought about this very moment? Aeron swallowed her desire and gave him a swift shove with her boot. "Move."

She led Orrin down a jungle path, nudging him forward with a touch of her blade against the back of his neck when she felt he wasn't moving fast enough. They broke through the trees into the makeshift village her band called home. Some huts and small cottages built of deck timber and tents made of old canvas sails dotted the land before them. There were women busying themselves with work and children running about the grounds. Aeron saw him gaping at the sight before him: entire families living there happily. Clearly this wasn't what he'd expected to find when he'd landed on the island.

Aeron nudged him forward with the cool steel of her blade against his spine and directed him into the tiny town square.

A child ran over to them, smiling brightly and clutching a doll tightly in her grasp. "Captain," she squealed, "thank you for my doll. She is so lovely." The girl cooed, rubbing her cheek against the face of the toy in her arms.

"You are most welcome, Rianna." Aeron's eyes softened as she smiled down at the girl.

"Does she have a name yet?" she asked, conversing with the child as if it were nothing to be standing in front of her with a sword against a man's back.

"Yes." The girl nodded. "I've named her Aeron, after you."

"I am honored, Rianna," Aeron replied with a nod of thanks and a warm smile.

Rianna giggled in return and skipped away.

"Aeron is such a lovely name," Orrin said, casting a glance over his shoulder at her, a grin lifting up one side of his mouth. "It's most unfortunate that its beauty is wasted on the likes of a pirate."

Aeron stretched up onto her toes, pressing her face closer to his. "I'd mind that tongue, sir. I would hate to have to cut it from that pretty mouth of yours, but rest assured I will, pirate hunter."

He smiled as she pushed him along the trail. He was trying to get under her skin and looked assured he was succeeding. Bastard.

"Brendon," Aeron shouted up into the trees as they continued down another vine-riddled path on the other side of the village.

"Aye, Captain," a voice shot down from above.

The pirate hunter looked up into the towering jungle trees, trying to see from which one the booming voice had come, and Aeron gave him a sound wallop on the back of the head. "Keep your eyes forward," she reprimanded before turning to the trees again. "What of the ship off the southern shore?"

"The bilge-sucking swabs have retreated, Captain," Brendon called down as he dropped out of the tree right in front of the prisoner. "Didn't much wait for you did they?" he directed at Orrin.

"My crew will be back for me," the prisoner seethed, "and all of you dogged pirates will be brought to justice." He practically spat the word "pirates" out of his mouth, as if the very mention left a bitter taste on his tongue.

"Arrogant bastard of a man," Aeron said with a laugh as she stepped around to stare her prisoner in the face. "You think because they've found the island once that they will find it again?"

"My men are highly trained and will seek out this poor excuse for an island within a few days' time, mark my word."

"Your word?" Aeron tossed her head back and laughed. "Your word means absolutely nothing to me," she said, "and your men, they may well be the most skillful men in the seven seas, but no one has ever found their way back to my island. Mark *my* word."

She could almost see his blood boiling with rage at her confidence.

"Will," Aeron called, waving the young man over. "Take this individual to the pen." The pirate hunter's sparkling blue eyes ignited fissures of heat deep in her belly as he glared down at her. "And see that he is not harmed," she instructed, running a finger across the bottom of Orrin's strong jaw as she licked her lips and felt his muscle twitch under her touch. "Anyone who harms him, will answer to me, understood?"

"Aye, Captain," William answered with a nod as he twisted the prisoner's wrists behind his back and shoved him forward.

Aeron watched as the young crewman led the despicable pirate hunter out of her line of sight. Walking back to the heart of her village, she prayed that no one saw through her bravado. That no one noticed her breath catching in the back of her throat whenever he looked at her, even in anger. She was playing with fire with this one, and if she wasn't careful about the flames, everyone on the island could get burnt.

Stepping into the square, Aeron gratefully took the plate of food one of the children had brought to her and sat at the large table along the perimeter, looking out over people milling about. Her people.

Her first mate, Darcy, sat next to her, turning his back to everyone as he propped his elbows on the table and leaned against it. He was a hulking man with closely cropped dark hair and tattoos from every corner of the world, and he was known far and wide for his specific methods of persuasion.

"What of their ship, Captain?" he asked, his voice low enough for her ears alone. "Sink or scrap?"

"Maybe it's time to start a fleet," she replied, a devious grin curling the corners of her mouth. "I hear it is a fine vessel, and I would hate to sink or scrap a brig of that quality. I think she would be just what we need for short runs, don't you agree?"

"Indeed." Darcy nodded with an equally sinister smile.

Aeron trusted Darcy implicitly, and she was confident that he knew if anyone could turn a crew to mutiny against another captain, it was her. This he would know firsthand, for that was how they'd met. She'd dressed as a man and boarded the ship he'd called home. When he had walked in on her changing one evening, he should have turned her over to the captain straight away, but he hadn't. She had pled with him and sworn to make him her first mate if he'd help her take over the ship, which he had done happily, stating that Brutus was a horrendous man with no business being a captain.

Darcy had also told her since then that it was something in her, some spark of fire in her eyes that had saved her. Aeron had spirit, a purpose, and Darcy had assured her that the men would be more than willing to get behind and follow her, though he did have to use his "talents" to convince a few of them. She was a woman, after all, and her mere presence on a ship had been believed to be bad luck by some, let alone her captaining the vessel.

"Shall I question the prisoner then?" Darcy now asked, scratching his stubbly chin. He had that look in his eye that he got when musing over what methods he might use to interrogate a prisoner, most likely elated to finally get his hands on the infamous pirate hunter.

She knew Darcy's methods and the order in which he employed them well. He'd start with thumbscrews and the breaking wheel before moving on to the knee-splitter and one of Darcy's tried and true favorites: rat torture.

"No questioning. I don't want him harmed in any way."

Darcy's fist cracked against the table with a thundering crash as he leapt to his feet, causing others around them to look in their direction. "You've never asked that of any other pri—"

Before he could finish his words, Aeron was on the move, the tip of her dagger against his neck.

"This is not the morning to question my methods, Darcy," she uttered. "I've already had my bath interrupted. Do you really wish to try my patience by interrupting my meal as well?"

"No, Captain," he replied, swallowing hard with the blade straining against his flesh as his throat flexed. "I was unaware you had plans for the prisoner. Forgive me."

Aeron pulled the dagger away from his throat and tossed it on the table. "Don't be absurd Darcy, you know I forgive you." She shook her head at her own reaction to the very legitimate question Darcy had posed. "I honestly don't know what's come over me…to threaten you, my dearest and closest friend. I've scarcely had a coherent thought in my head since Orrin Walsh stepped foot on this island."

She poked at her bread with her finger and shoved her plate away as Darcy's wife, Catrin, called to him from in front of their cottage at the edge of the village square.

"You'd better go." Aeron motioned to the beautiful blond woman with the swollen belly. "She may not be as forgiving as I am."

"Aye," Darcy agreed with a nod. "Her ire is far more frightening than any means of torture that I could dare to imagine, especially when she's with child."

They laughed as he pushed away from the table and walked toward the small cottage.

Aeron sighed to herself as she watched her friend enter his home, scooping his young daughter Rianna into his arms. She surreptitiously touched her belly as she then watched a group of children run through the village square, laughing as they chased a poor chicken past the pigpen. Aeron could have had a child with any of the men she'd taken into her bed, if she'd wished it.

But she didn't want a child with just any man.

With a heavy heart she left her untouched food on the table and wandered down the path that led to the pen where prisoners were kept.

Chapter Three

Orrin let out a grunt as Will pushed him through the trees to a small hut out of the village's sight.

"Inside, filthy pirate hunter," he spat as he gave Orrin a shove between his shoulders, causing him to stumble into the center of the hut and almost sprawl onto the floor. Will had a good amount of strength and anger for someone so young.

Orrin righted himself and stared at Will from across the cramped room; something about the boy was familiar. Where had he seen him before?

"I know you, boy," Orrin said, slanting his eyes at William and tilting his head this way and that in scrutiny of his features. Will's posture was staunch and proper, nothing at all like a pirate's slack carriage.

"I do not align myself with pirate hunters," Will said, his lip curled in disgust. "And I'm no boy."

"Come now," Orrin said. "You can't be more than eighteen."

William dropped his gaze for a moment before lifting his chin. "I will be nineteen this summer," he declared proudly.

Orrin laughed outright. "Like I said, no *more* than eighteen."

Finally, the boy's image clicked, placing the boy's face in Orrin's memory. He nodded and pointed a knowing finger in William's direction. "Yes, I *do* know you, you're—"

Will raised his hand, and Orrin was certain the boy was intent on striking him before he could utter another word, but a hand shackled Will's wrist. William's mouth gaped open when he whirled around, and he began to stammer. "Captain, I…I…"

"Which part of 'no harm is to come of him' was unclear?" Aeron asked coolly, flinging William's wrist from her grasp with a twitch of her lip. The young man started to speak, but she put her hand up, silencing him and waving him away. "Leave us now."

"Aye, Captain," he said with a bow of his head. "If there is anything I —"

"I said leave us, boy," she spat.

Orrin watched Will's face fall. The young man obviously harbored affection for his Captain, and the lack of reciprocation that now sent him skulking out of the hut like a wounded animal set in check the odd things Orrin had witnessed in the village. *This* was pirate behavior.

"Do you always wound the pride of your men to make a point, or is it just for your own enjoyment?" Orrin sneered at her.

The beautiful pirate shot him a scathing look in return.

"Ah." Orrin nodded, taking the opportunity presented to get underneath her skin again. He turned away from her and glanced back over his shoulder. "Perhaps it's just to make yourself feel more powerful, then?" He watched her jaw clench with rage as he turned his back, smiling ruefully in assurance he'd succeeded in striking a nerve. He needed to keep going, pushing her until she broke. His mind raced, but all he could think about was an overwhelming urge to grab her and kiss her into submission.

Orrin could practically hear her teeth grinding at his accusations and feel her gaze boring into his back. He heard her breathing grow more erratic and could only imagine what she was thinking. Would she really take the pirate way out and run him through while his back was turned, or would she be true to her nature as a temptress and use seduction to get what she wanted? His gut went with the first option, but his mind went with the latter, thinking for a moment how amazing her naked body would feel against his.

The creaky hut door opened, and a petite young woman slipped in with a plate of food in her hands. Orrin was more than thankful for the distraction; he needed to focus on the task at hand, not fantasize about ways to make his captor scream his name.

"Captain," the girl said quietly with a bow of her head. "Food for the prisoner, as you requested." Her cheeks had a tanned hue, and her long brown hair was haphazardly twisted into a messy knot. There was an air of innocence about her, and she kept her brown eyes cast to the floor the majority of the time. Orrin caught her braving a look in his direction, and he couldn't help but smile. The girl flustered, nearly dropping the plate of food she carried.

Orrin looked surprised to see meat, fruit, and bread on the dish and wondered what sort of foul libation could be tainting the meal.

"Thank you, Maura," Aeron said and took the plate from the girl.

Orrin raised an eyebrow at the two women as they laughed and whispered, stealing glances in his direction. How different they were from one another. Young Maura covered her face, and her cheeks colored when he gave her a small smile. But the other woman, she did not giggle at him or cover her face; instead, her eyes washed over him, sending a bolt of lightning through his veins. Orrin tilted his head, allowing himself to take in the vision that was her body, unconsciously licking his lips as they curled into a lecherous smirk. Oh, the possibilities in the company of a woman like this were endless. The thought of exacting his own justice on her, in his bed, made his skin prickle with excitement.

When Aeron cleared her throat and crossed her arms over her ample chest, he quickly turned his back to her, cursing himself for thinking her alluring at all.

Stop this ridiculousness, he told himself. *She is a pirate for God's sake, same as the rest.*

"That will be all, Maura. You may go," Aeron said, and she gave the sprightly young woman her leave. Maura gave a curtsy and turned to the door. "Maura," Aeron called after her. "See that we are not disturbed."

Orrin swore he saw the two women share a small wink.

"Yes, Captain." Maura nodded, pulling the door shut after her.

As Aeron set the plate of food on the dirt floor and stood at the other side of the room, she glared at Orrin. One of her thumbs looped into the belt tied around her waist, and the other lay poised on the end of her sword. She looked to be at odds with herself, and Orrin wasn't sure if she was going to slice him in half or rip all of his clothes off and have her way with him on the ground like an animal.

Orrin stared back, folding his arms across his chest and clenching his jaw, trying not to think about the latter or how soft those red lips of hers would feel skimming over his flesh as she did unspeakable things to him with her succulent mouth.

"Who commissioned you, pirate hunter?" she asked. Her voice was strong and sure and sent Orrin's blood coursing, burning with the wonder of what her hands would feel like on his body.

"My name is Orrin," he said, lifting his chin in outright stubbornness, challenging her. "If you are going to address me, at least have the common courtesy of doing so by name."

Striding across the room, her steps were fluid and sure as she floated over the dirt floor toward him. She reached out and pushed a lock of his hair behind his ear, admiring the cut of his jaw as she swept the back of her fingers across the light sprinkling of stubble along its edge.

"Who commissioned you, Orrin?" she purred, her tongue darting out to moisten her lips.

It took an immense bout of will for Orrin to back away from her warm caress instead of doing what he so wanted to do, which was lean his head into her hand and kiss the center of her palm.

"I don't know what you mean, pirate, I—" Before he could finish speaking, she was even closer, pressing her breasts against his arm, her lips brushing the shell of his ear as she spoke.

"Aeron, my name is Aeron. If you are going to address me, at least have the common courtesy of doing so by name." She ran one finger-tip lightly over the silk of his shirt. "I know that you were hired, and you are obviously well paid to be able to afford such a finely tailored garment as this." She toyed with the fabric along his chest, her touch barely grazing his bare skin. "So tell me, Orrin, who paid you and your crew for my head?"

Orrin stared into her eyes, their intense blue-green boring into his soul, and he held her gaze longer than what was proper between a man and a woman who had just met. *God, but I want to kiss that mouth,* he thought to himself.

"The port town of Sereph," Orrin said, blurting out the first village name that came to mind. Squeezing his eyes shut, he willed himself to pull away from her grasp and turn his back to her. He could not look at her at the moment without wanting to take her in his arms, brand her lips with his, and feel the contours of her body.

"Come now, you can do better than that." Aeron laughed outright. "That measly little town barely has a pot to piss in, let alone enough money to hire you and your crew."

Stepping back into his line of sight, Aeron squared off in front of him. "Tell me who hired you. Was it another pirate?" she asked. "They seem to take issue with my being a woman. Did they offer you untold riches or treasure?" She snorted and shook her head in disgust. "Which one of my depraved brethren paid you to kill me?"

"No one paid me to kill you," Orrin said coolly. "I was employed to capture you."

With that, Orrin lunged at Aeron, wrapping his arm around her neck and hoisting her feet off the ground. As he reached for her sword, he felt himself pulled away, and the next thing he knew, he was sailing into the hut wall, landing directly onto the plate of food.

Orrin shook the cobwebs out of his mind and saw a behemoth of a man bearing down on him. He was twice the height and width of any man in his crew.

"Christ," Orrin said, trying to get to his feet and out of the giant's reach.

"Gael, enough!" Aeron shouted at the large man, who obediently ceased his steps. "I won't get any answers from him if he is unconscious or dead. I'm fine. Leave us," she commanded. Gael growled a warning at Orrin before ducking out of the small door.

"I want to know who commissioned you to capture me," Aeron demanded, "and I know it wasn't a pirate, for they would most definitely have ordered you to kill me on sight."

Orrin saw no reason to be untruthful at this point, as he was most certain she'd eventually come to the conclusion on her own. Aeron was clearly a highly intelligent woman; she did not move or speak like any pirate Orrin had ever encountered.

"Her Majesty, Queen Winifred," Orrin said, wiping a trickle of blood off his face and spitting a mouthful of it to the floor before he continued. "She accused you of enticing her lover. I thought that was the true reason until I saw Prince William." He stood and brushed the dirt off his backside and glared at Aeron, shaking his head. "You took her son from her, and you are to be brought to justice, pirate."

Aeron's eyes widened as the barest hint of panic flashed across her face. Within seconds, she appeared to snap back into the moment, ripping her sword out of its scabbard and pointing it directly at Orrin's chest.

"You lie," she accused.

Orrin studied her face, her posture. Her shoulders were square and sure, her hand steady as a rock as she held the blade over his heart. Her delicate lips trembled, her nostrils flared, and tears welled in her eyes. Something was wrong.

"This isn't about William, is it?" Orrin asked.

Aeron exploded the breath she was holding and sheathed her sword as quickly as she'd drawn it. She strode to the door, practically yanking it down as she pulled it open. "Gael!" she shouted, standing in the open doorway, sucking air as if she couldn't bear to be inside the small room one more instant. "Blindfold him, and take him back to his ship."

"But, Captain—"

"I said do it!" she bellowed and took leave of the hut before she lost her composure completely.

Orrin raced to the door, only to be held back by the gargantuan man that was Gael.

"Aeron!" he called after her, but she did not turn. Instead, she practically ran through the jungle, lopping vines and branches out of her way with her sword.

What on earth could have caused that reaction? She had looked as if she'd seen a ghost when he mentioned the Queen. Orrin sensed there was more to this than a scorned monarch, something terribly dark. His gut twisted, and he raked his hands through his hair in desperation. This was not right; he could feel it in every part of his soul, and he could not…no, he *would* not leave without knowing the truth.

Aeron pushed through the jungle so hard and fast that Darcy heard the sound of her approaching before she broke through the vegetation and into the village, her brow creased in determination.

Something was definitely wrong.

"Captain," he called as he started after her.

She didn't even break stride, trudging forward along the outskirts of town. "Send him away, Darcy," she said as she bounded west. "Send him back to his ship."

Darcy stopped his pursuit for a moment. "Alive?" he asked, dumbfounded by this preposterous request.

"Yes, alive!" Aeron spun around and meet his questioning look. "And make haste before I change my mind," she said, turning on her heel and walking away again.

"But, Captain," he called after her, picking up his paces to catch up with her. "Captain," he repeated when he finally reached her and placed a hand on her shoulder, stopping her just outside the village boundaries. "Aeron," he said, speaking as her friend, not her first-in-command.

Aeron halted with an exasperated gasp, and she pulled her hands through her hair. "He was sent by the Queen, Darcy."

Darcy was the only one who knew the true history between Aeron and Queen Winifred, and he was fiercely protective of her as a result. Aeron knew he'd remove that cursed Orrin's head himself before he'd allow him a chance to turn her over to that wretched woman.

"What does it matter? Our plan still stands, no?"

She cast her gaze to a nearby rock, so he could no longer see the fear in them. "He's the man we drugged and left in that tavern in Oaksbridge, that cursed bastard I haven't been able to get out of my mind since that night two years ago." She pulled her shoulder away from his grasp.

"He's the one you speak of in your sleep, the one you compare all the others to since, isn't he?" Darcy asked.

"I need to be alone. I need to think," she said, still not looking her friend in the eye or answering his inquiry, merely turning back to the path she was set on.

"Aye," he said breathing a worried sigh before he turned with an angry growl and made his way to the man that had brought this unrest to his dearest friend. That cursed pirate hunter.

Orrin paced the floor of the hut, his hands pulling and tugging at his hair. He did not like to see pain of any kind brought upon a woman, not even a pirate, let alone be the cause of it.

But this was different, more. His stomach churned at the thought that he'd brought distress to *her* in particular.

He stopped in the center of the room, fisting his hands on his forehead. He felt like she was literally under his skin, scratching away at every part of him. He raised his face to the ceiling and cursed the very air around him for the essence of her it carried on it.

"What are you doing to me, woman?" he mumbled.

Orrin's mind was at grips with itself as if Aeron was curled up next to his brain, picking and wielding away at him ever since the night in Oaksbridge. He hated her for what she was, yet he yearned to take her into his arms every time she was near.

He clenched his teeth and kicked at the sand floor of the hut in frustration for allowing himself to think of her that way. However, he could not deny the warmth of her touch across his cheek, the feel of her lips against his ear, and the sweetness of her breath as it washed over him.

"Damn you, woman, get out of my head," he groaned.

The wooden door flew open with a crash, and Orrin whirled around. "Aeron, I…" He stopped when he saw a man standing before him, one he had yet to see. Good God, were all of Aeron's men gigantic?

This mountain of a man raised his eyebrow and glared at him; a thread of unease twisted in Orrin's gut.

"Where is your Captain? I must speak with her," Orrin pled, his near-desperation clinging to his voice.

"She has left you in my care. I'm her first mate, Darcy, and I am to see you are returned to your ship, unharmed," he stated, crossing his enormous arms over his barrel chest.

"No, I am not leaving until I speak with her myself."

"Are you deaf as well as stupid, pirate hunter?" Darcy asked. "She doesn't want you here."

"I don't rightly care whether she wants me here or not. I'm not taking my leave of this hole of an island until I speak to her," Orrin said, squaring his jaw.

Darcy narrowed his eyes and appeared to study Orrin, most likely figuring out which method of torture he would use first. While Orrin was lithe and wiry, he knew Darcy's reputation and knew for a fact that Darcy had made men twice Orrin's size soil their trousers with just a glance and a snarl. But Orrin had to stand his ground and show no fear whatsoever.

"Why?" Darcy's deep voice rumbled from out of his chest like a clap of thunder. "I already told you that she's ordered your safe return to your ship. Why else would you need to see her other than to beg for your miserable life?"

Why indeed. Orrin spat a curse under his breath. He'd never met a more irritating individual in all his life, pirate or otherwise. She was everything he stood against and everything he wanted all rolled into one infuriating woman.

"I do not know why," he said, twisting his hands in the air out of frustration as he squeezed his eyes shut. Everything used to be so simple.

Darcy looked at Orrin this way and that as he clenched and un-clenched his heavily bristled jaw. Orrin stood firm, toe-to-toe with one of the most feared men in all the surrounding oceans. He knew Darcy was capable of dismembering him in a dozen different ways, but he held strong.

"I cannot take you to her; she has asked to be left alone," Darcy said, and Orrin slapped his thighs in exasperation. "However," Darcy continued, "if one were to escape…" Orrin's head snapped up, listening carefully. "One might head to the west shore."

"Why are you telling me this?" Orrin asked, wary. He watched, astonished as the look in Darcy's eyes began to soften.

"Because she needs you as badly as you need her," he replied plainly, as if it were the most obvious reason. "And because if I don't get you out of my sight soon, I fear I may start to remove your limbs."

Orrin shook his head in disbelief. This man, this Darcy, this pirate, didn't even know him, and he presumed to know what he needed. The notion was positively absurd on the most basic level. And yet Orrin couldn't deny the pull that tugged at his insides, drawing him in the direction of the one he was supposed to be bringing to justice.

Aeron.

"And how would one escape?" he asked, half-jokingly.

Darcy shrugged his hulking shoulders and turned, leaving the door wide open and unattended.

"Gael," Darcy said exuberantly as he placed his arm around the enormous bald man watching over the hut and led him away from the door. "How is your wife, brother? Is she well?"

Orrin hesitated for a moment, making sure this wasn't a trick, a clever ruse devised to give these treacherous men the reason they needed to kill him without repercussion from their Captain. Perhaps this was all an elaborate trap of some kind; Aeron was nothing if not clever.

"Christ, I must be absolutely mad," he muttered as left, picking up a sword that was leaning against the outside wall and heading west into the jungle.

Hacking his way through the vines and the low-lying branches of the tropical trees, Orrin swathed a path toward the shore—or at least where he thought the shore to be—all the while contemplating what he would do once he found Aeron…the pirate.

His bounty.

The answer was simple; he would do what he was charged to do, capture her like he would any other pirate he was employed to seize. Pirates were a nasty breed of animal that would be just as likely to gut you as to look at you, depending on the day of the week.

But there was the rub. Aeron wasn't just any other pirate.

She behaved like one on the surface, certainly, captaining a vessel that robbed others and murdered in cold blood. Yet she'd had a village constructed for the family members of her crew. Pirates' crews wouldn't have wives and children. And Aeron was not only kind and generous to her men, but she'd also paid the widow of a man they'd just murdered for a rotting ship so the woman could buy food for her child once again.

Orrin stopped chopping and stood amongst the vegetation.

Did he do what he was commissioned to do and turn Aeron into the Queen for payment? Royalty or not, that woman reeked of corruption and, for lack of a better word, evil. Granted, there was no physical proof of such an accusation toward Her Majesty, and he could surely be strung up in the nearest tree for even thinking such a thing, but Orrin felt it deeply in his bones at the mere mention of her name. Likewise, Aeron's reaction when she learned of his employer did not bode well with him.

He wasn't sure what was what at the moment, but he would not blindly hand Aeron over to that woman, not without knowing the truth.

Chapter Four

*A*eron sat on the white sands of the west beach, gazing out over the crystal blue water as wave after wave washed upon the shore and the cool ocean breeze blew pieces of her fiery hair across her face.

Damn that pirate hunter for ever setting foot on my island, and damn him for affecting me the way that he does, she thought.

As she closed her eyes, images of Orrin immediately started to fill her mind. Images of his strong arms wrapped around her from behind and his golden brown locks as he pulled her close, nuzzling into her neck. Images so clear that she could practically feel the warm press of his chest and the tickle on her cheek as he'd leaned in to whisper in her ear. She could even smell him.

Aeron turned her head as she heard footsteps approaching. The wind from inside the jungle rushed by her face, and Orrin's scent washed over her. It was slight, but very distinct from any of her men—of that she was sure. She dropped her head into her hands with a heavy sigh before casting a glance over her shoulder.

"I will not go back to the Queen alive, so if you're going to run me through, just do it, please," she said, turning her eyes back to the sea in front of her. "Or at least lop off my head and be done with it. Your choice, but I grow tired of running."

She could feel Orrin watching her as the sound of rustling sand stopped behind her.

"Just promise me you'll leave my people be. Leave this island and forget what you've seen here. I assure you, you will have no trouble from them."

Orrin sheathed his sword. "I consider myself an honorable man, and if I were going to run you through, I would at least have the decency to do it face-to-face. There's not a lot of sport in catching someone unawares. And beheading? Horribly messy business if you ask me, and as you mentioned earlier, this is a fine shirt, and blood tends to ruin such a…how did you put it? 'Finely tailored garment' as this," he said, plopping himself down next to her in the sand. "Tell me, what made you so certain that it was me just now and not one of your men?"

Resting her hands on her bent knees, Aeron shook her head, trying her best to ignore the infectious grin on his face. His once white silk shirt was torn and splattered with jungle muck and blood from his scuffle in the hut with Gael. He was a complete mess, yet he smiled at her as if he hadn't a care in the world. This man was going to be the death of her if she wasn't careful.

"Because you move through the jungle like a rhinoceros," she said, turning her head in his direction, the smile breaking through, "and you smell just as bad."

Orrin raised his arm and took a whiff of himself. "It's not that bad."

"You spent the day locked in a brig hut, and you've been at sea for God knows how long before that. Yes, it's bad." Aeron chuckled, resting her head into the crook of her arms as she looked at him. He was her enemy, for all intents and purposes, but he was a stunningly beautiful creature no matter which way one looked at him.

Orrin bellowed with laughter, tossing his head back as his broad shoulders rolled up and down. The sound was utterly contagious, and Aeron couldn't help but laugh harder herself. When the hilarity subsided, she noticed he was staring at her thoughtfully.

"Is that why you are sending me away then?" Orrin asked, the sadness deep within his blue eyes lifting ever so slightly with every passing moment.

Any trace of humor slid off Aeron's face immediately, and she turned away from him to once again focus her attention on the ocean in front of them.

Orrin stared at her, and Aeron would have been lying if she said she didn't enjoy his eyes inspecting her every feature. Could he see the tension in the set of her back as her hands clenched into fists so hard her knuckles turned white? Or in the line of her jaw stretched taut and her eyes squeezed shut as she breathed in and out slowly, trying to stay in control of her emotions?

He raised a hand and swept a lock of hair behind her ear. "I'm sorry," he said.

"For what?" Aeron asked, her brow relaxing at the momentary feel of his warm hand on her cheek before she looked at him. She shouldn't enjoy this. Aeron knew that, logically, she shouldn't have even let him sit next to her. But as his fingers moved across her cheek, tenderly stroking down the side of her face, she couldn't deny this was what she had craved.

"For putting that look in your eyes." Orrin ran his thumb over her chin and back, circling it across her cheek. His body moved closer to hers; she could feel his breath in her hair, and it felt divine. "Aeron," he said, moving closer still, "what on earth did she do to you?"

Before Aeron could answer, she noticed something odd. Without warning, her hand whipped up between their faces, grabbed a lock of Orrin's hair, and she inspected it. She rolled the silky strands between her fingers as she examined the rest, spying patches of hair clumped together all over his head.

"I don't know how you managed it, but you have a ridiculous amount of sap in your hair," she said, pointing to at least a dozen spots matted together. "Come, we must get it out before it sets. Otherwise, it will never come out."

"And if it doesn't come out?" Orrin asked while Aeron rose to her feet and dusted the sand off her buttocks.

"You remember Gael, don't you?" she asked, indicating the large bald man that had tossed him around the hut like a rag doll.

"Yes," he said.

"Yesterday he had hair."

Orrin's eyes widened as he vaulted to his feet. "For Christ's sake, let's go. I'm not shaving my head," he said, disappearing into the jungle.

"You're going the wrong way!" Aeron called after him before ducking into the brush to steer him in the right direction through the maze of vines and palm trees that dotted the island. She needed no path; she knew this terrain like the back of her hand and could find her way to the private lagoon behind her cottage from anywhere on the island in the middle of the night with her eyes closed.

Neither pirate nor hunter, it seemed, was quite sure what to make of what they felt for the other at the moment as far as Orrin could tell.

They should be enemies. By rights, Aeron should have eviscerated Orrin there on the rocks along the edge of her lagoon this morning. And just moments ago, Orrin should have snatched the opportunity to take Aeron as his captive, delivering her to the Queen as promised and claiming his bounty.

But they'd done neither of these things nor explained their actions, or lack thereof. Instead, Orrin felt tension and feelings of ambivalence charge the air around them as they moved silently through the dense underbrush, stepping over roots and fallen coconuts along the way.

When the jungle before them started to open up into a clearing, Orrin recognized the sparkling water of the hidden pool he'd found Aeron floating in upon his arrival on the island.

"I'll be right back. Wait here," Aeron announced as she walked away.

Orrin lashed out and grabbed her wrist, pulling her back to him before he knew what he was doing. She clearly was allowing this to happen, for he was certain if she didn't want to be moved, come hell or high water before anyone could move her. Looking into her eyes, Orrin snaked his hand around her waist, drawing her closer to his solid frame.

"You're leaving me alone?" he asked, tightening his grip and pulling her against his body. "Aren't you afraid I'll run away?"

"No," she said assuredly. "I've yet to have a man run away from me."

"Fair enough, but there is a first time for everything." Orrin dragged the pad of his thumb lazily up and down her spine. He could feel her heart beat, hammering wildly against his chest.

"True," she said, nodding, "but you'd be lost twenty feet into the brush. You'd starve and attempt to eat one of the many poisonous fruits that grow wildly. Cunning warrior or no, you would undoubtedly die a most unpleasant death alone in the jungle."

Orrin thought about the real danger he was in at that very moment. He was also smart enough to know when his wits had been bested. He smiled down at her as he licked his lips and leaned forward, his mouth but a breath from hers.

"The sign of a good warrior is knowing which battles to concede," he said, taking a step back and sliding his hand down Aeron's arm until he grasped her fingers in his and turned her knuckles to the heavens. "This round to the lady."

He bowed his head and pressed his lips to the back of her hand. When he released her, Aeron hurriedly disappeared down a path carved into the jungle.

Curious, Orrin wondered as he watched her hurry away. Had he managed to offend her with his bold behavior, or perhaps...excited her?

Orrin hoped for the latter as he stripped the shirt from his body and released the tie from his hair at the back of his neck. He unbuckled his belt and scabbard and placed them on a nearby rock as he pulled his boots off and slid into the water, leaving his trousers on. The water was just warm enough to soothe the muscles that ached from hacking his way through the jungle.

"Mmm," he groaned, submerging his whole upper body and trying to figure out what the hell he was going to do about his feelings for Aeron. He remembered scoffing at the silly stories his sisters would spin about finding true love, how he'd tease them about the absurdity of falling in love at first glance.

He laughed, for he could think of nothing else from the moment he'd set eyes on Aeron, even when she was threatening him with her sword. He was playing a most dangerous game indeed, one that could end in his swift death, but still he couldn't stop. He'd never felt so alive in all of his life, so whole and complete as he did in this moment.

"Christ, I've gone mad," he said to himself, "completely mad."

Aeron's steps flew over the path to her cottage until she shoved through the back door. She rifled through the few chests she had, grabbing a fresh shirt and a pair of trousers that looked like they would fit Orrin nicely. She picked up some soap and a small colored glass bottle from the table against the wall. Suddenly, thoughts began to run rampant through her mind, and she stopped dead in the center of the room.

She pulled her bottom lip between her teeth as uncertainty creased her brow. Perhaps this was all a ruse, a way to capture her so he could collect his bounty from Queen Winifred? Orrin was certainly clever, but was he so clever a pirate hunter that he would use her own tactics of seduction against her? Would he dare be so cruel as to make her fall in love with him for a sack of gold?

No, she would not let her heart be crushed ever again at the hands of the Queen. She would take control, seduce what she could out of him and be done with it. Orrin was just a man, just like all the others. Wasn't he?

As Aeron made her way back to the lagoon, she paused just outside the line of trees that secluded her pool to loosen the tie of her blouse. She spread the fabric open a touch to allow an alluring hint of her bosom to peek out before she pushed through the barrier and saw his shirt lying on the rocks.

Aeron swallowed hard, as lying a few paces from his shirt was his belt. She carefully stepped over his boots, which were haphazardly discarded on the rocky shore.

Heavens, is he naked? she wondered, touching the back of her hand to her forehead to wipe away a bit of perspiration that had accumulated. This was going to be a lot harder than she'd thought. Orrin smiled at her from the water, and as he swam over to where she stood, a million butterflies took flight in her belly. *Damn him. Damn him straight to hell.*

She squared her shoulders and commanded her voice to remain steady. "Where are your trousers?" she asked him.

"On my arse," he said. "I didn't think I needed them off to wash tree sap out of my hair, but if you insist…" Orrin's hands dropped beneath the surface of the water.

"No!" Aeron said and thrust her hand out to stop him from going any farther. His smug grin infuriated her; the bastard did that on purpose just to rattle her. She collected herself and quietly cursed him as she set the clothes she brought down at her feet. "Here is everything you need," she said, walking over to the edge of the lagoon to place the soap and glass bottle on a flat rock there, well within his reach.

She watched out of the corner of her eye in caution as he swam closer to her.

"Forgive my forwardness, my lady," he said, "but I'd hoped you'd be joining me. Won't you?"

Aeron's heart leapt, and her breath caught in the back of her throat. The sprinkling of hair across his bare chest swirled with the water as it moved around him. *Curse him for looking so bloody inviting,* she thought.

"That is quite forward, indeed, but a fair assumption given my reputation, I'd imagine," she responded.

"Then you'll join me," he said confidently, extending a dripping hand to her. "I assure you I won't bite." A lecherous smile spread across Orrin's lips, and Aeron believed he might indeed bite and that she might like it. "Please?" he asked, and she'd be damned if he didn't look sincere.

"Very well," Aeron said, rolling her eyes and trying to sound indifferent to the offer. "It *is* basically impossible to remove the sap completely without assistance."

Doing her best to keep her wits in check, Aeron untied her belt and slipped off her boots before she slid into the warm lagoon, fully clothed and turned to face the bank. She heard the distinct sound of water moving as Orrin swam in behind her. He ran the tips of his long fingers over the cloth covering her arm.

"You're cheating," he purred into her ear. He circled around in front of her, leaning lazily against the stone bank.

"I am not." She leaned forward, sliding her body against his as she reached for the bottle on the rock behind him. "You assume far too much, sir. I hardly know you," she said with her lips just a breath from Orrin's neck. Using every bit of restraint, Aeron took a step away from him and twirled her finger in the air. "Turn around."

He seemed to hesitate for a moment, but slowly he turned and waited for more instruction. As Aeron moved in, she could feel the warmth of his body on hers. Her eyes fluttered in her head, and her skin ignited as she pressed against his back.

"What are you going to do to me?" he asked as he looked over his shoulder at her, a smile curling one side of his mouth. "Should I be worried? What is that you have there?" He nodded to the glass bottle.

"This is a mixture of oils. It helps to remove the sap," she explained as she opened the ornate bottle and poured a small amount into her hand. She spread the oil between her palms and worked it into the sticky patches, pulling the tree sap free of his hair. As she slid her fingers over his scalp, massaging from front to back to make certain every trace of residue was removed from every strand, she heard Orrin sigh at her touch.

Placing the bottle back on the rocky bank and picking up the soap, Aeron moved in behind him once again. "Do you trust me, Orrin?" she asked, skimming her finger up the length of his spine.

"Yes, Aeron, I trust you." He answered without hesitation, to her surprise.

Her lips brushed tenderly against his neck as she said, "Lie back."

Closing his eyes, Orrin took a deep breath and released a quiet sigh as he lay back in her arms. Aeron held him in the water and rubbed the bar of soap over his head, washing the traces of oil out of his hair. His hand reached back to slide around her waist, and his fingers spanned across the small of her back while his thumb rubbed up and down her lower spine. Aeron tried to hold onto her composure and resist offering herself up to him to do with as he saw fit.

Lowering his head into the water, she rinsed the suds from his hair. When all the soap was washed out, she pulled him up and motioned for him to stand facing her. Orrin watched her work the bar in her hands, the suds spilling over her fingers.

"Now what are you doing?" he asked, closing the small gap between them. "I thought you were just helping me get the sap out of my hair."

"I thought *you* said you trusted me."

"I do."

"Then shut up and raise your arms out of the water," she said.

Obediently pulling his arms out of the water, Orrin held them out at his sides. Aeron began at his fingertips, running the soap up the length of his arm, over the top, and swirling the soap around his elbow. She pushed the bar around his shoulder and beneath his underarm, slowly dragging it across the underside of his bicep, down along the crease of his elbow, and all the way to his wrist. Methodically, she lowered his arm under the water, rinsing the suds away and splashing water onto his shoulder to do the same. She enjoyed the way Orrin watched her carefully as she moved to the other side, repeating the process with slow strokes and gentle touches.

When Aeron was through with his arms, she slid behind him, out of his line of sight. She lathered the soap between her hands for a moment before she swiped it across his back with one hand and spread the lather with the other. She stayed well above the surface of the water and noticed that Orrin had risen up onto his toes, getting as much of his torso out of the water as possible.

She leaned forward and slid her hands across his chest and down his corded belly along the soft trail of hair below his navel. A barely audible moan escaped from him as her fingertips brushed the top of his trousers, and her resolve almost cracked. Steeling her will, she turned away. She laid the soap on the rocks and took a moment to catch her breath. Suddenly, she felt his arm curl around her waist and his wet hand push her hair away from the back of her neck.

"Is it my turn now?" he asked in a husky voice, his hot breath washing across the spot of flesh just below her ear. "Do you trust *me*, Aeron?"

Time slowed to a crawl as he pulled her ear lobe into his mouth, lightly grazing it with his teeth.

"Yes," she breathed and tilted her head, awaiting the touch of his mouth against her skin, but instead felt him release her and move away.

Aeron had never felt more devastated or foolish. She had dared to want something for herself, something she had no right to.

She slowly opened her eyes, expecting to see Orrin's men surrounding the secluded lagoon. Instead, she was more than surprised to find William standing in front of her with his sword aimed at Orrin, who, she now saw, was standing behind her with his hands high in the air.

"Are you all right, Captain?" Will asked, never taking his eyes off the pirate hunter. "This filthy bastard escaped, and…"

Aeron sighed with relief and raked her wet hands through her hair. "Yes, William, I know." She looked up at the boy, who still had his sword poised to run Orrin through at the first opportunity he could see. "Put your sword away."

"But, Captain—" Will said, lowering his weapon.

Aeron pulled herself from the water and rubbed her hand across her forehead in frustration.

"Not now, William. I'm hungry, as I'm sure our guest is as well."

William stood and blinked at her. "Guest? But I...he..."

Aeron's patience had grown thin, and she glared at the young man. "Yes, guest. Is that going to be a problem with you, Your Highness?" she asked with acidity in her voice.

"No, no, Captain," he answered, shaking his head vehemently.

"Good. You will remember that it is your choice to be here, and so you will remember your place. Now make yourself useful and find our guest a place to stay."

With a deep bow, William scurried off down one of the paths surrounding the lagoon.

Aeron bent down and picked up her things and saw Orrin was still in the lagoon, watching the exchange take place. "Are you coming?" she asked him as she started walking toward the path that led to her cottage, hoping he wasn't horrified to see her acting like such an arse. However, William had to be kept humble if her plan was going to work.

"In a moment, if you please. I need to find an, um"—Orrin cleared his throat—"cold patch of water first, if you don't mind."

She pointed to the clothes she brought for him. "There are some dry clothes to put on when you're ready," she said and nodded toward a path. "My cottage is just through there when you're done. I'm going to change into something dry, so be sure to knock." With a wink she picked up the bottle of oil and bar of soap before disappearing into the jungle.

Orrin shook his head as he swam toward the waterfall where the churning water was cooler. He needed to calm himself and get his mind in the right place before he could even think about following Aeron down that path.

There was more to her than piracy; that much was clear to him. Women had bathed him in the past, but while always pleasant, it had never been like this. Incomparable to anything he'd ever felt from anyone, the tenderness and care made his heart ache. She'd also had more than ample opportunity to end his life; on numerous occasions today alone she could have sliced him from Adam's apple to arse but didn't. He believed that if she wanted him dead, he would have been so already.

The cool water of the fall beat down on his shoulders as Orrin stared into the carved-out section of jungle. He was certain there was more down that path than he could ever imagine.

Chapter Five

illiam's boots gouged the earth as he tromped into the village, spewing venomous curses.

How dare that pile of filth place his hands on my captain, he thought as he headed straight for Darcy. "The Captain wants a place for our guest to stay," he seethed to him.

"Mind your tone when you speak of our captain, boy," Darcy warned. Darcy had never cared much for Will's joining the crew, and Will knew it; the man wasn't exactly the subtlest of people.

"One moment he's our prisoner," William spat, "and the next I find him half-naked with his arms tangled around her."

"I will not say this again, Will. Mind your tone." Darcy took another step forward, towering menacingly over the young prince. But Will chose not to hear him.

"I left my throne for her, to serve her." William's lip twitched as he pulled his hand through his straight, sandy blond hair. "To love her," he said before clenching his hands at his sides in anger. "And to see her give her affection to that…that…"

Darcy's hand flashed up and grabbed him by the throat. "You are testing my patience, boy," he growled.

Will struggled under the vice-like grip, sputtering and turning purple as Darcy's fingers squeezed tighter and cut off the flow of air. When Darcy finally released him, the prince staggered back a few steps, his normal color returning.

"I am not a boy," he choked out as he rubbed his hand over his throat. "I have had more than my share of women."

Darcy responded with a bursting laugh. "What, handmaidens and ladies of the court? Those women only share themselves to gain footing on the social ladder, to brag that they bedded the Prince. Nothing more," he said.

William's blood boiled with embarrassment and anger as he tried to think of something to say in return, only to come up with nothing at all.

"Why would our captain give her affection to you? Because you were a prince?" Darcy continued. "Because of the intense hatred she rightfully harbors for your mother?" Darcy closed the gap between the two of them in one powerful stride. "You are not worthy of her," he said. "You never were, and you never will be…*boy.*" He spat the last word directly at young Will's face, driving the point home in the young man's mind.

William feebly attempted to shove Darcy's massive frame aside, but he'd have had just as much luck trying to move an oak. Frustration overtook him, and William charged out of the village among curses and vows that he'd had enough of this treatment as he disappeared into the jungle.

After getting himself under control, Orrin dragged himself out of the water and removed his wet trousers. He pulled on the dark brown breeches Aeron had left for him and slid into his boots, fixing his belt around his waist. Taking a deep breath, he gathered his courage and followed the path to the north of the lagoon, the one Aeron had disappeared down. It was a clear, winding trail with no low-lying branches or vines in the way; this was obviously an oft-used route. When the back of her cottage came into view, Orrin stopped and thought about what she could be doing behind those walls.

Was she dressed yet, or was she still standing naked in the middle of the room? He licked his lips at his fantasy, and a smile curled his mouth. As he got closer, he noticed the door to the cottage was open just a crack.

She had asked him to knock, hadn't she? He couldn't remember, or chose not to. He paused where he was and wondered what she might do to him if he were caught. Did he dare look in? Curiosity got the better of him, and Orrin crept closer, trying to be as quiet as he could while he peered through the crack.

He saw her naked backside just before the tail end of her shirt fell over it. His blood surged through his veins as she pulled a pair of black trousers over her sleek, bare legs, lifting the back of her shirt as she slid the dark cloth over her mouthwatering rump. His eyes fluttered closed as he held back the groan building in the back of his throat. He had to stop this, now. His reputation as a bounty hunter was at stake, and a man who was not worth his reputation was worthless.

Pulling his bottom lip between his teeth and squeezing his eyes shut, he cleared his throat loudly and gave the door a swift knock.

"Come in," Aeron called over her shoulder as she finished tying her breeches.

Pushing the door open slowly, Orrin entered the room. His eyes washed over Aeron's sumptuous form as she twisted her long hair behind her head. "Could you hand me that belt?" she asked around the two ivory sticks held between her sultry lips, motioning to the settee next to him.

Orrin picked up the belt and noticed the scabbard on its side with a mermaid carved into the thick leather. He recalled the first moment he'd seen Aeron in the lagoon and had wondered if she was such a mythical sea creature. As he lifted the belt, he saw something else sitting on the sofa's red brocade fabric, glinting in the sun that shone through the window. His father's brass compass.

"I believe that belongs to you, does it not?" she asked as she plucked the ivory sticks from her mouth and worked them into her hair to hold it in place.

"Yes." He picked up the trinket and turned it over in his hand; it had been polished to a bright sheen, clearly well cared for. "It was my father's," he said. "It isn't worth much. Why did you take it?"

"Taking it afforded me the opportunity to get close to you," Aeron answered as she arranged her hair around the ivory sticks in front of an ornate mirror. Orrin carefully tucked the compass into his belt and noticed that Aeron was watching his reflection in the mirror.

He walked across the room, her belt spread out in his strong hands as he approached her.

"Thank you," he said, and he stepped up behind her and spread the belt across her lower back. Before he could stop himself, he closed his eyes, dipped his head to her body, and dropped soft kisses up along her shoulder and onto her neck as he reached around, tying the supple leather belt into place. His eyes opened as his lips reached her ear, and he looked into the mirror at their reflection.

Aeron's eyes were closed, and her head tilted to the side, allowing him to lavish her with his kisses. Her mouth hung slightly open as she breathed a quiet moan. Her skin was warm and tasted sweet. When he stopped kissing her, he watched her eyes open and stare at his reflection.

His strong hands circled around her waist, pulling her flush to his body. Before she could protest, Orrin spun her in his arms. His palms smoothed up her back to the sticks fixed in her hair. With a swift tug, he pulled them free, and her silky hair tumbled down her back like fire. He tossed the two pieces of ivory to the floor and leaned his forehead against hers.

"Aeron," he breathed, his lips brushing over hers, barely making contact.

"Yes." She nodded, her eyes closing with a sigh.

Orrin smiled as he continued to tease her with featherlight touches.

She reached up, sank her hands into his hair, and pulled him closer. "Either kiss me or leave," she panted.

Orrin gripped her body tighter, pressing her breasts hard against his chest as he pulled her hips into his. He felt Aeron's body tremble before he covered her mouth with his.

The kiss was firm, hot, and wet. Aeron tugged on his hair as she slid her body up the entire length of his arousal. He savagely squeezed her buttocks as he overtook her, claiming her mouth with his tongue; she was wild and delicious.

Aeron ripped her hands from his hair and planted them on the center of his chest. Suddenly, she shoved him back, but not before sucking his bottom lip into her mouth as she pulled away.

"Why did you stop?" Orrin gasped in confusion as she slid out of his embrace. She ducked under his arm and crossed to the other side of room to pick up her boot.

"I'm hungry," she said over her shoulder as she pulled the boot up her thigh, seductively tracing her fingers farther up her leg than she needed to.

Orrin gaped at her, near panting from the state she'd left him in as she coolly yanked her other boot on. The sneaky little pirate was trying to get the upper hand back—and succeeding.

We'll see about that, he thought as he calmly walked to her and teased his lips against her ear.

"I'm hungry as well," Orrin said, and he reached around and slid his finger under the cuff of her boot. He watched her bite her lip as he traced along the inside of her thigh, indicating in no uncertain terms what he was hungry for. Before he could reach his destination, however, she turned and daintily took him by the hand. She looked deep into his eyes as she lifted his hand to her mouth and slid her tongue across the pulse in his wrist, then up through the center of his palm and took one of his fingers into her mouth.

His entire body felt as if it was going to explode, but, all too quickly, Aeron released him and strode confidently across the room to the door.

"Are you coming?" she asked as she pulled the door to her cottage open.

Orrin glanced down at himself and back to her. Once again he'd found himself in quite an uncomfortable predicament. "Do you intend to leave me like this every time I'm around you?"

"You may have to stay awhile and find out, won't you?" Aeron answered as she turned to exit.

Crossing the room with lightning speed, Orrin wrapped his hand around her waist, holding her against his body as he tunneled his face into her hair, inhaling the scent of sweet, ripe mangos.

"I'm trying to behave like a gentleman should, but you test my control," he confessed against her ear as she melted into him.

Aeron turned in his arms and placed a finger at the base of his throat.

"Control…" she mused, and she ran the tip of her finger through the hair that sprinkled his chest, across his belly and below, pulling away just as she reached the tip of his arousal. "I find it to be highly overrated," she said, just before she stepped away and left him panting again.

Orrin's nostrils flared as she sashayed down the path. He was furious with himself for letting Aeron get the better of him three times in a row, two of which were just moments ago.

Damn her.

He knew he should go back to his ship, assemble his crew, and take the island. But as he looked down the winding trail Aeron had taken, that direction tugged hard on his heart. Orrin scrubbed his hands over his face as he mulled over his two choices. He reached down into his gut, took a deep breath, and chose a path.

Chapter Six

Aeron listened for following footsteps as she rounded the corner, her cottage completely out of sight. When she didn't hear anything, she leaned against a palm tree to catch her breath. This man kept her on her toes.

She wiped the beaded sweat from her brow, trying to remember the last time she'd been kissed that soundly, but she couldn't recall any such instance, ever. His lips were gentle yet demanding.

Aeron patted her face on her sleeve and steeled her nerves as she headed into the town. She'd just left Orrin a more than ample opportunity to flee the island if he so chose; however, she desperately hoped that he would not. She wanted him to stay. She needed him to stay.

When Aeron entered the village square, she immediately saw Darcy sitting at the table closest to the cottage he shared with his wife, Catrin, and daughter, Rianna. He waved Aeron over to join the family in their meal, which Aeron happily obliged.

"You look…well, Captain," he said as she sat next to him.

Aeron quirked her eyebrow at her first-in-command. For all his menacing attributes, there was a softer side to Darcy that not many got the pleasure of seeing; she was thankful she was one of those treasured few.

"I am well, Darcy," she replied, before leaning over and placing a kiss on his cheek. "Thank you."

Darcy scoffed. "I don't know what you're thankful for, I didn't do a damned thing, and make no mistake, I'm right bloody pissed that I didn't get to torture anyone." He made a horribly sour face.

"Are you trying to seduce my husband, Captain?" Catrin asked with a wink as she stepped up to the table with her burgeoning belly. There was no doubt Catrin knew better than anyone that the love between Aeron and Darcy was only that of a sister and brother, nothing more.

Aeron laughed, slapping the table with amusement. "Catrin, you should sit down before you drop that child right here," she said, motioning to the chair next to Darcy. "Besides, you know he only has eyes for you." She patted her friend on the back.

"It's the God's honest truth. No other woman sets my blood on fire like you, my beautiful Catrin," Darcy said as he wrapped his arms around what was left of her waist. "It's not every woman that can keep up with the likes of me, ay?" he asked, giving her a hearty smack on the backside. He then suddenly leapt to his feet and swept Catrin up into his arms, showering her face with kisses as she squealed to be let down.

Aeron watched the love that radiated when her friend kissed his wife.

I want that, she thought.

No sooner had the thought crossed her mind when Orrin practically appeared before her. The radiant smile he wore reached all the way up to his eyes, and Aeron wondered how long he'd been standing there, looking at her.

Clearing her throat, Aeron nodded to the empty seat on her left. "Will you join us?" she asked. "If it's all right with Darcy. This is his family's table."

The enormous man glared at Orrin and appeared to size him up with a sneer. He uttered some semblance of a response, at which Aeron smiled and motioned Orrin to the empty chair.

"It would be my honor, lady," he replied as he sat next to her.

She shook her head. "Thank you, but I'm most assuredly no—"

Before she could finish her thought, Orrin had taken her hand in his and raised it to his mouth to kiss her knuckles.

"But you are," he said. Aeron felt a warm blush stain her cheeks, and she tried to look away, but Orrin leaned in closer so that only she could hear the words. "It's an honor as well to have such a lovely effect on you, as I would assume not many things in this world could bring color to those cheeks anymore..." He brought her fingers to his lips again. "Lady," he said before he kissed her hand again.

As the meal commenced, Orrin surveyed the village before him.

This was not what he had expected a pirate village to look like. Granted, this was the first one he'd ever laid eyes on and the only one he'd even known to exist, but there were no piles of jewels, no mountains of gold—hell, not even a sack of it. Not even in Aeron's own cottage, where there were only a few small trinkets and what looked to be mementos from her travels.

He looked around the heart of the community, where it seemed everyone was gathered to eat together. There were no servants of any kind—no one seemed to be in a higher authority than anyone else. Every table was set with jugs of wine and large platters of food. If a jug of wine went empty, whoever was holding it simply got up and filled it; if food was needed, they passed their plate to the person sitting closest to the platter. It was quite a refreshing change from what he'd observed the few times he'd gone to court, to say the least.

When Orrin had approached the table earlier, he couldn't believe what he'd seen before him. The sheer joy coupled with tremendous heartbreak that wracked Aeron's face. That one look spoke to him more than any words she could have uttered aloud. He'd seen a semblance of that face many times over…staring back at him every time he looked in a mirror.

Halfway through the meal, Darcy moved in to address Orrin.

"You will be staying with my wife and me," he said as he leaned in closer for Orrin's ears only. "I want you close, where I can keep my eyes on you at all times." Darcy sat back in his chair and placed a hand on his wife's large, round belly. "I should warn you, however, this woman snores like a wild boar."

Aeron tossed her head back and laughed as Catrin narrowed her eyes and walloped Darcy in the back of the head. Orrin didn't dare crack a smile, no matter how amusing he found the moment, but he believed that he could listen to the sound of Aeron's laughter for the rest of his days.

While ranting and cursing every person on the island, William stumbled upon Orrin's boat on the east shore, the bow peeking out from under the carefully arranged palm fronds. Will glanced out at the sea, deducing that the pirate hunter's ship and crew must be out there somewhere waiting for their captain to return.

He looked up at the sun to gauge the time of day and decided it was far too late to row out. He wasn't certain the ship he'd be looking for would even be out there, and trying to find something in the dark of the impending night would be near impossible. Leaving at first light was the smart choice. He would show them all that he was no boy.

He was a man. A prince.

And he would have what he felt he should, what was owed to him—Aeron, for his own, no matter what it took.

Even if it meant going back to the life he'd left, the life he loathed. He would dare a dance with the devil to have the company of an angel.

Aeron watched Orrin as they partook in their meal. Every rumor of him she'd ever heard had spoken of his foul temper and cold heart. Even in the brief encounter they had shared in Oaksbridge years ago, she'd seen for herself his stern demeanor and that his eyes were only on his catch. The man she saw in front of her now was very different indeed. She liked the way he seemed so comfortable on the island, and she felt just as content, as if he'd always been there. She also noticed that Catrin and Rianna were taken with his brilliant smile and charming manner. Darcy, however, was less than convinced. She saw the way her second-in-command brooded while Orrin interacted with their people.

After the meal was complete, Aeron walked Orrin around the square, conversing with every inhabitant of her little island. She knew the name and trade of every single person and pointed out who he should go to for any need he could possibly have. She often found him staring at her instead of listening, something she normally would have been irritated with, but every time their eyes met, she could do nothing but chew on her bottom lip like a fool.

As they approached the farthest end of the village, they came upon a woman with a babe swaddled in her arms, and Aeron noticed that Orrin gave pause. Did he recognize the woman? Did he know this was the widow of Cormac Doyle, the man she'd dealt with in Oaksbridge?

Luckily, before he had a chance to ask anything, Rianna came running through the square and tugged on Aeron's hand.

"It's Momma," the excitable young girl practically yelled, yanking hard on Aeron's wrist. "She says the baby is coming!"

"Christ, I knew it was going to happen soon, but not this soon," Aeron said as she ran after Rianna with Orrin half a step behind them.

When they reached Darcy and Catrin's cottage, Darcy was sitting in a chair against the outer wall looking horribly anxious.

"Stay here," Aeron called over her shoulder to Orrin as she pushed through the door without knocking.

Orrin took up the seat next to Darcy as the man fisted his hands in his dark brown curls while Catrin bellowed inside.

"Hell, I hate this part," Darcy said out loud to himself as he rocked back and forth in his chair. His hardened face contorted with every shriek he heard, and he made a few cries of his own.

"You feel her pain," Orrin said, and he placed a tentative hand on Darcy's massive shoulder. "Despite the rumors to the contrary, you are a good man."

Darcy shrugged his shoulder out of Orrin's grip. "You may have Aeron fooled, but make no mistake. I still don't trust you further than I can throw you," he said. "And if at any moment I feel she or anyone on this island is in danger, orders be damned, I will kill you where you stand. Are we clear?"

Orrin swallowed hard; one of the last people on the planet he wanted to cross was Darcy. "Perfectly."

"Good. Now tell me, you've had ample opportunity to flee the island like the coward that you are. Why are you still here?" Darcy asked.

Orrin mulled the question over for a moment. He could lie and risk Darcy's wrath, or he could be honest, which in and of itself could bring on a completely different punishment. He weighed his options carefully before he answered.

"I don't trust the Queen," he said truthfully. "Her son ran from her to join your crew, and as beautiful and alluring as Aeron is, I find it hard to believe that even she could tempt a spoiled prince out of his birthright. I can't explain it, but there is something about that woman."

"That's a bold statement," Darcy said warily. "One might even say those were words of treason. You should take care who you say them to. I've heard the Queen pays well for reports of such acts."

"You are more than welcome to turn me in, then," Orrin challenged.

"Tempting," Darcy said, arching his brow as if he were seriously considering the option.

As the hours passed, Darcy took to pacing well into the night, wearing a path in the ground while Orrin nodded off in the chair outside the door. When Aeron stepped out of the cottage, Darcy practically knocked her over.

"How is she? Is the baby here? Is it a girl? Is it a boy? Do I have a son?" he rambled as he wrung his calloused hands.

"Easy, my friend, there is still a while to go yet," Aeron said calmly. "This babe is stubborn. It's most assuredly a boy." She immediately saw the flash of panic in Darcy's eyes, and she gave him a reassuring pat on his shoulder. "Catrin is a strong woman, Darcy. She'll be fine. They both will."

Darcy nodded and put on a strained smile as he took up pacing again.

Aeron turned around to see Orrin sleeping in the chair. Yes, it had been a long day, and it was going to be a long night. She silently studied his face. He looked like an angel with his dark lashes against his smooth skin, his full lips pursed together as he slept. She couldn't help but reach out and ghost her fingers over the shadow of his cheek.

With impeccably quick reflexes, Orrin snatched Aeron's wrist before she could pull away, without even opening his eyes. He brought her hand to his lips and placed a kiss at the bottom curve of her palm. Her entire body ignited as his mouth connected with her flesh, making every inch of her skin tingle and setting a fire inside of her.

"How is Catrin, is she well?" he asked as he opened his eyes.

"It'll be a long night," she said. "The child is stubborn, just like its father."

Orrin laughed lightly while his eyes appeared to drift closed of their own accord with exhaustion.

"Go back to my cottage and sleep," Aeron said as she ran her finger along the side of his unshaven face.

"No, I want to stay here, in case I can help with anything," Orrin said. He straightened in his chair, clearly struggling to stay awake.

"Help with anything? Look at you." Aeron laughed. "You can't even keep your eyes open, let alone be of any use to anyone right now. When was the last time you even slept in a proper bed on dry land?" Orrin shook his head and started to protest, but Aeron stopped him with a quirk of her brow. "You can go back to my cottage and sleep, or I can fetch Brendon and have him drag you back to the hut and you can sleep on the dirt floor. Your choice."

Orrin looked as though he was about to argue but sighed in defeat. "Very well." He yawned as he stood and stretched toward the night sky and took a step toward Aeron, his chest nearly touching hers. "But I'm keeping all my clothes on, in case your pirate ways get the better of you and you decide to ravage me in the night," he said with a cocky waggle of his eyebrows.

Aeron rolled her eyes. "And what makes you think I want to ravage you?"

Orrin leaned over closer, his warm breath blowing against Aeron's ear as he spoke. "I can see it in your eyes," he said before he turned on his heel and headed down the moonlit path to her cottage.

In the moments before daybreak, when the sky was just beginning to lighten, Aeron finally left Darcy and Catrin's home. The child was very large, which had made the birth very difficult on Catrin.

As she slipped through the door of her cottage, she approached the bed and saw Orrin's bare chest peeking out from under the blanket. She stood and stared at him as the morning light spilled through the window and illuminated his magnificent shape. There was a pull, an urge to crawl into the bed with him that she could deny herself no longer.

Moving with the silence of a cat, she changed into a chemise and slid into her bed, trying not to wake him. Slowly she began inching backward, moving closer and closer until she was next to his sleeping form. Orrin groaned loudly in his sleep and rolled over, flinging his arm over her body and nuzzling the back of her hair with a sigh.

Aeron closed her eyes with a warm, content smile on her face. She allowed herself a few moments to enjoy the feeling of his arms wrapped around her before she drifted off to sleep.

Chapter Seven

*L*ater in the morning when Orrin finally awoke, he found Aeron nestled in the crook of his arm with one of her feet tangled around his. It felt as natural as breathing, lying with her like this. He was thankful he'd made the decision to keep his trousers on; otherwise, with Aeron lying this closely, he might not have been able to control his urges.

As gently as he could manage, Orrin worked his way out of the bed, grabbing his shirt, belt, and boots. Leaning over, he captured a lock of her deep red hair and twisted it around his finger before he carefully snuck out the door.

He stood at the fork in the path and again contemplated fleeing. He could head back to his ship and forget this island ever existed. That part would have been simple. However, forgetting Aeron would have been something else altogether. It would be all but impossible.

There is only one clear choice, he thought as he took the path to the village square. He knew Aeron had had a very long night, and he wanted to see about scaring up something for her to eat before she woke.

Stepping into the village square, Orrin saw the same woman he'd recognized the previous night now setting bowls of fruit onto the tables and struggling with a squirming baby tied to her waist.

"Here, let me help you," Orrin said as he ran over, taking the bowl from her hands just before it slipped out of her grasp.

"Thank you, sir," she said with a bright smile.

The battered woman he'd seen before in Oaksbridge was gone, and he began to wonder if it was the same person.

"My name is Orrin," he said with a nod.

"Thank you, Orrin. I'm Lenore, and this is little Sarah," she said, cooing at the child.

"Forgive me, Lenore, but I feel as if I've seen you someplace. Have you ever been to Oaksbridge?" he asked.

"Aye," the woman said, nodding, "born and raised, and I'd still be in that pit if it wasn't for the Captain. She freed me."

"Really? How so, if you don't mind my asking?"

The woman weighed her words carefully before she spoke. "Not all men are as kind as my Peter," she said, gazing over at the blacksmith who pounded away on a piece of iron. "My former husband was a horribly cruel man who met a very deserving end. However, he left me and our son with no money and a pile of debt," she said, adjusting the baby she held. "Aeron assisted me in getting his debts paid and offered me and my son a life here on the island."

"You left everything in Oaksbridge? What of your family, do you not miss them?"

"I had no family to miss, sir. Cormac saw to that as soon as he purchased me from my father." She looked around the village square at all the people starting to mill about and prepare for the morning meal. "This is my family now."

In a strange way, Orrin knew exactly what she meant.

He hurried back to the cottage with a plate full of food and found the bed was empty and the back door slightly ajar. Setting the plate down on the settee, he headed out the door and down the path to the lagoon.

As he broke the trees, he saw Aeron standing on a rock in front of the waterfall, washing her hair. He gazed longingly at her naked body. The scars that striped her back seemed to melt away in his mind's eye, and all he saw was perfection, a slice of heaven right here on earth. She stepped into the waterfall to rinse the soap, and he shed his clothes and dove into the pool.

Aeron heard someone dive into the lagoon behind her as she emerged from underneath the rushing water of the fall. She quickly submerged herself up to her shoulders and scanned the waters around her for the miscreant invading her bath. Her heart stopped when she saw Orrin's hard, wet body crest the water, breaking the surface like a magnificent dolphin.

"What are you doing in here?" she called across the water. An odd sense of modesty got the better of her, and she crossed her arms in front of herself.

"I believe I owe you a bath," Orrin said, smiling as he slowly swam toward her, the rich baritone of his voice resonating off the water and into her body.

Aeron started to back up toward the rocks behind her as he moved closer and looked for a means of escape. "Where are your trousers?" she asked nervously as her back hit the rock behind her. She had nowhere else to go, and he was headed right for her.

"Over there, with your night dress," he said, glancing over to the large pile of clothing lying on the rocks along the shore.

Before Aeron could even think of what she could do, Orrin was there, rising to his full height right in front of her, crystal beads of water glistening off his chest.

Aeron had been with many men in her day. Seduced them and taken them to her bed without a second thought. But now she was the one being seduced, and the idea thrilled her, making her heart race like never before. It also frightened the hell out of her, especially with a man she couldn't resist such as this one.

Orrin leaned forward and stared down into her eyes as he picked up the soap from the rock. "Turn around," he said in a husky voice, twirling his finger in the air as she'd done to him the day before.

Aeron froze, suddenly very aware of the dark red scars across her back. "No," she said, shaking her head. "I don't want to play anymore."

She pulled her mouth into an uncomfortable line as she sank back against the stone and tried to move away from him any way she could. She was beginning to panic as she had never done before.

"Don't you trust me?" he asked. Aeron averted her gaze, refusing to answer or even look at him. "Aeron, you can trust me. Please turn around."

She frowned uncomfortably and bit her bottom lip, shaking her head. "No, I can't," she said. "I don't want you to…" Her voice trailed off as she struggled with herself, trying desperately not to cry in front of him.

"This is about Queen Winifred, isn't it?" he asked as he placed a gentle hand on her cheek and wiped away a tear that had escaped.

Again, Aeron couldn't say anything in response; she just stared down at the water. Her shoulders immediately tensed, and all of her confidence melted away at the mere mention of the Queen.

"My God, Aeron, what on earth did she do to you?"

Aeron's bottom lip trembled as tears rolled freely down her face. Her time in service of Queen Winifred was something she rarely spoke of. The horror Aeron had endured in the palace would haunt her for all of her days and was only known by one other person: Darcy.

But there was something about Orrin. For someone whose lot in life was to end hers, she felt oddly safe with him, and for reasons she couldn't place, she trusted him. She glanced up and saw the hurt on his face. It reflected her own on some level, and she couldn't shake the feeling that, God's knew why, he genuinely cared.

"She let me live," Aeron said.

The tall barriers she had built around herself began to crack as Orrin closed his arms around her, pulling her close and stroking her hair, comforting her. His arms were warm and welcoming as he held her tightly, rocking her as he sprinkled her hair with tender kisses. Aeron felt innately protected. For once, she allowed her body to unclench and sank fully into his embrace, sobbing against his shoulder.

She wasn't certain how long they'd been holding each other, but when Aeron finally calmed, it was a calm like she'd never known before.

"I brought you breakfast," Orrin said as he pulled back and kissed the back of each of her hands.

"Thank you," she said quietly.

"Go on, get your things." He nodded to the clothes on the rock.

Aeron could feel that uncomfortable feeling creep up her back again. She didn't want to tell him she was afraid for him to see her right now, that she couldn't bear for him to look at her bare back in the bright morning sun. But she didn't have to.

"I'll turn around," he said as he turned his back to her.

She was certain any other man would have feasted his eyes on her naked flesh, welcomed to or not. Aeron's heart melted like ice on the hot sand at this simple gesture of kindness.

William had left the island at first light that morning and rowed all day, pulling the oars through the water over and over again. His rage and jealousy were the driving forces that kept him going, even at such a slow pace, long after his body wanted to stop.

Just when the sun was about to sink into the ocean, he heard a voice in the distance. Turning in the wooden seat, he saw a brig bobbing in the water. It could very well have been his mind playing tricks on him because he'd been rowing in the hot sun without a drop of water or a bite of food since dawn. His eyes squinted against the setting sun, and he saw a person on the deck waving wildly and shouting, "Ahoy!"

He pushed past the pain in his arms and the rumbling in his belly as he rowed toward the vessel. "You will be sorry you ever turned me away, Aeron," he said.

Kale was sitting below deck when someone yanked the door to his cabin open.

"There's a boat in the distance, sir," the crewman said. "The Captain returns."

That was oddly fast, Kale thought. Orrin was a man of skill when it came to hunting scoundrels down, but Kale hadn't expected to see him for at least another day.

He climbed up to the deck as the man perched in the crow's nest shouted down, "It's not the Captain, sir!"

"Well then, who the hell is it, Gerard?" Kale called up to him. Watching Gerard look through the telescope again, Kale heard his lookout mutter something about not touching the likes of liquor again.

"Well?" Kale called again, growing impatient.

"You're not going to believe it, sir, but it looks like the prince!" Gerard hollered.

Kale grabbed the closest telescope he could find and peered through it. This was something he needed to see with his own eyes.

"What the bloody hell?" he said in disbelief.

The man in the dinghy clearly looked like His Royal Highness, or at least a dehydrated version of him.

Iona's crew pulled Prince William aboard, and all of the men gave him a respectful bow. His naturally blond hair looked stark white against the sunburned flesh of his face, his lips cracked and blistering. A scrawny cabin boy shoved his way through the crew, offering His Highness a full bag of water.

"Your Highness," Kale said with a bow of his head as Will greedily drank from the sack, "it is an honor to have you aboard —"

"I require you to take me to my home port," William croaked, cutting Kale off. "This instant."

Kale looked around at the men before addressing the Prince again. "We would be happy to, Your Highness. However, we have a man on that island, my brother Orrin, the captain of this vessel."

"Your brother is gone," William said dismissively, wiping water off his chin with the back of his arm.

"Orrin…" Kale said, staggering back. "My brother is dead?"

"No," Will answered, "it's far worse. He has been bewitched by that she-pirate, Aeron. I know how strong her hold on him is, for I was captivated by her as well. She has him and all of her men under her spell."

Kale and the crew stood staring at him in disbelief, their mouths agape at what they'd just heard.

"What the devil are you waiting for?" Will bellowed in agitation. "Make haste before she tires of your brother and casts him out as she did with me. Take me to port so we can devise a plan to take that island and the sea witch that calls it home!"

Kale nodded woodenly, his mouth suddenly going very dry. Something about William's tale did not set right with him, but he could not place what it was. He wanted to stay and launch an attack on the island, but he was bound by His Royal Highness's wishes.

"Make port!" Kale called to his men as he bound across the deck toward the helm. If he was going to save his brother, it would have to be this way.

Chapter Eight

There was a new member of their pirate family, and the entire village was preparing for an evening of celebration to welcome Darcy and Catrin's new son, Owen.

It had taken a fair amount of cajoling from Catrin—and an order from Aeron—to convince Darcy to stay inside for the day to take care of his wife and their new babe. Orrin could see that Darcy was a proud man and disliked the idea of shirking his duties as a member of the community. What made matters worse, Orrin himself would be stepping in and doing Darcy's work for him. That had put an even nastier scowl on Darcy's face, and even though he'd argued, in the end he relented.

"Damned women," Darcy said. He scooped up the baby, and Orrin laughed to himself as he overheard Darcy lecturing his new babe. "My first lesson to you, my son, is don't try to argue with women. They always win."

With Darcy settled, more or less, Orrin followed one of the many winding paths that led to and from the heart of the island and headed to the shore where twenty of the largest men he'd ever seen were hauling in nets of fish for festivities. Though Aeron's second-in-command had put up one hell of a fight about Orrin taking his place, Orrin was more than happy to lend a hand. He figured the best way to find out more about Aeron was through her men.

He arrived on the shore and saw Gael, the large bald man Orrin had encountered in the small hut. If he was being honest, Orrin was not looking forward to working side by side with him. Their last and only encounter resulted in Orrin lying flat on his back and bloodied from a sound arse-whooping.

"What are you doing here? Where's Darcy?" Gael asked as he peered down his nose at Orrin.

Orrin swallowed back the memory of having been flung into a wall by this very man standing before him, who looked larger-than-life and stared Orrin square in the eye as he crossed his arms over his massive chest menacingly. Orrin squared his shoulders, looked Gael in the eye, and stood his ground.

"He is with his family," Orrin stated, picking up a length of rope near his feet. "I'll be taking his place today."

"By whose order?"

"Your captain."

Gael twisted his features as he eyed Orrin up and down, seeming to size up whether his lean build was up to the task. "Very well," he snorted, slapping Orrin on the back and nearly knocking him over. "Try not to get tangled up in the rope and pulled into the ocean, hunter." Gael took up his length of rope. "The captain would skin me alive if you wound up dead…or worse."

With determination setting his brow, Orrin dug in his heels, and he managed to keep up with Gael and the others. It had been a long time since Orrin had put in a good day's worth of hard labor like this. Granted, he worked side by side with his men on *Iona*, but hauling a sail up and bringing in a net full of fish were two entirely different kinds of work. Even steering his ship through a vicious storm didn't break his back like this did.

They worked until dusk, hauling in the nets and cleaning and gutting the fish for the feast. It was solid work, and Orrin made the most of it. In that time working side by side with her men, he learned a great deal about Aeron.

He learned the ships she and her crew conquered were sailed or towed back to the village and stripped down for utilization. Every cottage and the tables in the square were constructed from decks, and the tents and tarps made from sails. No piece of a vessel went to waste—she'd even devised a rope and pulley system in the trees using old crow's nest baskets for picking fruit and keeping watch over the island.

He learned of how she would spread what they had in excess, gold and treasures, to those who needed it to trade for food in the nearby ports and on the mainland.

Moreover, he learned that she took in those who had nowhere else to go. He knew these things to be true from talking to Lenore this morning. He'd even spoken with several men who'd escaped the slavery of the palace and taken asylum on the island, giving them purpose once again. Everyone who lived there had a task, a duty, even the children. The entire village was a true community, a family. Every one of them would lay down their lives for her, without a moment's hesitation.

By the end of the day, his back ached, his hands hurt, and he smelled to the heavens of fish and God knows what else. He was allowed to walk with the men to a large lagoon where they went to bathe. En route, he almost collided with young Maura, knocking a bundle of clothing out of her hands. Orrin scooped up the garments and dusted them off, happy to finally see a friendly face.

"I'm terribly sorry. Maura, right?" he asked as he began handing the bundle back to her.

She nodded her head with a giggle and pushed the clothing back at him. "Yes, Maura is correct, and these are for you. The Captain asked me to bring them to you," she said with a wink. She was a sprightly young lady, with eyes full of life and wonder, and her spirit reminded Orrin of his sister, Iona.

"Did she now?" Orrin asked as he pulled the string off of the tied bundle. He found his black trousers had been laundered, and there was another fresh shirt, folded neatly into a pile. But it was something on the shirt lapel that caught his eye, a pair of blue whale fins embroidered on each side of the collar. "This is beautiful work, Maura. Did you do this?"

"Part of it." She smiled, tucking a piece of mahogany hair behind her ear. "I made the shirt, but the Captain did the embroidery this afternoon." Orrin traced his index finger over the delicate blue thread. "You should have seen her," Maura said, leaning forward as if she were sharing a grand secret. "She picked every piece of thread out herself, making sure it was just the right color."

"The right color?"

"Yes," Maura said, nodding, "to match your eyes."

"Thank you, sweet Maura," Orrin said, his heart clenching so tight in his chest that he felt it just might burst straight through his ribs. "It has been an honor to be in the presence of a lady such as yourself." He grasped her hand and pressed a gentle kiss to her knuckles. With a sweeping bow, he then turned to find his way to the lagoon to wash the fish stench off himself, leaving a giggling Maura in his wake.

Orrin spent more time bathing and dressing than he ever had before in making sure he'd sufficiently rid himself of fish smell and that he looked acceptable for Aeron. His mind kept wandering to the way she smiled and the sweet feeling of her lips against his. He hoped that he would have the opportunity to kiss her again, this night and every night after.

As he walked into the village center, the many tables were beautifully decorated with flowers wrapped in brightly colored ribbons, and it appeared as if everyone in the square dressed in their best clothes for this wondrous occasion. Every face exuded such joy and happiness that the air practically filled with it and warmed Orrin's soul, and he couldn't help but smile. The only thing missing was Aeron.

The festivities were in full swing, with plenty of music and dancing and echoes of rich laughter, when Orrin swept his gaze across the square.

There she was, Aeron, ducking out of the path that led to her cottage. She was stunning. Her gown was the same shade of blue as the embroidery on his shirt, but modest, nothing fancy or courtly; it wouldn't have been her way. Her fiery red hair was loose from its normal braid and flowed down her back, the sides swept up and anchored with two small silver combs.

She smiled at him from across the way, and he almost clutched his chest. He had traveled the seas from one side of the world to the other and had seen things of great and staggering beauty, but he was certain he had never laid eyes on a more beautiful sight, dreaming or awake, as what he beheld before him now.

Go to her, a voice inside his head prodded him.

He desperately wanted to, but wasn't certain he could make his feet move.

As if fate itself was working with him, a villager brushed passed him, giving him the momentum to finally move from the spot where he stood ogling her.

Once Orrin's feet were in motion, they carried him through the maze of tables and benches and right to Aeron. He stopped in front of her and took a ragged breath, his mouth gaping open as he shook his head at her, stunned into silence by her ravishing beauty.

The brilliant smile melted from Aeron's face. "You don't like it," she said, casting her eyes away for a moment before she gathered the skirts in her hands and turned on her heel. "I never should have worn a goddamned dress," she muttered as she started to walk away.

Orrin caught her wrist before she could bolt from him. "No, please," he pled, "it's just…" He raked his eyes over her body and pulled her closer. "I've never seen anyone so beautiful."

She glanced down, a blush dancing across her face.

Curling a finger under her chin, he raised her gaze back to his.

Aeron drew in a labored breath as Orrin's eyes met hers, and he lifted her fingers to his lips and placed a kiss on the back of her hand.

The gesture appeared to fluster Aeron, and he was certain she wasn't accustomed to being treated like a lady.

To put her more at ease, Orrin gestured toward the dinner table where their friends were seated. They dined on the fish they had caught, the roasted wild boar they had cooked in a pit underground, a multitude of native island fruit, and more jugs of wine and rum than Orrin could keep track of, especially with Aeron distracting him with her very presence.

Orrin sat and watched as Aeron walked over to a beaming Darcy and held the new little baby in her arms, carefully cradling him as if he were her own. She bent her face to place a gentle kiss on his little nose. There was a gleam in her eyes just then as she held the child that he was certain wasn't there before. A sudden thought startled him, but at the same time the idea felt natural and almost calming. A child, with Aeron. A girl. A sweet, red-headed little angel with his blue eyes and her glorious smile. *Yes, that would do nicely,* he thought.

Their eyes met across the square for a moment, and the smile she gave him made him wonder if she felt the same.

One thing he knew: falling in love with Aeron was definitely not in his plan.

Aeron carefully handed the baby back to Darcy and headed straight for Orrin, mesmerizing him with her grace and fluidity. Time seemed to slow to a crawl as she floated across the square, the hem of her skirt ghosting over the ground. Along her path, she passed no one without the acknowledgment of a smile or delicate incline of her head.

She stopped directly in front of him and took his hands in hers. "Stay with me tonight?" she whispered into his ear as she leaned in and planted a kiss on his chin.

The smallest hint of a smile teased at the corners of his mouth. "I thought I was to stay with Darcy and his family," he replied.

"You were." Aeron nodded. "But they have the baby now and…" Her eyes danced over his features, and she seemed to momentarily lose her train of thought. "And I…I…"

Orrin leaned in closer, as if he was trying to hear more clearly. "And you what?" he asked her, teasingly, inhaling her warm breath as it washed over him.

"Make love to me, Orrin." She pressed her cheek to his.

He would have assumed she was intoxicated, but he knew for a fact that she hadn't had a drop of wine or rum all evening. With one quick glance around, Orrin noticed that all of the villagers' attention was centered on the new family member.

"I thought you'd never ask," he breathed. He took Aeron by the hand, slipping away unnoticed as he led her to her cottage.

Aeron and Orrin didn't speak as they wound down the path. They were afraid even to breathe, terrified that everything would blow away like a dream in the night right before their eyes.

When they approached the cottage, Aeron stepped inside and moved to snuff out the candles in the room.

"No, please leave them," Orrin said before she could squelch a single light.

Aeron stopped where she stood, her vulnerable back turned to him. Her fingertips curled over the top of her shoulder as she hugged herself in uncertainty. She'd been with countless men in her career as a pirate and never thought twice about the marks that crisscrossed her entire back. Yet she didn't want Orrin to see this part of her; she didn't want to spoil the allure of her beauty with the hideous truth that ran across her back.

"Aeron, please, you can trust me," he said, wrapping his arms around her waist and nuzzling his face against the back of her neck.

"They look repulsive," Aeron said solemnly. "It's better with no light."

"No, they don't," he said as he slid the blue fabric of her dress over her shoulder. "They're part of you." He kissed her exposed shoulder, where the slightest hint of a pink line whispered over her skin. "Trust me, please?"

Her body tensed under his touch. She took a long, deep breath and released it slowly. "I trust you."

Backing up slightly, Orrin pulled the ties that secured the back of her gown. He loosened the laces just enough to allow Aeron to pull her arms free of the sleeves as she held the bodice in place.

He began to caress the top portion of her back, from one shoulder to the other. With her eyes squeezed shut, she steeled herself for his reaction, waiting for Orrin to finally see her scars. She listened closely for his gasp of horror, but there came none. Only sweet kisses as he traveled the length and width of her back. He slid the dress down an inch at a time, lavishing each newly exposed sliver of bare flesh with kisses and slow swipes of his tongue. When Orrin placed the last tender kiss at the base of her spine, Aeron turned to face him. Her gown still hung at her waist, and she looked at him with wonder. Tears filled her eyes and spilled down her cheeks as her mouth opened and closed to say words she couldn't seem to utter.

He cupped her face in his hands and wiped the tears away with his thumbs. "You are so beautiful, every part of you," he said as he peppered her face with kisses.

"You're insane." Aeron choked out on a sob, shaking her head.

"Only when it pertains to you."

With a newfound sense of confidence, Aeron slid her gown and undergarments off her body and stood naked in front of him.

Orrin looked her bare flesh up and down, and Aeron could see his breathing accelerate. Before she could speak, he scooped her up into his arms. Whirling around on his heel, Orrin strode across the room and set her down on the bed. He licked his lips hungrily, tracing the line of her body with his fingertip as he stepped away from the bed.

Aeron's chest heaved with desire as he began to undress for her, captivated by every move that he made. She noticed that as he pulled his shirt over his head, he moved slowly, deliberately, a wicked smirk gracing his perfectly carved mouth while he pulled at the ties of his breeches. The surface of Aeron's skin prickled, her nerve endings sizzled, and she literally shook with need for him as he slipped his hands into his trousers and swiftly slid them off his slim hips with one fluid motion.

A light sheen of perspiration covered his body and glistened in the candlelight, accentuating the long, lean lines of his taut abdomen as he stood proudly at the foot of the bed.

He was male perfection incarnate.

She watched brazenly as he crawled up onto the mattress, lowering his head and dropping open-mouthed kisses along the tender, smooth flesh on the inside of her leg. His lips were so soft, so close, suckling the skin of her inner thigh while his strong hands curled around her hips and he moved up her body.

Aeron quivered as he gave her one salacious lick after another, coaxing her legs father apart. He stopped briefly, pausing to dip his tongue into her navel before he made his way up her belly. His hands crawled across her flesh, reaching for her breasts, squeezing them, rolling her nipples between his nimble fingers, making her gasp loudly and arch her back into his touch. She reached down and sank her hands into his silky hair, crying out in pleasure as he wrapped his warm lips around one of her rosy buds.

As he continued to move his body over hers, she slid her hands down over his back. She could feel the muscles in his shoulders flex, his biceps tense under her fingertips, and his steely erection pressed against her center.

She watched his face as he loomed over her, drawing his bottom lip between his teeth as he stared down at her and entered her, slowly, inch by agonizingly pleasurable inch.

Aeron gripped his back and pressed her hips up into his, begging him to take her in a manner she was accustomed to…a wild, savage rut.

"No," Orrin breathed, his lip twitching as he sat still inside of her. "I want you to feel me," he rasped, rolling his head back with a sigh as he pushed into her completely. "Feel *me*."

Aeron's soul, which had been numb for so long, sprang back to life as Orrin began to roll his hips forward and back at a slow, measured pace. Her body enveloped him easily, caressing his length from base to tip like rich velvet. She breathed his name as his hands roamed up and down her body, and he moved in and out of her lazily, like the tides of the ocean washing up on the shore.

Her mouth gaped open, gasping for air, whimpering a semblance of his name as he picked up the pace of his thrusting. She gripped his firm backside, her fingers squeezing hard with the need for more, driving her hips to meet his as she teetered on the edge of complete and total ecstasy. Aeron felt his hand slide deftly between them, his fingers brushing over the jewel at her thighs' apex. Her body began to quake, and her eyes fluttered back in her head with pleasure.

Aeron's nails scraped across his back as every thrust brought her to a higher plane of orgasmic ecstasy. She squeezed and gripped him as he slid in and out of her until his control evidently snapped and he started moving faster, harder, deeper. She heard him curse and grunt under his breath, and she felt the muscles in his body coil like springs beneath his skin.

Aeron watched his climax overtake him: his eyes closed, and his lips pursed together on the push in and opened with a breath on the retreat. The corner of his mouth twitched up as he started to come down. She'd seen more than her share of men lose themselves in bliss before, but none of them had managed to look as beautiful as the sight before her.

Orrin's body collapsed on hers, and Aeron welcomed the weight as he wrapped his arms around her like a cocoon and buried his face in her neck. She heard him deeply inhale her scent as he lavished kisses along her collarbone.

Aeron closed her eyes, pulling her fingers through his hair and stroking down his sweat-covered back. A slow, content smile spread across her face.

"My love," she whispered.

They spent the remainder of the evening lying on their sides and simply gazing at one another until there were only a few candles that continued to burn in the room, casting a dim light on their naked bodies.

Orrin rose up onto his elbow and traced the lines of her body, feeding the gnawing urge just to touch her skin again. His finger slipped down over her hip onto the top of her thigh where he slid his finger into the indentation of a scar. This one was nothing like the ones across her back; it was clearly from a puncture wound of some kind, and she didn't seem to try to hide it like she did the others.

"Dagger?" he asked, rubbing across the thin, shiny skin.

"Yes." She nodded and turned her hip toward him, showing the back of her thigh where a mark half its size branded the other side of her leg. "The tip went straight through," she said. Her tone had an air of pride to it when she spoke; this was clearly something she considered a badge of honor. "When Darcy and I took over our first ship, there were members of the crew that didn't take kindly to being led by a woman. Some spoke of their unease while my back was turned, but most of them stayed quiet out of fear of Darcy," she said, her brow creasing with irritation as she recounted the events. "This coward crouched in a dark corner of the ship and waited for me. He attacked and tried to subdue me and have his way. When I fought back, he thought he could take me out by stabbing me in the leg with a dagger, that I'd go down quietly." She laughed, shaking her head as she recalled the incident.

"What did you do?"

"I pulled out the blade, of course." Aeron shrugged. "And then I buried it into his heart, to the hilt." She rolled onto her back, pulled her hair over her shoulder, and splayed it across her chest, arranging it neatly around her breasts. "There was no more trouble from the crew after that."

Orrin raised his hand and pointed. "See there." He nodded to his raised hand as Aeron grasped it to inspect the practically invisible scar on his finger. Giving her a sideways glance, he saw her concern and added, "From my mother's spinning wheel when I was five."

"God, you are a miserable bastard, do you know that? I thought you were serious," Aeron said as she playfully shoved at his chest.

Orrin laughed as he pulled her into his embrace and held her tightly. She made a good show of attempting to struggle against his strong grip before she gave up and nuzzled against him, inhaling deeply. He eased up his hold on her and stroked her back, leisurely tracing his fingers over the thick marks that ran across it. Within moments, Aeron's body went limp, and her breathing fell into a pattern as she drifted off to sleep.

Aeron's dreams were filled with things of her past, things she hadn't thought about in years. Memories she'd locked away tightly.

Pain licked at her back. She was feeling the sting of the barbed cat-o'-nine-tails again, she realized, as if she were in the middle of that hell all over again. Her eyes washed over the nightmare, the purgatory she'd inhabited for a portion of her life. One thing was different, however, something that wasn't there in reality, a presence in the distance. Orrin.

She fixated on him, on his image and the memory of what they'd just shared. The pain started to melt away, and the horror around her dissipated like an apparition until all that was left was the two of them, standing alone in her room.

Aeron awoke with Orrin's arms curled around her protectively, as if he knew what she needed, even in his slumber. She buried her face into the crook of his arm and wept at the warmth she felt in her heart for him.

She was going to have to tell him the truth, sooner rather than later. As much as she wanted to swallow the past, something inside her that she couldn't explain knew that Orrin was her only chance at true peace. He would understand. He had to.

Chapter Nine

eron slid out from under Orrin's arm and began to ready herself for the day. She couldn't stop sneaking glances at his reflection in the mirror and the way the bright morning sun shone on his sleeping face. She watched the way he blinked into the light, his half-open eyes searching the room for her. A lazy smile stretched across his face when he finally found her standing there pulling on her trousers. Her body quivered as he stretched across the bed, the shape of his nude form moving over her sheets before he rose and strode over to her.

"You're not getting dressed, are you?" he asked against the back of her neck, wrapping his hands around hers to stop her from dressing. The morning scruff on his chin tickled her skin.

Giggling like a girl was not a common practice of hers, but she'd been finding herself doing it more and more with Orrin around. She caught their reflection in her long mirror: Orrin stood behind her, trying his best to undo the laces of her breeches as soon as she could get them tied. She was thankful that she couldn't see the reflection of his naked backside, for that might have persuaded her to give in, and it was all she could do to keep her thoughts about her as it was. *Damn this man,* she thought.

"Orrin, stop, I have to get dressed," she said grudgingly.

"Not if you come back to bed." He nipped at her neck.

She bit her lip and enjoyed the feeling of his warm mouth on her skin for one more moment as she turned and wrapped her arms around his waist. "I'm the captain of this isle, and I have business to attend to. However, I will need some assistance in my bath tonight." She gave a saucy wink and reached down to grab a healthy handful of his bottom.

"Very well, tonight every inch of your body will know my touch, and my tongue," he said, the most devilish of grins plastered on his face as she felt the backs of his fingers dragging along the side of her breast. Her body thrummed, and she watched him saunter over to his clothes and pull them on.

"Can I ask you something?" he asked as he tugged his shirt over his head.

"Of course." She nodded, picking up her sword and belt. "I may not answer, but you may *ask* me anything."

Orrin pulled on his trousers. "I've yet to see a ship anywhere along the shores of this island."

"That's not a question," she replied with a wink.

Orrin stood and started to pace the room. "Lenore's little boy, Felix, took me up into the trees yesterday and showed me the entire island."

"That's still not a question."

"Blast it all! Where in God's name do you keep your ship, woman?"

Aeron laughed at his frustration and tied on her belt. "That is a very good question," she said as she slid her sword into its scabbard, "and it's good that you finally spit it out, because that is where we are going today, if you can keep up." Without another word, Aeron flung the door open.

"Damn bloody pirate," she heard him mutter as she headed down the path to the village.

Aeron stepped into the square, watching as the people went about their morning. She spied Darcy speaking with one of their crewmen, Brendon. When the two men saw their captain, they immediately made their way over to her.

"Brendon just informed me that William found the boat," Darcy said only loudly enough for her ears to hear as he took his seat next to her.

"Good, let's hope the dumb bastard found his way back to Orrin's ship." She filled her cup.

"Aye, he left yesterday morn," Brendon said, looking around the village and scratching his dirty chin.

"Excellent," Aeron replied, casually taking a drink and looking around the square for Orrin. "Now let's see if he goes running back to Mother. Good work, Brendon."

"Yes, now go take a bath, for God's sake," Darcy chided him as he clapped the man on the back. "You stink to high heaven."

When the crewman headed off, Aeron saw Orrin emerge from the jungle. Darcy screwed up his face as he stood and excused himself from her company. Aeron shook her head at her surly first mate as she rose to check in on Catrin in her nearby cottage.

"You look very well this morning," Catrin said with a weary but knowing smile. "Have a good night's rest, did you?"

"Indeed," Aeron said. Color rose up her neck and burned her cheeks. She gingerly sat on the edge of the bed and took Catrin's hands in hers. "I've truly never been this happy. I don't know how I know it, but he is my peace, Catrin. I can feel it in my very soul."

"I know," Catrin said with a nod. "I think we can all feel it as well."

Not a moment later, Orrin knocked at the cottage door. "Good morning, Catrin," he said with an enormous smile. "You look very well. How are you faring on this glorious day?"

"Wonderfully, thank you." Catrin beamed, cuddling baby Owen close to her. "The boy does nothing but eat and sleep."

"Just like his father," Aeron added as Darcy stepped in the door and pushed past Orrin to take the seat in the chair on the other side of the bed. He briefly groused at Aeron, and she could tell he was swallowing his pride just to be next to his family. She watched his face soften as he reached over and gently stroked his infant son's head.

Orrin stared in wonder as Darcy interacted with his newborn infant. This was the first time he had really seen this giant of a man show any hint of tenderness. He'd heard many a tale about Darcy over the years, and had seen his handiwork with his own eyes on more than one occasion. But he could also see why Aeron had so much love and trust for this fiercely loyal person.

As Orrin looked around the village he was still stunned at how things were there. Every man, woman, and child had stopped their tasks—save for the ones keeping watch—to eat as a community. It reminded him of his home before the pirate raid, and he thought this was a practice he could get accustomed to.

What the bloody hell was he saying? He couldn't stay here. He had a ship and a crew that needed him. Once he learned the truth about the Queen from Aeron he would—

The sound of Aeron's laughter filled the square. Her eyes shone brilliantly, sparkling bits of blue and green.

Dear God, give me the strength to do what is right.

After they'd eaten their morning meal, Orrin walked with Aeron into the jungle. She moved briskly, pushing vines and branches out of the way. As he took in the scenery, Orrin couldn't tell if they were getting deeper into the wilderness or coming out of it. He wondered for half a moment if she was leading him into a trap, into the thick of the island only to leave him to die.

But he shook the thought from his head. He hadn't heard her tell anyone where they were going, and his skin tingled at the thought of being alone with her on her ship. His gaze traveling the body of the woman before him, Orrin watched her move from behind; the gentle sway of her hips and the absolute certainty behind every step she took made his heart pound in his chest.

Aeron glanced over her shoulder at him, as if she could feel his blatant appraisal of her form. Her eyes sparked a ravenous and hedonistic fire at him before she took off running through the tropical wilderness, dodging and ducking through the greenery.

Orrin, more than eager to lay chase, attempted to follow her as quickly as he could. But as he was not at all familiar with his surroundings, he promptly smashed face-first into a low-lying branch and fell to the ground with a dull thud. He heard her immediately skid to a stop and rush over to where he lay, clutching his nose and groaning in pain.

"Are you all right?" she asked as she knelt at his side.

Peeking through his fingers, Orrin saw the amusement in her eyes, as well as genuine concern. He almost felt bad for what he was about to do.

Almost.

Orrin whipped his hand around her waist and rolled Aeron under him, pinning her to the jungle floor. "Oh, I'm quite fine," he assured as he settled his hips over hers. "How are you?" He leaned down and started to kiss along her exposed collarbone.

The feeling of her body underneath his and the taste of her flesh against his tongue was beyond delicious. Hell, he'd be content to spend the rest of the day with her underneath him…and on top of him.

As if reading his mind, her arms curled around his neck, and she tossed a long, lean leg around his waist. Orrin groaned in pleasure as she lifted her hips and pressed against his body. The next thing he knew, she gripped him with her thighs and turned him onto his back with one swift, smooth motion.

"Nice try," she purred into his ear, and before he could gain his bearings, Aeron leapt to her feet and continued walking along the path.

Orrin pounded the ground with his fists in frustration while he watched her stride away.

God blessed devil woman.

"We're almost to the ship. You should really pick your arse up off of the ground before a snake slithers up your trousers," she called over her shoulder.

At the mention, he popped up off the ground like he was spring-loaded, scanning the ground for any slithery reptiles. "You're going to pay for that, woman," he called.

"Indeed, I'm counting on that," she replied with a waggle of her brow as she led him to the edge of the jungle near the coast.

They started up the slope of a hill that appeared to overlook the ocean. When they reached the top, Aeron stopped at an opening in the ground near her feet where there was a length of rope tied off to a large rock. She picked up the thick line and gave him a wink.

"Follow me," she said as she disappeared through the hole in the earth.

"What the devil?" Orrin wondered out loud as he walked to the edge. He looked into the hole just as Aeron's feet set down into the crow's nest of a mighty ship. "Clever pirate," he said, picking up the rope.

As he lowered himself down, he noticed the mouth of the cave. It opened right out into the ocean, and he imagined that, if the tide was right, the magnificent vessel could shoot out into the island lagoon like an iron ball out of a cannon.

He shimmied down the mast and touched down onto the deck of Aeron's galleon, taking in the sight around him. This was the most beautiful vessel he'd ever seen, including the monstrosities the Queen employed in her Navy.

Orrin watched silently as Aeron approached the railing and whispered to it as she gently stroked her fingers along the sturdy oak. She then bent her head to the railing and kissed it, embracing it as if were flesh and bone, born of her own blood. He'd never seen so much love for a craft in all his days. He loved his ship, make no mistake, but there was a bond Aeron had with her galleon that transcended captain and vessel; they were one.

"She is beautiful," Orrin said, sliding his hand up the sturdy mast. "Nearly as beautiful as her captain."

Aeron ducked her head and turned her back to him as a blush stained her cheeks.

Orrin's blood zinged and skin prickled with delight every time he caught sight of the effect he could have on Aeron. A smile, a dusting of pink in her cheeks, a giggle, a sigh—all of these things made him want to tear out his heart and serve it to her on a silver platter to do with as she pleased.

After the heartache of his wife Helena's unfaithfulness and the loss of his beloved family, it almost pained him to admit that it was a pirate awakening feelings within his soul that he had assumed long dead.

"What is she called?" Orrin asked as he strode across the deck, leaning against the railing next to her.

"The *Mermaid,*" Aeron replied, her fingers absentmindedly tracing the mermaid engraved in the leather of the scabbard dangling at her side. "When Darcy and I commandeered her five years ago, she was in such disrepair I was surprised she managed to stay afloat." Aeron wandered across the deck. "I suppose any other would-be captain would have left her and found a more suitable means of transport, but there was something about her, something in her soul that spoke to me, and I couldn't leave her to die."

"Her soul?"

"Yes," Aeron answered with a nod. "I suppose you think that's as ludicrous as Darcy did."

Orrin smiled. "On the contrary, my father used to speak of his ship the same way," he said. "He used say she was his mistress, a love second only to Mother."

"I completely understand that."

Aeron took Orrin around the entire ship, pointing out all she had done to turn the sinking wreck into a mighty galleon fit for the most ferocious of pirates. They gathered the few items they'd come aboard for and headed back to the village while the sun was still high in the sky.

They were quiet as they walked through the jungle. Orrin glanced over at Aeron and saw the strong and proud woman walking next to him, all the while thinking of the trembling girl she'd become in the lagoon the other morning, vulnerable and petrified. He thought about how he'd held her in her sleep, how he'd silently tried to count her scars, but there were so many that they all overlapped and merged into one mass of marred flesh. He wanted to confront her so badly, but he had to be patient. When she was ready, she would talk to him. He could feel it in his gut so held on to that. When she was ready to talk to him, he'd be there for her.

Chapter Ten

eron and Orrin reached the village when the sun had just passed its highest point, and Aeron saw Darcy was pacing like a cat, waiting for her return. With a sharp flick of his head, he signaled to Aeron that he needed to speak with her, and that it was of the utmost urgency.

She immediately turned to Orrin and handed him the bundle she had carried from the ship. "Can you take this back to the cottage, please? I have some ship's business to attend to."

"Um, of course." Orrin nodded as he leaned over to kiss Aeron on the cheek. "You do know that if there is anything I can help with—"

"No," Aeron said, shaking her head, "not yet."

"Of course," Orrin said, smiling politely as he kissed her on the cheek. He took the bundle from her and headed down the path to her cottage.

With a heavy heart, she watched him lope out of her sight. His face had fallen when she'd dismissed him, and it almost buckled her. She so wanted to include him in her plans, but couldn't bring herself to do so, not yet.

Aeron walked with Darcy through the lush green jungle to the other side of the island, where her scout, Roderick, was sitting at a small table, wolfing down a plate of food as fast as he could. He hadn't eaten since the day before, when he'd set out to follow William rowing toward Orrin's ship.

Aeron pulled the chair out across from him and sat. "Well?" she asked, folding her hands on the table.

"Aye, Captain," Roderick said in his thick brogue, swallowing a large bite and nodding. "Their brig picked him up just beyond the horizon. They left for land like the Devil himself was at their stern."

"Very good." Aeron rose and clapped her scout on the shoulder. "You've done well, Roderick."

"It is an honor, Captain," he said with a nod of his head. "Anything to bring down Queen Winifred."

"We will bring her down, my friend," Aeron said with a reassuring pat on the back before she turned and headed out the door. "Even if it's the death of me."

As Aeron traipsed down the twisting path through the palm trees, pushing stray vines out of her way, she thought about Orrin. She smiled to herself as she remembered how many times she'd pictured him in her mind's eye, fantasizing about that shallow dimple in his chin. How she'd longed to kiss that one spot and the curve of his bottom lip. He had the most magnificent mouth, full, ripe and exquisitely shaped, and it tasted better than she could have ever dreamed it would. Ever since seeing him in Oaksbridge, she'd known she wanted a taste of the man whose beauty transcended the dark tavern atmosphere. Naturally, she had foreseen this physical attraction, but she'd never imagined she would feel the way she did about him.

Aeron arrived in the village square, and she half-expected to see Orrin sitting there, engaged in some lively conversation with one of the villagers, but he was nowhere in sight. She smiled as she made her way down the path to her cottage, hoping to find him lounging naked on her bed, but as she pushed the door open, she found the room was empty, as was the bed. Panic filled her, and she wondered if he'd finally seized the opportunity to flee until she spied the open back door.

Her heart thundered in her chest as she wandered down to her private lagoon. Would he be waiting for her, or had he simply taken this route for his escape? Worry, sadness, and anticipation wracked her body with every step she took as she wondered what she would find at the end of the trail—a sad, empty pool or one filled with wonder beyond her wildest dreams.

She closed her eyes as she stepped out into the open. She couldn't bear to see it if he wasn't waiting for her; the thought alone was all but devastating. The air felt lonely, and the only sound she heard was the churning of the waterfall. She swallowed the lump in her throat and steeled her nerves as she opened her eyes.

Her heart leapt in her chest when she saw Orrin smiling and staring back at her; he was already in the water.

"There you are," he said with only his head above the surface. "I was wondering if you'd changed your mind and found somewhere else to take your bath."

"I thought about it," Aeron lied, "but I would have come straight away had I known."

"Had you know what?" he asked.

"That you were already undressed," she said with a sultry pout, toeing her boot over the rocky shore. "I very much enjoy watching you take your clothes off."

Orrin swam to the ledge and pulled himself out of the water. "Fully clothed as per my lady's desire," he said with a sweeping gesture to the soaking clothes that clung to his body.

"How did you know?" Aeron was dumbfounded that he'd predicted what she would want.

Stalking toward her, he looked like a tiger about to pounce on its prey. His white shirt, turned practically transparent from the water, allowed her to see his tawny brown nipples, and the wet black cloth of his trousers accentuated every bit of manhood. He bent over and picked up the soap from a nearby rock as he moved closer, tossing it in the air and catching it again. He stood toe-to-toe with her and swept a lock of her long red hair behind her ear.

"I know you, Aeron" he said simply, his voice so smooth and rich. "Now, I believe I owe you a bath."

"Yes, you do," she said, confirming both statements with one answer. She was surprised how effortlessly those words fell from his lips and how easy they were for her to hear and accept.

He smiled at her as he tossed the soap over his shoulder and into the lagoon and began to strip his drenched shirt off. Aeron watched unabashedly, thoroughly enraptured by the movement of his finely sculpted muscle and the fabric that clung desperately to his flesh as he pulled it over his head. Her eyes were trained on his long, skilled fingers twisting around the ties of his trousers, and she raised a finger to the hollow of his throat.

"All day long, I've thought about you and how delicious you look when you're naked," she confessed.

The tight groan Orrin released as he wrapped his arm around her waist made her shiver. Aeron caught her breath when he pulled her body into his embrace, and his lips descended to her upturned mouth and kissed her hungrily, greedily consuming her.

She felt him gather her shirt in his hands as he tugged it over her head and tossed it away before he set to working the ties of her belt and trousers. Kneeling on the rocks in front of her, he slid her breeches down her legs, the tip of his tongue darting out to taste her skin as he stood before her.

Seizing him by the laces of his trousers, Aeron yanked the ties open hurriedly. She slid her hands down between the blazing hot skin of his hips and the cool wet fabric as she peeled the drenched clothing off his body. An excited squeal erupted from her as Orrin swung her up into his arms with one swift motion. The way his mouth curled up at the corners made her toes curl, and she couldn't help but think he looked like sin itself embodied in earthly human form.

He carried her into the water and set her on her feet as he picked up the floating bar of soap and commenced washing her thoroughly. His gentle touch was unlike anything Aeron had ever felt before, and as he rinsed the suds away, he lavished each clean patch of skin with kisses.

Aeron felt his arms wrap tightly around her, pulling her close. "Dine alone with me tonight," he said while his hands moved along her body under the water and over the swell of her breasts. "I know that isn't customary, but I don't wish to share you tonight," he continued, his fingers slipping between her legs and petting her into a near frenzy. "Greedy bastard that I am, I want you all to myself."

"Please," Aeron groaned, gripping his hand and holding it between her thighs.

He lifted her out of the water and set her onto the edge of the lagoon, near the waterfall where the rocks were covered with soft moss. He smiled up at her and began to nibble his way up the inside of her leg. His wet hair tickled her belly as he rolled his head between her thighs, sliding his tongue back and forth over the hot button of flesh there. Aeron curled her leg around his shoulders and gripped his hair, drawing him closer as her entire body shook with the force of the orgasm he gave her.

She watched as Orrin rose up out of the water and picked up the drying cloths. He tied one around his waist before wrapping the other around Aeron, helping her to her feet and drying her with soft, loving touches. He gathered her in his arms again and carried her down the path back to her cottage, and Aeron smiled deliriously; she buried her face in the crook of his shoulder, peppering his neck with tender kisses the entire way.

Aeron carefully watched as Orrin made his way around the cottage, lighting its candles one by one. She was mesmerized by the way he moved, the round fullness of his naked buttocks, the muscles of his perfect, unmarred back flexing and pulsing as he moved. She sighed to herself, again painfully aware of the unsightly marks that practically covered the entire span of her back. She thought about the time she'd spent with him and how safe and secure she felt with him.

Sitting in the bed, she hugged her knees tightly to her body. How she wished she could hug herself so hard that she'd disappear into nothingness so she didn't have to tell him what she was about to tell him.

Orrin smiled as he lit the last candle; he loved the way Aeron's naked body shimmered in the candlelight. As he turned back to the bed, he saw her huddled in the center of the mattress, and his smile all but evaporated. Over their brief time together, he'd already noticed her hard exterior melting away with every gentle caress he could bestow upon her, but this was the most vulnerable he'd ever seen her. He sat beside her and brushed her hair away from her face. Tears welled up in her eyes, and his heart shattered for her.

"I need to tell you the truth about what happened to me," she said, lowering her gaze as though in shame. She pulled part of the sheet around her body and tucked her hair behind her ear.

Orrin's heart weighed heavily in his chest as he wrapped the other end of cloth around his waist. Aeron was so strong and sure of herself, all of the time, and he knew it could only be the work of deep sadness that could reduce that strength to what he saw in front of him.

"I've only ever spoken about this to one other soul. Darcy. He's my second-in-command, and there are no secrets between the two of us. He's been the only other person I've ever trusted…until now."

"Aeron, you don't have to do this, it does not matter," Orrin said, cupping her face in his hand and stroking his thumb across her cheek. "You've given me ample opportunity to flee, to leave without a word, and yet I stay. I'm here of my own free will. I'm here with you because I want to be."

"Which is why it matters even more now," she said, closing her eyes and leaning against his warm palm. She looked down into her lap and turned her fingers this way and that as she took a deep breath and began.

"Eight years ago, an offer was made to my parents for me to serve in the castle. My family didn't have a lot of money for a dowry, and my mother and father were told that I would be able to find a decent husband there. Working in the castle could give me a better life than marrying a struggling farmer or fisherman.

"I was informed upon arrival that the Queen had asked for me directly. Apparently I'd caught her eye when she passed by my parents' farm on her way into the village for a visit. I didn't know what to say to such an honor. I thought a simple farm girl being handpicked by the queen herself was a good thing, an answer to my parents' prayers for me to have a better life. I was very naïve once," Aeron said with a strained chuckle.

Her expression was bemused as she recounted how Queen Winifred had been very kind to her, paying special attention to her and spending time with her directly, personally. The king, Richard, was kind as well, but Aeron had seen sorrow hidden deeply in his eyes, a loneliness lurking well under the surface that he had tried so desperately to conceal behind warm smiles and words of encouragement.

One of the first things Aeron had noticed in the castle was that the king and queen did not share sleeping chambers. Aeron had thought this was quite odd because her own parents shared a bed, but she also knew that was just how things were done in such social circles. They were always polite to one another when they dined or came upon one another in the castle, however, she'd never even seen either the king or queen anywhere near each other's chambers in the evening, or any other time of the day, for that matter.

Aeron had enjoyed the interest the queen paid her, but as the weeks went on, she also noticed that no matter where she was or who she was with, the queen had never been too far away. If Aeron was out of Her Majesty's sight for any length of time, she'd be immediately summoned back to her side, often for the most ridiculous and bizarre reasons. Aeron had been unable to help the feeling that she was being smothered by Queen Winifred's attention.

Aeron took a long, slow breath as the memory flooded over her.

"For as long as I breathe air on this earth," she said, looking around her cottage, "I will never forget the day that I was called into the queen's chambers. I'd been there many times before, so I had no reason to question my summons then.

"I'd barely entered the room when her lady-in-waiting left, closing and bolting the door behind her. I should have suspected something was amiss, but I had no reason to. Her Majesty had never been cross with me, ever. She had always regarded me with a sense of admiration. As I said, I was very naïve."

Aeron had stood silently, just inside the door, looking around the massive chamber. The room was decorated elaborately with sweeping gold curtains hanging from the canopy over the bed. There were gilded mirrors and combs on the dressing table, a massive oak wardrobe with more drawers in it than Aeron had ever seen before, and an ornately carved trunk tucked away in the corner.

"Your Majesty?" she had said quietly, taking an uneasy step further inside, her stomach twisting in knots for reasons she couldn't explain. She'd had nothing to fear; she'd been alone with Her Majesty in her chambers before many times, but never with the door bolted.

"Over here, my child," Queen Winifred had called from behind the lavishly painted screen that surrounded her bath.

Aeron had been able to see the elongated shadow of Her Majesty's form and hear the movement of water. Making her way around the screen, Aeron gave a curtsey and respectfully averted her eyes as she tentatively approached the bath.

"How may I be of service, Your Majesty?" she had asked, the knot of nausea twisting tighter in her belly as she focused on the items on the shelf across from the queen's bath.

"Would you hand me that cloth, my sweet?" Queen Winifred had asked as Aeron saw, out of the corner of her eye, her motioning to a square of fabric sitting high up on the shelf.

Nodding her compliance, Aeron had stretched up onto her toes and plucked the washing cloth from the top shelf and passed it to Her Majesty.

Aeron had gasped as the queen grasped her wrist. Her touch was light at first, what she imagined what a lover's touch might feel like, making Aeron feel extremely uncomfortable. As she tried to pull away Her Majesty's grip tightened, twisting Aeron's arm until she was forced to look in her direction. The sickeningly sweet smile that stretched across the queen's face made her skin crawl as the hairs on her arms pricked up in unease. The look in Winifred's eye was one Aeron knew quite well. She'd seen it many times before in lecherous, repulsive men.

"I cannot reach my back, child. Will you wash it for me?"

The request had seemed sincere and Aeron knew she had no choice but to do as she was asked. Perhaps she'd misread the queen's look and harsh manner from just moments ago. With a trembling hand, she took the cloth and dunked it into the warm water as the queen sat up, exposing her naked back. As Aeron moved the cloth over Winifred's shoulder and started to pull away, the queen shackled her wrist again, her icy, vice-like fingers biting into Aeron's flesh.

"Your Majesty—" Aeron had cried in surprise as she began to struggle, squirming and trying desperately to yank her arm free. She didn't expect this level of strength from a woman as pale and thin as Her Majesty.

To her horror, the queen had moved Aeron's hand over her breast and forced it down her body without a word. Aeron tried to pull away, only to have the queen's grip tighten further, her nails pressing against the bone of Aeron's wrist.

"Don't fight me," Queen Winifred had purred, and she proceeded to push Aeron's hand under the water. Tears streamed down Aeron's face, and she shook her head violently, curling her fingers into a fist as Winifred tried to force them between her legs.

Growing agitated with Aeron's refusal, the queen had suddenly risen from her bath and pushed Aeron back onto her bed. She tore at the terrified girl's clothes frantically, stripping away everything until Aeron was completely bare and exposed before her.

Aeron had lain crying and terrified as the queen retreated to a trunk in the corner and, after methodically picking through its contents, returned and forced an object and herself on Aeron's innocent body.

From that point on, she had belonged to the queen and was brought to the royal bedchamber on a near nightly basis. It was horrid, brutal, demeaning and at times confusing. Her Majesty would be kind and loving toward Aeron in one instant and then threatened her and, worse, her family, if she were to breathe a word of what went on behind the closed doors of the queen's room. Aeron was to act as if everything were normal, and she did, to the best of her ability, for weeks on end.

One trying evening, Aeron had lain in the hall outside the queen's chambers, huddled against the wall crying, with blood staining the left corner of her mouth and the front of the nightdress she wore. She'd all but resigned herself to a life of hell. She clung to the stone in fear as she heard footsteps approaching. As the king's slippered feet appeared beside her, Aeron was petrified that he would also exercise his royal rights and take her as the queen had, but he didn't.

"Come child, let's get you washed up," he had said softly as he helped Aeron to her feet and down the hall to the washing room. He gently wiped the blood from her face and fetched her something clean to wear before he walked her to her cot and tucked the blanket around her carefully. Aeron couldn't help but feel that she wasn't the first girl he'd found in the hallway outside of Winifred's room crying, terrified, and covered in blood. She was certain that, for the most part, he chose to ignore Her Majesty's fondness for beating and forcing herself on young women, most likely out of fear of what the queen would do to him. But why risk helping Aeron? Aeron didn't care; she was thankful for his kindness.

As the months had worn on, Aeron had grown to almost welcome her time with Winifred, for she knew Richard would be waiting for her afterward to comfort her. They had become lovers, biding their time in secret until they could figure out what to do to get away.

That was, until the queen had gotten wind of their trysts from one of her maids who happened to spot Aeron and the king in an embrace in his drawing room. Winifred was beyond livid; Aeron was her lover, hers and hers alone.

Shortly after Her Majesty learned of the affair, Aeron had slipped into Richard's bed after a particularly bad, unusually cruel night with the queen. She slid over against her king and noticed that his body felt deathly cold, and as she turned, she raised her hand to his face. It was like ice.

"Darling, you're so cold," Aeron had said, rubbing her feet against his in an effort to warm him. She sat up and reached for the thick fur blanket at the foot of the bed and caught sight of his face. His mouth was agape and his eyes open, staring into the night. "Your Majesty, Richard, are you—" Then she saw the blood soaking the sheet down the side of the bed.

Aeron had gasped in horror, a strangled scream stuck in her throat as a figure stepped out of the darkness.

"I'm so sorry, my sweet, but he cannot answer you," Queen Winifred had said coolly as she stepped away from an opening in the wall beside the fireplace, twirling a blood-soaked blade in her hand. Her Majesty must have utilized one of the many secret passageways that ran behind the walls of the great castle while Aeron had cleaned herself and recovered from the evening's beating.

Aeron had wanted to scream and alert the guards, but before she could work the sound out of her throat and past her lips, the queen lunged at her and clamped a bloodied hand over Aeron's mouth.

"You belong to me, only me," Winifred had snarled through her teeth. "Are we clear?"

Aeron had been stunned and terrified. As she nodded under the queen's iron grasp, she could feel Richard's blood, cold and sticky on her skin, and it was all she could do not to vomit.

"Good girl, I love you so much," the queen had crooned into Aeron's hair as she swept her into an embrace. "However, you know I can't let this go unpunished."

Aeron now took a shuddering breath, and Orrin was sure she was remembering that punishment and all the others. Orrin's thumbs cradled her face and wiped the tears away, jolting Aeron back into the present.

"The queen slit his throat, like she was slaughtering some lowly animal," Aeron said as she stared blankly at the wall. "The next day, when his body was found by a page, she chose a knight at random, blamed an innocent man for murdering the king and had him hung from the battlements with her morning tea, as if it were nothing."

Aeron's memories continued to spill from her mouth. "It was the night of Richard's murder that the beatings really began."

Henceforth, on the third night of every week, Aeron had been whipped by Queen Winifred herself in the royal bedchamber, and she came to know that Her Royal Majesty had many torturous devices at her disposal, her favorite being the cat-o'-nine-tails. Her Majesty had several cats in her loathsome collection, including one that was fashioned with silver barbs on the end of each tail that ripped at Aeron's back.

In the months to come, Aeron's belly had begun to swell with Richard's child. She was frightened that Her Majesty would do something awful to end the pregnancy; she didn't want Aeron's attention to be diverted from her in any way. But to her surprise, Winifred had allowed her to carry the child to term.

In that time the queen had given her little rest, keeping Aeron tucked away in a dark alcove hidden inside her room. Even on the night Aeron went into labor, she couldn't be free of Winifred's presence. The queen insisted that Aeron labor through the night in her royal chamber as she loomed in the background like a demon waiting to feed.

Just before the new day had broken, Aeron had given birth to a healthy baby girl. She'd never been happier in her entire life as when she saw Richard's eyes staring back at her.

Foolishly, Aeron had thought the queen would let her keep the child, but she saw seething hate in Her Majesty's eyes as she skulked toward her and ripped the child from her arms.

"She took my child across the room, to the open window, and she…" Aeron's words halted as she choked back a sob at the horrific memory. "She dropped my child into the ocean below, without the slightest hesitation. She told me that no one would have my affection above her, ever."

Orrin immediately took her into his arms. She was wooden and distant in his embrace and tried to squirm away, but Orrin held tightly as she sobbed against his chest. He didn't know what to say to her, or even if there was anything to say. So he held her, stroking her hair and rocking her in his arms in the middle of the bed as he let her cry.

"I ran from the castle at the first chance I had, and I stowed away on the first ship that I came upon. That's where Darcy found me." Aeron smiled as she remembered. "I stabbed him in the arm with a knife I'd stolen from a sleeping crewmember because I thought he was trying to have his way with me," she said with a chuckle.

Orrin listened intently as Aeron went on to tell him how she and Darcy had turned the ship on its captain during its next voyage. Orrin was amazed at Aeron's innate flare for leadership. It made him smile to hear how she'd used it—along with her feminine wiles and the sword skill she'd learned from her father—to become a pirate, taming the seas and the men that sailed them.

"I'd gotten word that upon learning of my escape, Winifred went completely mad. When we found this island, we knew straight away that it would be our home. We needed some place out of the royal grasp in order to gather our numbers. I intend to take my revenge for what she did to me and my child and anyone else she has harmed, and I need your assistance, Orrin," she said. "Help me bring down this demon of a woman and send her back to hell where she belongs."

Orrin looked deeply into Aeron's eyes as he stroked his thumb along her cheek. His suspicions about the queen had solidified in his mind; he'd sensed she was a vile woman, but he'd had no idea of the extent.

And he was all but certain that it was the queen who had laid hands on his sister Iona, marking her back with the two scars she'd carried after her brief service in the castle.

"I will help you, if it takes my very last breath. Even if I have to carry her to the gates of hell myself, she will pay," Orrin vowed.

Chapter Eleven

Kale stood on the deck of the ship, looking out over the water in the very spot where Orrin had stood what was now a week ago. He still did not fully believe what the prince had told him about his brother. Orrin was a pigheaded and ill-tempered man, not one who was easily swayed by anyone, even a beautiful woman. At least not while he was in his right mind.

Could Orrin indeed be under some spell cast by this whore of a sea witch? They both knew the stories that surrounded Aeron Lynch and her ways. Tales of how she easily enraptured the most steadfast of men and robbed them blind were common knowledge amongst seafarers.

On the other hand, Kale himself might be inclined to embellish on the truth in order to save face were he to be found floating in a dinghy in the middle of the ocean and left with nothing more than the underclothes on his arse.

However, Aeron had coaxed Prince William right out of the palace, for God's sake.

A knot formed in his stomach as he thought about what the prince had said. William had told them how Aeron had persuaded him to leave his family and his throne, only to force him into her servitude. He'd spoken of the slaves she had to do her bidding around the island and that their beloved Captain and brother was following her around like a lost puppy hoping for a petting and scrap of meat.

Kale's brow creased and his nostrils flared at the very thought of his brother being made a fool of in any way. If this pirate had indeed bewitched his brother, she would pay dearly. Woman or not, he would hunt her down like the rest of the pirate vermin and free his brother from her. He'd end her life if he had to, without hesitation or regret.

The churning white, frothy water in the wake of the ship captivated him as they sailed toward the mainland.

"Have no fear, my brother," he said. "I have your back."

"Land on the horizon!" one of the deck hands called, breaking Kale out of his trance.

Taking up a telescope, he calculated that they would make port just before nightfall. Once they had delivered Prince William safely, Kale would regroup with his crew and go back for Orrin, bringing the queen's own fleet down on that scurvy she-pirate if need be.

The second the *Iona* made port, William jumped off the ship and bound up the docks toward the palace, hell-bent on getting his revenge on Aeron.

"We must stop her, Mother!" he shouted as he burst into the castle and strode up to the queen. "Aeron is planning to overthrow you, and we must take her out before she strikes."

He watched, catching his breath as his mother, Queen Winifred, slid her icy gaze across the room. "No, we must catch her," she said, "catch her and break her. Make no mistake, I will have what is mine again."

William bowed obediently to his mother before he continued. "Then I shall need more ships to —"

"Done," she responded, cutting him off before he could finish with an elegant sweep of her hand.

"Mother," he said, standing proudly before the queen. "I will capture her, and I will deliver her to you broken and —"

"You will not touch her!" The queen's voice boomed, echoing off the stone walls as she rose from her throne, walked directly to William, and grasped a handful of his hair. His face twisted in pain as she pulled his head back at an unnatural angle. "You will capture her and bring her directly to me," she said, her lip twitching in anger. "Rest assured, I will know if you've laid even one finger on her."

"Yes…Your Majesty," William mumbled with a grimace.

Winifred flung her hand from Will's hair. He watched as she wiped her palm on the dress of a nearby lady-in-waiting. It was as if she were trying to rid herself of some unspeakable disease.

"It was bad enough that I had to take a man into my bed in order to conceive you," she spat coldly as she headed back to her dais. "Do not make me regret not doing away with you before you were born by being insolent with me now, boy." She flipped her robes behind her as she sat in her ornately carved throne. "Remember, it's not too late to rectify that issue. Just ask your father."

The following week, when Orrin woke with the bright morning sun on his face, he stretched across the bed in search of Aeron. Finding nothing but empty space, he spied the open back door and smiled to himself.

Without even bothering with trousers or boots, he slipped silently down the path to Aeron's private lagoon, naked as the day he was born.

As he came upon the pool, there she was, floating on her back like a water nymph, all decadence and creamy skin for his eyes to feast upon. She looked as if she hadn't a care, as if the weight of a world had been lifted from her shoulders.

Perhaps that was how she did feel these days, ever since sharing her most intimate secret with him. He couldn't imagine having had to bear the weight of that on his soul, knowing every day that the beast of a queen was still walking the earth.

"When you've finished gaping at me, you should really get in. The water is quite lovely," she said, without opening her eyes, a playful smile teasing at the corners of her succulent mouth.

Orrin slipped into the water and made his way over to her. "How could you possibly know I was here?" he asked as he pushed along her flesh, tracing a long finger across her bare stomach.

Aeron cracked open one eye and peeked up at him. "I heard you tromping down the path from the cottage," she said, giggling.

His mouth gaped open, and he stared at her in mock astonishment. "I did not tromp."

She righted herself in the water and stood before him. "You are skilled in many, many fine things, sir," she said, trailing her hand down his chest and sliding it under the water to tease him. "However, I will have to teach you the proper way to stalk through the jungle."

Grabbing her by the waist and pulling her to him, Orrin pressed her against his body, and a low, quiet purr erupted from her. "I am more than ready for your teaching," he murmured as he descended on her neck, nibbling his way down to the top of her shoulder.

He was rousted out of his reverie by the sound of someone clearing his throat loudly.

Darcy stood on the rocky banks of the lagoon, glaring at him. Orrin swallowed hard. The man looked as if he were seriously considering picking up a rock and heaving it at him. Orrin felt Aeron tilt her head in Darcy's direction, likely to cut him a glare, for Darcy took a precautionary step back.

"Ahem, Captain," he said, averting his eyes from the amorous couple. "The crew is waiting."

"Very well," she grumbled, "we'll be there in a moment."

"Aye, Captain," Darcy said, clearly forcing a respectful nod to Orrin as he disappeared into the jungle.

"I want you to come with me. You should be an active part of our plans from this point forward," Aeron said as she raked her fingers through Orrin's wet hair.

"Are you certain you want to do that? I don't think your man, Darcy, thinks much of me."

"Then it's a good thing he's not the captain, isn't it?" Aeron wrapped her arms around his lean torso. "Darcy can be thick, but you'll win his favor, I know it. And yes, I'm very sure I want you at my side."

"Then I shall stand by your side proudly, Aeron," he said as he bent to kiss her forehead. "Now, let us go, for the sooner we get dressed and go, the sooner we can be back here and naked," he said. Orrin surged his body against hers one last time and gripped her backside, teasing her before he pulled himself away.

He could feel her following close behind as he made his way to the shore and hauled himself out of the water. But before he could right himself, Aeron bit his backside.

"What on earth was that for?" he howled as he rubbed his right ass cheek.

"I'm sorry, I couldn't stop myself. I've been dying to do that since I met you," she confessed.

"I thought you hated me when you met me," Orrin said.

"I did," she said as she sidled up next to him. "For a moment, anyway."

"Correct me if I'm wrong, but you pulled your sword on me and held a dagger to my throat within the first ten minutes of our meeting."

"Naturally," Aeron responded matter-of-factly. "Honestly, Orrin, how else do you think I meet men? Trust me, if I truly hated you for any length of time, you'd be long dead by now. I am a pirate, after all," she said with a wink.

"That you are, but you are *my* pirate." He wrapped his arm around her waist and placed a kiss on the end of her nose.

As Orrin followed Aeron to the meetinghouse, he squelched his growing nerves. He'd been on the island for a good couple of weeks now, and this was the only place he hadn't been allowed as of yet. Truthfully, before Aeron's confession last night, there still would have been a part of him that wondered if this was all an elaborate trap, but no longer. At least not by Aeron's hand.

Darcy was another matter altogether. Orrin knew the man loathed him, but what of the rest of the crew? Yes, they glared in his direction and muttered curses under their breath when Orrin was around; however, he noticed that the looks had eased and the cursing gave way to friendly nods and the occasional ribbing by all but Darcy. The man was terrifying.

As they entered the meetinghouse, buried deep in the center of the jungle, the evident change in Aeron's demeanor was instantaneous. Orrin saw her back straighten tall and strong, and the air around her took on a different feel. She went from the swooning woman he'd held in his arms moments ago by the lagoon to calculating pirate, all right before his eyes. It was nothing short of amazing.

She quickly introduced him to the crew, most of whom he'd already seen and worked with in the past weeks. When the meeting started, Orrin tucked himself against the wall and listened as she began to lay out her plan to overthrow the queen by drawing her out, using William as a lure.

A decidedly odd and uncomfortable feeling washed over him as she gave out orders to the crew, for they seemed to be directed at him as well.

Was she really intending to take this battle to sea?

He wanted to speak in protest. As he scanned the men in the room, he could see the unease on their faces, and yet no one was man enough to stand up to her. This was contrary to everything he believed. A captain should want to know every possible perspective before mapping out a plan of action and jumping to a decision half blind. His jaw tightened and his fists clenched as he swallowed his objection to her plan. He would have to speak to her about his concerns when they were alone.

"Is there a problem?" Aeron asked him directly.

He didn't want to openly question her orders in front of her men, but, damn it all, he was a captain as well, and he was not accustomed to holding his tongue, no matter how hard he tried.

"I can't help but think that if we wait for them to come to shore we will have the advantage of familiar territory and more time to prepare," he said. "Whereas the sea is terribly unpredictable and can muck up a good plan of action in a heartbeat."

Aeron visibly bristled and glared at Orrin for a moment, her nostrils flaring as he saw the rage burning in her eyes.

"There seems to be some sort of question to my authority here," she said calmly to her crew before she turned back to face Orrin. "Let me make this as clear as I possibly can. We will take them on the open sea. That is an order," she said curtly before she flew out the door and into the jungle.

"Bloody fucking hell," Orrin mumbled, and he pushed through the door behind her, following as fast as he could and praying he didn't get lost. "Aeron," he called as she hurried into the brush.

Luckily, he was a very quick learner and followed her every move, calling after her incessantly and catching brief glimpses of her before she ducked out of sight again. She never answered, not a single word, but he tracked the sounds of her slicing through the jungle as it started to thin and he could hear the ocean.

Orrin barely got a boot out onto the open sand before Aeron lunged at him, sword and dagger drawn. He knew this attack was a warning, for she would have otherwise run him through instantly, no mucking about.

However, he was not the type of man to give in and run away at the first sign of trouble. He drew his sword, and it met hers with a thundering clang to parry her second advance.

"I'm not one of your men, Aeron. You cannot order me about like you do them," he said, holding his position.

She grit her teeth as she pulled back and sliced through the air at him, dagger in one hand, sword in the other. Their weapons clashed as she moved on him, driving him down the beach.

"No, my men would never question me," she shouted as she moved in for another attack.

Orrin defended himself and made an advance of his own. "They should!" he shouted back with a swipe of his sword. "If they had, I may not have found your island so easily."

Aeron spun at him, forcing him into the waves lapping at the shore. "I wanted you to find it, you twit!" she screamed and made another mighty lunge.

He blocked her attack with quite a bit of effort and stared down at her, swords tangled together and arms stretched in the air over their heads.

"Why?" he asked, the steel of the blades squealing in protest as they fought to occupy the same space. She was trembling ever so slightly and trying desperately to hide it. If he hadn't grown to know her so well he never would have seen the slight quiver of her lip or the hint of a waver in her stance.

Aeron shoved him back, breaking away from him. "I told you last night, because I need your help!" she shouted in frustration, throwing her weapons into the sand and stomping through the surf away from him.

Orrin trudged through the waves after her.

"Don't walk away from me, Aeron," he said, grabbing her by the wrist to stop her. "As I told *you* last night, I am giving you my help, willingly, but I will not follow you blindly like your men do. I'm not knit that way."

"Let me go," Aeron growled, struggling against his grip, but he only tightened his hold on her.

"No, not if you're going to run away from me," he said as he tried to shackle her free arm, to no avail. She'd managed to wriggle around and crack him across the nose with her elbow. Orrin's grip broke, and Aeron sprinted down the beach.

Thoroughly exasperated, Orrin ran after her. He caught up with her and hooked her around the waist, tackling her to the sand below. She fought relentlessly beneath him like a hellcat, cursing him and trying to kick him off. Orrin laid more of his weight onto her body and managed to pin her arms over her head as she seethed under him.

Instinctively, Orrin lowered his mouth on hers, pulling the fury from her with a single, voracious kiss until he felt her begin to relent. As he lifted his head, he smiled victoriously at the drunken state Aeron appeared to be in; however, within moments she began to struggle again.

"Get off of me," she spat up at him.

"Aeron, if you would just listen for one moment—"

"It is my ship, my crew, and I will listen to no one," she snarled as she continued to wiggle, almost breaking free of his grip.

Orrin bent his head and kissed her again, longer, harder, until he felt her moans reverberate against his tongue. As he slowly released her hands, he slipped his palms down to her face, cradling it and letting the magic of their lips work against her iron will.

He felt her fingers sink into his hair, clamping it in a death grip and tugging with all of her might. As she pulled, he groaned into her mouth, kissing her deeper, harder, hungrier. She'd somehow managed to wiggle her legs from underneath him and lock them around his waist, frantically pushing her hips against his and digging her heels into his back as she squeezed her thighs tighter around his body. His erection began to grow harder as she ground it between her legs. He cried out as her teeth sank into his shoulder and ripped through the fabric of his shirt in a fit of pure lust.

Orrin rubbed his body against hers and tried like hell to slip his hand between them. He had to have her, right now and on the sand, and he could feel her need for him as well. He tried to reach the ties of his trousers, but her body was pressed too tightly to his; not even a breath could have gotten between them at this rate.

"Aeron," he rasped in frustration as he reached behind himself, grabbed her by the foot, and tried to loosen the grip she had on him. He yanked her boot off and flung it up onto the beach before digging inside his own boot to find the dagger he kept there. When he found the small blade, he slid it up the leg of her breeches, minding her delicate skin as he cut the cloth away from her body in desperation. He cut away enough of the fabric to allow himself access to her soft, wet flesh. He eased two of his fingers into her, slipping his thumb over her sweet bud. She clutched the back of his shirt, nearly ripping it to shreds as he worked to bring her to the very edge of release, only to deny her total satisfaction.

With a fierce growl, Aeron broke the grip she had on his shirt and tore at the ties of his breeches, pulling and tugging at the knotted string caked with seawater and sand.

Orrin chuckled arrogantly as she frantically worked to get his trousers open. He enjoyed seeing her like this, as ravenous for him as he was for her.

"Either help me or get off of me." She glared up at him, burning with a rage he knew only he could squelch.

"Well, I'll just get off of you then," he purred in response as he let her go and started to get up.

Aeron grabbed the waist of his trousers with one hand and his shirt with the other, pulling him back down on top of her. "Don't tease me, Orrin. I am not in the mood." She released his shirt and ripped the dagger from his hand, cutting the knotted ties open before she hurriedly tossed the knife aside and reached into his trousers to pull his length free and position the tip against her hot, wet entrance. "Do it, now," she demanded.

Orrin's breath rattled from deep within his chest as he easily slid into her to the hilt with one smooth thrust. His breath caught at the sight of Aeron beneath him, arching off the sand in ecstasy as a rogue wave suddenly washed over their bodies. They were immediately soaked to the skin, allowing Orrin to feel her hard nipples against his chest through their two layers of wet fabric. Bending his head to her, he started to thrust unabashedly as he raked his lips and teeth across the tender skin of her neck.

He could feel the sand in her hair when he curled his fingers in it, pulling her closer, protectively, possessively.

"Aeron," he breathed as he started to move with the tide sneaking up around them, slowing the pace to a steady rhythm that made his head reel with pleasure. Never had a woman, not even his wife, made Orrin feel so willing to give up every ounce of control like Aeron did.

He knew the tells of her body like they were his own. He felt her body tense under his; her legs pressed against his back, and her fingers dug into his flesh, shuddering beneath him as her breath came in short bursts against his neck. He knew his own defeat was approaching rapidly, for he couldn't contain feelings of complete and utter bliss as he felt her body gripping his rigid flesh, pulsing around him as each thrust made her cry out louder and breath harder.

Rearing back, Orrin drove deep within her, and his mouth gaped open as he gasped for air and found his own release. He collapsed on top of her when he could no longer move, blowing grains of dry sand against her neck as he panted, all of his energy completely spent and sated. Aeron slowly turned her head to look at him, her blue-green eyes sparkling and drowsy with satisfaction.

"Damn you," Orrin said. "You make me want to agree to anything when you look at me like that." He tried to brush the sand from her cheek with wet fingers

"I was about to tell you the same thing," she said with a laugh as she pushed a sweaty lock of hair off his forehead. Orrin reached around his back to tickle her bare foot. "Stop that," she giggled, trying to wiggle her foot out of his grasp. "What in the devil did you do with my boot?"

Orrin lazily looked up the shore and spied her boot hanging off a branch. He laughed; he hadn't realized he had thrown it that far.

"What is so bloody funny?" Aeron asked, craning her head around. "My, but you *were* quite eager, weren't you?"

Rising to his feet, Orrin offered her his hand to help her up. "You made me insane," he admitted as he pulled her into his arms, running his hand down her back to cup her bare buttock.

Aeron pulled back, and they both looked down at her state of undress. Her trousers were hanging from one leg only with the other pant leg splayed open, revealing everything they were meant to hide. A blush rose on her face as she buried it in his chest, giggling incessantly.

Orrin, ever the gentleman, peeled the wet shirt from his body. He could feel her eyes on him as he moved, carefully sliding his shirt over her head, the ends of it falling to just below the curve of her backside. He knelt in the sand in front of her and stripped off what was left of her breeches before fetching her boot from the branch and helping her pull it on.

"My God, woman," he said, looking her up and down as he stood. "How in heaven's name do you do that?"

"Do what?"

"Look so incredibly tempting in my shirt." He grabbed her around the waist and pulled her close, nipping the decadent flesh of her neck as his hands roamed freely.

"Orrin, we have to get back," she giggled and half-heartedly shoved him away.

"We'll get back…eventually," he said, pursing his lips as his eyes traversed the curves of her body.

"Do you really think that's wise?" she asked, the distinct look of mischief sparking her eyes. "Darcy has been searching for a reason to throttle you but good since you crossed his path."

"Indeed," he said, taking a step toward her with a naughty grin spreading across his face, "but moments alone with you are well worth a good beating."

Aeron smiled and turned on her heel, taking Orrin's hand and leading him through the jungle.

Contrary to his nature, Orrin didn't ask any questions about where she planned to take him; he simply followed wherever Aeron was going to lead him. They could have been heading back into the village for all he knew, but as long as Aeron was with him, she could have led him off a cliff and into an abyss, and he wouldn't have cared one iota.

It had been two hours since Aeron had stormed off into the jungle with Orrin chasing after her. She should have been worried that her crew was searching for them, but the only thing that concerned her at the moment was staying out of Orrin's grasp. They'd chased each other from one of the ship's rooms to another before ending in her cabin. He was now kneeling on the small bed, trying to grab her and pull her back, but she knew they needed to get back to the task at hand: planning to defeat Queen Winifred.

Orrin lunged at Aeron as she whipped the sheet off the bed, knocking him off balance. She cackled with victory as she slung the sheet around her body and bound up the stairs to the deck.

As she laughed manically and flung the door open, she stopped dead, almost colliding with Darcy, who had his sword drawn at the ready

"Darcy, what are you doing here?" she asked, out of breath and clutching the sheet around her naked body.

"Searching for you," he scolded. "The entire crew is worried sick that the filthy blackguard has kidnapped or killed you." Just then, Orrin burst through the doors, wearing nothing but a smile.

She watched his smile disintegrate as he casually reached down and grabbed the bottom half of her sheet. He promptly cleared his throat and covered his important bits, most likely in fear of getting them lopped off by her sword-wielding first mate.

"Darcy," he said with a nod.

Darcy shot a scathing glance over Aeron's shoulder at Orrin as he asked her, "Have you reached a decision on which course we are going to take, Captain?"

"Yes, we are going to wait for them to come to shore," she said with confident nod.

"What? No," Orrin said, shaking his head vehemently. "You were right. We should attack them on open water and take them by surprise."

Darcy arched an eyebrow at Aeron before he rolled his eyes and shook his head at the pair of them. "Christ," he mumbled. "Blasted woman captain." Darcy stuffed his sword into his scabbard, grabbed the line, and hoisted himself up the rope.

"He's going to kill me one day, isn't he?" Orrin asked as he looked up at the large man ambling up the rope as if it were nothing.

"I'd sleep with one eye open if I were you." Aeron gave a playful wink. "Time to get back," she said, slapping on his naked backside as she headed back down below the deck. Luckily, she had some of her clothes on board and was able to dress herself before they returned to the crew.

Aeron could see the curiosity building inside Orrin as he watched her move about the cabin. She watched him try to sneak peeks inside her wardrobe. It was only a matter of time before that curiosity would get the better of him, and she knew it.

"Hmm, interesting," he said casually as he pulled on his boots.

"What's that?"

"You don't have any men's clothing in your locker."

"No, as a matter of fact, I don't," she said as she tied her belt into place. "To be truthful, there has never been a man in this room before. Other than Darcy, of course, but I don't think he counts."

Orrin immediately stopped tugging on his boot and looked up at her strangely. "Are you saying I'm the first man to lie with you in this bed?"

"Yes, you are."

He seemed to be thinking on that as he finished putting on his boot and rose from the bed. He sauntered across the cabin to her in that way that made her knees turn to butter, and he took her face in his hands. "You are the captain," he said thoughtfully. "You tell me how you would like to run the attack on Queen Winifred, and I will follow your lead." He leaned his forehead to hers and kissed her nose.

"Thank you," she breathed, touching the side of his face. Did he have even the smallest idea what that meant to her? "We shall—"

"Captain!" one of her men shouted as he landed on the deck with a bone-rattling thud, followed by a thunder of men landing one after the other.

Aeron and Orrin ran to the deck, opening the door to her crew spilling onto the ship like a ravenous plague.

"What the bloody hell going on?" Aeron demanded as Darcy landed solidly behind her.

"A ship on the horizon, Captain," he said before turning to Orrin. "Your ship."

Aeron drew in a breath as betrayal flooded through her. Had she been duped this entire time by Orrin and all of his promises of love? Tears welled up in the back of her eyes, but she willed them not to fall. If this was his doing she would not let him see how much he'd hurt her.

"This is not by my order, I swear it," Orrin said, obviously seeing the look in her eyes; she should have known she could hide nothing from him, not anymore. "Aeron, you know me." He grabbed her hand and placed it on his bare chest. "You know my heart," he said desperately. "I made a promise to you that I would help you defeat the queen, and God as my witness, I will do just that. My brother Kale could be a great help in our quest, but you have got to trust me right now."

Aeron looked around the deck; every eye was on them, waiting for her order. Did she trust Orrin or wish him slaughtered right then and there? His heart thumped against her palm as she let his words sink in. A reassuring warmth seemed to spread between them, passing through his body and into hers.

Sliding her hand from under his, she rested it on his cheek and looked deep into his blue eyes. Yes, she trusted him, not only with her life, but the lives of her people.

"I trust you," she said.

"Captain?" Darcy asked, his hand flexing on the hilt of his sword.

"You heard me. If Orrin says this order does not come from him, I believe him."

"Yes, Captain," Darcy said, his jaw clenched as he nodded his head in respect. "What is your order?"

Aeron gave Orrin a soft pat on the cheek and turned to her waiting crew.

"We sail!" she shouted as she bound across the deck and barked orders to her crew.

Chapter Twelve

William walked through the halls of the castle. He'd been spending his time preparing his ship and the rest of the fleet for the attack on Aeron. As he climbed the steps to his room, he saw men taking trunks from his mother's chambers past him. He followed the corridor on her floor to her room. The heavy wooden door was ajar as he rapped his knuckles against the oak.

"Come," he heard through the panel.

When he stepped in, she looked in his direction briefly before she clucked her tongue against the roof of her mouth. "What do you want?" she asked, her tone conveying her sheer annoyance with him.

"I saw trunks being carried from your chambers, Mother. Are you going to the country until I return with your prize?"

"No," she said plainly, coldly. "I'm going with you."

"On the ship?" he asked, his mouth dropping open in surprise.

"Of course on the ship," Winifred replied. He shivered at how cold and hard her eyes were, as if he meant absolutely naught to her. "Do you really think that I would trust you to carry out this task on your own? Really, William," she scoffed before he could even answer. "You can barely take a shit without assistance."

The hair on the back of Will's neck stood on end with anger. She didn't know him anymore; she had no idea what he was capable of. But she was his mother and his queen, so he held his tongue despite the rage roaring inside him.

"It really is a shame that you got your brains from your father. He was an emotional dolt as well," she snapped coolly.

"Just tell me what to do to please you, Mother, and I shall do it," William said, forcing himself to obediently drop his gaze to the ground in front of him and bow his head to her.

Her sigh of frustration and utter disgust cut through the air like a knife slicing through William's skin.

"Your very presence on this earth displeases me," she spat as she pushed past him and out the door without a glance in his direction.

William was left standing alone, abandoned, with the few threads of pride he'd managed to keep a hold of. He'd show her. He'd show them all. He'd make his mother proud of him if it killed him.

Orrin stood at Aeron's side at the helm of the *Mermaid*, the wind whipping past them as the ship sailed through the water at a staggering speed. Orrin looked out at *Iona*, growing larger on the horizon as they moved closer.

"I know my brother," he said to Aeron. "Whatever he learned from William didn't set well with him, so he comes to seek the truth for himself."

Aeron nodded. "Aye, Will has most likely spun quite the tale for him."

An uncontrollable urge came over Orrin; he protectively wrapped his arm around Aeron's waist as the ships approached each other. With subtle and gentle pressure, he coaxed her to turn in his arms. "No harm will come to you, I vow it," he swore.

"And I shall protect you as well, my love," she replied, stretching up onto her toes to kiss the slight dimple in his chin.

His arms immediately felt empty as Aeron pulled free to address her men. "There will be no weapons today," she called out. "This is not a fight. We need the trust of this captain and his crew, and we will not gain that with a sword, not this day."

Aeron's words died on the wind as the two mighty vessels faced off in the middle of the open sea, sailing within twenty feet of each other. Faces Orrin knew well stared back at him with confusion from the decks of *Iona*. He prayed they would understand.

"Kale," Orrin called across the water when his brother came into sight. "Come over and let us talk."

Just as the last word left Orrin's mouth, he heard the distinct sound of cannon doors opening and the heavy iron weapons rolled into place.

"Captain?" Orrin heard Darcy ask cautiously as he took up to Aeron's right. Orrin saw his discrete nod to the actions of Kale's craft. This was clearly a sign that his brother did not intend to talk.

"No," Aeron answered, "no cannons, not even so much as a fist, Darcy. Understood?"

Orrin watched her eyes scan *Iona*'s decks. She was a devilishly smart woman; he could almost hear her mind humming.

"I think not, my brother," Kale called back. *"You* come over, and bring that scurvy sea witch with you, or we shall open fire."

The men behind them grumbled, and Orrin could hear them readying their weapons. Aeron turned to them instantly and glared fiercely at her men.

"I said no weapons, of any kind," she reiterated as she removed her sword and pulled the dagger out of her boot, handing them both to Gael. She reached around him and took the rope Darcy offered to her.

Orrin saw the worry creasing the man's mighty brow as his soulful eyes flashed over her shoulder to the opposing vessel.

"All will be well, my friend," Aeron said with a reassuring smile. "I can feel it." In a measure of good faith, she firmly gripped the line and swung across to Orrin's ship, alone and unarmed.

When she was safely across the water, Darcy shoved another length of rope to Orrin, none too kindly. "If she dies, you die. Of that you can be sure."

"Duly noted," Orrin said with a quick nod as he took his leave and swung over, landing directly in front of Aeron to effectively block Kale's sword-drawn approach.

"Lower your sword, little brother. She means you no harm," Orrin said as he stood to his full height and squared his shoulders.

"Stand aside, Orrin," Kale said as he reared his blade toward Aeron. "She has bewitched you into serving her, and I intend to break her hold on you. By removing her head."

"I'm merely a woman——" Aeron said, craning her neck to look around Orrin's body.

"Hold your tongue, witch!" Kale shouted.

Taking a step toward his brother, Orrin brazenly placed a gentle hand on the hilt of Kale's sword. "Kale, you are my brother. No one knows me as well as you do. Look at me," he said as he pushed the blade aside. "No one has bewitched me."

He saw his brother nervously glance over at Aeron's ship. Orrin knew Kale was observant and could see that the cannon doors were still closed tightly and that her men held no weapons whereas Kale's men surrounded them with swords at the ready.

"Blindfold and gag her," Kale said with a nod of his head in Aeron's direction. "Then I will speak with you, brother."

Orrin started to protest the ridiculous request when he felt Aeron's hand on his shoulder.

"It's all right, I understand," she said. "He's being smart. Lord only knows the outlandish tales William has spun about me to him." She looked at Kale. "Agreed."

The heat of Darcy's murderous gaze was palpable and bore into the back of Orrin's head. Orrin turned to see the mammoth of a man glaring across the waters at him while Kale's men blindfolded, gagged, and bound Aeron.

Orrin swallowed hard. He prayed that he knew his brother as well as he thought.

Following them below the decks, Orrin cringed as Aeron was dragged down the stairs and roughly shoved down into a chair.

"Mind yourself, Kale," he ground out, taking the empty seat next to Aeron. "Our mother taught you better than that. Aeron is still a lady."

Kale stared across the table at his brother with a look of sheer and utter shock on his face; he clearly couldn't believe what he was hearing.

"What the hell has she done to you?" Kale asked Orrin.

"Other than try to kill me on several occasions?" Orrin asked, catching out of the corner of his eye Aeron's grin under the strip of cloth that kept her quiet. It made him smile, too. "She showed me what it was like to live again." He took Aeron's hand and stroked the back of it with his thumb as he gazed at the blindfolded woman. "She freed me."

"She has bewitched you," Kale accused, and he slapped the table in frustration, surprising Orrin with such an outburst. "She has tempted you with her flesh and made you her slave to do her bidding."

"No, Kale," Orrin said, shaking his head and trying to keep his cool while his own brother spoke hateful things about his beloved. "No one, not Aeron or any member of her crew has made me do a single thing that I did not want to do. I have always been free to leave the island at any time I chose."

"I don't understand," Kale said, looking from Orrin to the bound woman next to him. "You come to me, on a pirate's ship, and you speak as if your loyalty lies with her, this godforsaken…*whore,* and not with your own brother, your own blood."

"It does," Orrin said calmly, though he leaned across the table menacingly, his lip twitching. "And if you speak ill of her one more time I will remove your tongue from your head with my bare hands."

Kale leapt to his feet, knocking his chair over as he grabbed for his sword and aimed it at Orrin. "Then *you* are not my brother," he spat.

Orrin moved with lightning speed, jerking Aeron to her feet and spinning her around in front of him, her vulnerable back to Kale. "Do you remember Iona?" he shouted, his knuckles turning white as he fisted the back of Aeron's shirt in his hands.

Kale remained frozen where he stood, the color draining from his face and his sword lowering at the mere mention of their beloved sister's name. Orrin continued. "Our sweet, innocent little sister craved the courtly life and worked to earn a place of service in the castle. Do you remember?"

Kale nodded. "Yes, I remember," he said quietly.

"She returned home in a month's time, different than when she left."

Kale's eyes welled as Orrin evoked the memory of their darling sister, who had been so vibrant, so full of life before she'd left, as compared to the shell of a person she'd returned as, empty and broken. The light that had once shone in her eyes had been squelched by events she would never speak of but over which they'd heard her crying in the night when she'd thought them asleep.

Orrin reached into his belt and pulled out the dagger he'd smuggled aboard. "Do you remember that one time she accidentally fell into the stream? When you and I could see the marks on her back through her wet shirt? Do you?" he shouted, his entire body vibrating with emotional pain.

Kale's nod was short and tight, the look in his eyes tinged with the wretched recollection.

"Forgive me, my love," Orrin said to Aeron a moment before he pulled the dagger across the fabric of her shirt. The material opened easily, exposing the dozens upon dozens of nasty scars marring her flesh akin to the two equally hideous marks on Iona.

"Look at her!" Orrin shouted when Kale tried to turn away. "This," he said, gesturing to the scars, "is the work of Queen Winifred. Not one of her lieges, but by her own hand."

Kale's mouth gaped open as he fell back against the wall behind him, unable to look away from the twisted flesh. "Good Christ, you two intend to take on the queen, don't you?"

"Yes, we do," Orrin answered. He helped Aeron back into a chair, kissing her on the forehead as he untied her blindfold.

"That's treason," Kale said quietly, wisely not speaking of such a thing too loudly.

"Yes, that it is," Aeron croaked as Orrin pulled the gag free of her mouth.

Orrin finished untying her, carefully pulling off his shirt and slipping it over her head, since her torn garment was now useless. He noticed Kale staring intently at his movements and saw his face twist with the conflict Orrin was certain brewed inside him.

"We ask your assistance in our efforts," Orrin said as Aeron stood by his side. "However, if you cannot give it, we ask that you at least stay out of our way, because we intend to drag Her Majesty down, no matter what the cost."

The truth of what would happen to them should they fail was left unspoken, for they all knew the punishment for treason was immediate death. Orrin knew his brother was as loyal a man as he, bound to his country and his queen. But would the ties of family hold Kale's heart and soul as tightly as they did his own? Would his promise to take down the devil that had harmed their sister win over?

"Treason be damned," Kale said with a treacherous smile, the one Orrin had seen many times when they'd headed into a fight, the one he reserved for only the vilest of creatures. Kale reached across the table, extending an open hand to Aeron and asked, "How can I help send this demon back to hell?"

With Kale's allegiance to the cause sealed, they came to the agreement that he and his crew should come to the island for a full briefing of the plan and leave for port at first light. Aeron knew these waters and how to sail them as well as she knew the terrain of her island. So when she confidently promised she could plot a course that would shave an entire day and a half off the trip back to the queen's port harbor, Orrin didn't even question her claim.

As they emerged onto *Iona*'s main deck, Aeron grabbed the line handed to her, ready to swing back to the *Mermaid*. Orrin strolled up behind her and fit his palm over the flare of her hips.

"If you wish to sail back on your own ship, I will understand," she said over her shoulder, gripping the rope in both hands.

Orrin smiled, snaking one hand around her waist and wrapping the other around the rope above hers as he hoisted her body against his.

"I will be where I belong, wherever you are."

"You are incorrigible."

"Incredibly," he replied gripping the rope as they swung across the water.

"Welcome back, Captain," Darcy said as the pair landed on the deck of the *Mermaid*. He looked down his nose at Orrin, but the harsh edge to his stare had waned from what it had been before. "Maybe you aren't so bad after all," he said with a nod to Orrin.

"Thank you, my friend."

"I said you weren't so bad. I didn't say I was your friend." Darcy snorted, and he strolled away.

Orrin's mouth quirked up; something in the clipped tone of Darcy's voice gave him hope that they might indeed be friends one day. He liked that thought very much.

"Try to keep up," Aeron called over to Kale as she ran across the decks, beaming with pride and shouting orders to the crew. She took hold of a bowline and leaned into the wind with her entire body. A salty gust of sea air blew her hair, whipping it around her shoulders as she tossed her head back and laughed with abandon.

Orrin watched intently, captivated by this most beautiful creature before him. With her eyes closed and her chest thrown out against the wind, Aeron stood illuminated in the brilliant sunlight; her red hair danced like fire behind her, and the most glorious of smiles graced her perfectly formed mouth.

"She cannot be tamed," a familiar voice boomed behind Orrin. As he turned, he saw Darcy towering over him, watching him watch Aeron. "She is a force of nature that won't be held down, and only a fool would dare to try."

"I do not want to tame her. I couldn't imagine her any other way than she is," Orrin said thoughtfully. "No, I love Aeron just the way she is—stubborn, strong-willed, unpredictable, and more alive than anyone I've ever known in all of my life."

Darcy grunted a response, and Orrin swore he caught a hint of a smile on the large man's face as he nodded his head in agreement. "Just remember, break her, and I will break you," Darcy said as he clapped Orrin on the back, knocking him forward a step.

As the two vessels approached the island, several of Aeron's large men leapt from the ship and swam to shore, alerting the village of visitors.

The *Iona* and her crew were welcomed with open arms onto the island as they disembarked. This gave Orrin a sense of pride like he'd never felt before.

He pointed Kale and his men toward one of the lagoons where they could wash up before the evening's feast. They'd had a long journey, and Orrin knew all too well that they could all stand for a good bathing.

"Brother, I have to be honest with you," Kale said solemnly as they walked to the edge of the lagoon. "I get the sense that you will not be leaving with us on your ship tomorrow."

The pit of Orrin's stomach stung with guilt over what he was about to say. "No, Kale, I won't be returning with you."

"What about the men?" Kale asked as he turned to face him. "They need their captain."

Orrin had seen the way the men responded to Kale on the ship, had watched as they'd followed his every order and command without hesitation. "They have a captain," he said, swinging his arm over his brother's broad shoulders and ruffling his dark hair. Kale swatted Orrin's hand away and scowled playfully at him.

Orrin laughed. He looked across the large lagoon and saw Aeron, who smiled and winked at him as she ducked into the surrounding jungle and disappeared from sight.

"These are your men now," Orrin said, patting Kale. "I know where I belong."

"Do you love her?" Kale asked, looking at where Aeron had been.

"Yes," Orrin answered honestly. "With all of my heart."

Kale felt a twinge of jealousy as he watched Orrin take off into the jungle after Aeron. He'd never seen Orrin so happy and full of life, and it made his heart swell with joy. He hoped that one day he would find such bliss.

He couldn't recall the last time he'd bathed in water this fine; it was crystal clear and warm like a summer spring, easing his sore muscles and aching bones.

His mind then wandered suddenly to a place he hadn't intended it to. When the *Iona* had pulled up to the dock, scads of the villagers had come out to help moor the vessels and greet their beloved captain. There had been a girl amongst them with light caramel-colored hair and eyes of the deepest brown. It was her eyes that had caught his attention; for a shade so dark, they had a brightness about them that captivated him. Part of him tried to put the girl out of his mind as he washed away the grime, while the other part plotted a variety of ways that he might go about finding her.

After he bathed and dressed, he tied his shoulder-length hair back with a leather strap. Pieces of it slipped free and hung in his face.

Damn.

He did his best to push it behind his ears and keep it out of the way; it would have to do.

Following some of the others down a jungle path, he was surprised when he walked straight into the village square. So many people milled about that he couldn't believe it. How on earth was he going to locate one woman amongst them all?

A petite woman to his left struggled to see around a bundle of cloths she was carrying and was about to trip over one of the benches that hadn't been tucked into place. Kale raced over, easily scaling a table, and plucked the large pile of tablecloths from her arms as if it were light as a feather before she could fall.

It was her, the beautiful brown-eyed girl from the dock. He found it hard to believe that this delicate flower of a girl was a pirate or even in leagues with one. This was certainly the most peculiar band of pirates he'd ever seen.

"Oh, thank you," she said quietly, nervously pushing a stray lock of hair behind her ear in the same way Kale had done with his.

"It is my pleasure, my lady," Kale replied with a bow of his head. Surely this fair maiden was not in any way associated with the ball-scratching bilge rats he'd seen aboard Aeron's vessel.

She giggled, covering her mouth with her hand. "I'm not a lady, sir, I…" She stopped. She looked into his eyes for a moment, and Kale felt the world around him grind to a halt. She looked away just as fast, apparently forgetting what it was she was going to say. The most fetching shade of pink dusted her cheeks with embarrassment.

Kale was instantly taken with her. He'd had his share of women and then some, but none had melted his heart with one look and a half-spoken sentence like this woman had. He wanted to sweep her up into his arms and kiss the hell out of her more than he wanted his next breath. He cleared his throat dramatically.

"My name is Kale, Kale Walsh," he said with a full, sweeping bow. "May I have the honor of knowing your name, my lady?"

"Mauralynn Sullivan," she said with a tiny curtsey as her blush deepened, turning her skin a crimson that was even more breathtaking than the pink. "But everyone calls me Maura."

Taking her hand in his, Kale lifted her knuckles to his lips. "I am truly honored to make your acquaintance, sweet Lady Maura."

Chapter Thirteen

Aeron paced impatiently from one side of the cottage to the other, waiting for Orrin. He should have joined her by now. The way he had handled himself today, the sure way he'd taken up her cause in the face of his own brother had made her body tingle with need for him. She was anxious to have him and have him now.

Exasperated, she started up the path toward the village in search of Orrin and nearly collided with him not ten feet from her door.

"There you are. I was just coming to find you," she said with a bright smile.

Without a single word and without breaking his stride, Orrin scooped her into his arms with a mischievous gleam in his eye.

"What the devil, have you gone mad? Put me down!" Aeron commanded as she squealed, kicking her feet and flailing about.

"Absolutely not," Orrin laughed.

He hefted her over his shoulder, gave her a hard slap on the backside, and navigated his way back to the cottage. She heard his boot connect with the wood of the door as he kicked it open. He deposited her on the bed with such force she practically bounced back up onto her feet again. He flashed her a lopsided grin, walked over to her wardrobe, and began rifling through her clothes.

Aeron leaned back onto her elbows on the bed and watched as Orrin carefully inspected each of her dresses. The man was up to something, but what on earth could he be about?

"Fancy a dress to wear tonight, do you?"

Orrin pulled a crimson gown from the cabinet and held it to his chest. "I think I would look stunning in this color, don't you?" he asked, batting his eyelashes playfully at her as she cackled hysterically. Heavens above, how she adored him.

"Put that silly dress down and get your arse over here and make love to me, damn it," she demanded, patting the mattress next to her.

He looked over at her, thoughtfully, for just a moment.

"No," he said in return as he placed the garment back into the cabinet and continued through the remainder of her gowns.

"No?" she asked with a shock. *We'll see about that, sir,* she thought as she turned over on the bed and rose up onto her hands and knees, moving her hips from side to side and wiggling her rump temptingly, certain she knew his game. "Are you going to make me beg?" she asked with a sultry pout, skillfully playing her part.

"No," he said, calmly glancing over his shoulder at her. "I'm simply not going to make love to you right now."

That did it.

"What?" she asked, straightening up on her knees and fisting her hands on her hips as she narrowed her eyes at him.

"You heard me, woman," he said. He casually pulled a lavender gown from the wardrobe and crossed in front of her over to the settee, where he laid the dress and smoothed out its silky fabric.

"What the bloody hell are you doing?" she asked.

Orrin walked over and sighed as he knelt on the bed before her, taking her hands in his. "Do you have any idea how much I love you, Aeron?"

"Clearly not enough to take me when I offer myself to you," she snapped, not even trying to mask the irritation in her tone.

Orrin took a deep breath. "In less than a week we will go into battle, and…" He stopped. She could see the anguish on his face; he appeared to be struggling to find the right thing to say to her. Gently cradling her face in his palms, he started again. "I do not wish to tame you, Aeron. I only want…damn, this isn't coming out right." He scowled and cursed himself.

Her heart melted at his visible frustration. She felt the uncontrollable urge to soothe him.

"Don't be absurd. You and I, we have nothing to hide from one another. You can say anything to me, you know that."

As he took her hands in his again, he sucked in a deep gulp of air. "Marry me, Aeron," he blurted.

She stared blankly at him for a moment, eerily silent as she took in the words.

"Marry you," she said finally as she blinked at him in uncertainty. "You want to marry me?"

"God help me, I want nothing more in this life than to spend every waking moment making yours the best it can be. I want to fall asleep each night with you in my arms and wake each morning to your warm breath on my neck."

Everything in her chest clenched as tears streamed down her face. Almost immediately she felt Orrin's touch, wiping the tears away with his thumbs.

"Marry me, Aeron. Please."

The urgent pang in his voice stabbed at her, making her eyes squeeze shut as she shook her head slowly. "I can't."

"Why?" he asked, looking thoroughly wounded, as though she had just twisted a dagger deep into his heart.

Aeron slipped out of his grasp and rose off of the bed. She crossed the room hastily, needing the physical distance to think clearly. "Queen Winifred…"

"Damn the queen!" Orrin spat as he jumped from the bed, racing over to Aeron and turning her to face him. "I don't give a shite about the queen, nor do I fear her like you do. The only thing I fear is not having your love in my life."

"You have no need to fear *that*," she said with a sexy smirk in an attempt to distract him with her feminine wiles from the conversation at hand. She trailed a finger down to his trousers.

"Damn it, Aeron, do not treat me like one of your conquests. That is not what I meant by 'your love' and you know it," he said as he backed away from her, casting a disgusted glare. He turned and walked to the window, and she immediately felt horrible for making light of his feelings for her. She'd never felt more like the whore she'd been accused of being than she did in that very moment.

Her stomach roiled at the thought of Orrin seeing her that way now. She loved him more than she had any right to, more than she'd ever loved anyone in her life, more than she'd ever thought she *could* love another. She stepped up behind him, tentatively wrapping her arms loosely around his waist and leaning against his strong back.

"I'm sorry," she whispered, rubbing her lips against the muscles pulsing along his spine. "But you have to understand how much she frightens me."

He turned without hesitation and wrapped his arms around her protectively.

Clamping her arms around his waist, she pressed her cheek into the hard planes of his chest. "But it frightens me even more so what she would do to you if you were to be captured by her. You don't know her like I do, like Iona did." Aeron closed her eyes at the mere thought of anything happening to Orrin as a result of loving her. The image of Richard's lifeless body in the moonlight flashed before her, only instead of Richard's face in her mind's eye, it was Orrin's.

Orrin's strong fingers tilted her face to his. She tried to hide the fear welling up through the tears in her eyes, but one look from him—one hopeful, caring look—and the tears spilled over.

"My love, *you* have to understand that if I have you by my side, I fear nothing and no one, and that includes that wretched demon that passes herself off as queen." He kissed her forehead, as if that one simple act sealed them together. "I will see her fall for what she has done to you and Iona," he continued. "God himself will not be able to help her if she ever tries to harm you again."

Orrin's words resonated down into the very core of Aeron's being. He was her savior in every sense of the word, body and soul. How in heaven could she deny him?

The answer was simple: she couldn't. Nor did she want to any longer. She wanted him more than she'd ever wanted anything in her miserable life.

Her eyes cut to the settee, and she nodded to the lavender gown he'd laid out on it, all her apprehension melting away. "So am I to assume that *if* I say yes, that is that what you'd like me to wear for our wedding?"

"You assume correctly." He smiled and tightened his grip around her waist. "Is that a yes, then?"

"Is the dress a must?" she countered.

"Absolutely," he said with a teasing wink.

"Ugh, very well. If I must," Aeron groaned and rolled her eyes playfully. She loathed wearing a gown, but she would suffer the hell of being trussed up like a goose if it made him happy.

Elated, Orrin hoisted her into his arms, laughing. "Thank you," he whispered into her hair as he spun her around and kissed her neck.

After a brief discussion on when they would announce their engagement, they agreed that the evening's feast would do fine.

The pair then glided down the path, hand in hand, into the heart of the island village to meet with Kale and his men. In a jungle clearing just off the square, Kale's men were at swords with Aeron's, sparring for sport and practice.

Kale turned to face her, his arms crossed over his broad chest. "Your men are very good, Aeron, I'll give you that. Very disciplined and well trained," he said as she and Orrin approached the practice area.

"Thank you," Aeron said with a proud smile, "as are yours, from what I can see."

"I will say, I am horribly curious who your best swordsman is." Kale's violet blue eyes narrowed as he surveyed the men battling in front of them.

Aeron shook her head. "You may stop looking, for my best is not out there."

"Well now," Kale said with a grin as he pulled his sword from his belt, easily spinning the weight in his grip. "Bring him on. My curiosity is thoroughly piqued."

"Maura," she called over her shoulder to the petite woman arranging plates on a table across the square.

"Yes, Captain," the woman replied with a respectful bow of her head when she approached.

Aeron nodded toward Kale as she yanked her sword free and tossed the blade to Maura. "Please show our guest how it is done."

Kale's eyes widened as he saw sweet, shy Maura change into a warrior once the sword was in her hands. Her gaze locked onto his, her shoulders squared, and her jaw set for battle. She twisted the heavy blade over her head and raised a challenging eyebrow at Kale.

"Well?" she asked, waiting for him to advance.

"You're joking with me?" he asked with a laugh, lowering his weapon.

Maura pursed her lips and swung out with her sword, forcing his hand into defending himself.

"Do I look like I'm joking?" she asked from behind their crossed blades. Her voice was clear and sure, not quiet and meek as it had been before in the square. She no longer looked away blushing when he stared down at her.

Pulling his sword back, Kale blinked in disbelief when he saw the warm brown of Maura's eyes harden. He looked at her, her weapon poised above her head, and a slight twinge of fear skittered up his spine.

"What's the matter? Are you afraid?" she asked, a hint of a snarl in her voice as she egged him on with a slight flick of her sword and a smile.

"No, but I will not fight a woman," Kale said, narrowing his eyes at her.

Kale lowered his weapon again and turned to walk away. He heard her feet moving across the ground as she began to advance on him, swiping her blade through the air and forcing him to defend himself once again.

"You *are* afraid," Maura said, pulling her weapon away as she glared at him. "Afraid to lose to a woman." She threw the words back over her shoulder as she walked away from him. She was baiting him, and he knew it.

"I am not," Kale bristled, unable to hold his tongue any longer as he watched Maura turn her back to him outright. "However, I do not believe that swords belong in the hands of women."

Orrin burst out laughing and shook his head. "Little brother, that has got to be the single most preposterous thing I have ever heard you utter."

"What is so bloody preposterous about it?" Kale asked innocently, sliding his sword into its scabbard. "A woman's place is in the home with a babe on her hip, not a blade in her hand."

Orrin shook his head in disbelief and set a gentling hand on Aeron's shoulder as she riled. "Kale..." he began in a clear warning.

"Our mother and sister only picked up a sword to hand it to a man, never to wield it," Kale said, ignoring his brother's warning as he looked to Aeron and Maura.

"That is true." Orrin nodded, discreetly stepping in front of Aeron and putting himself in the line of fire. "However, had they learned to use a weapon, they may have been able to defend themselves when they were attacked."

"It wouldn't have mattered," Kale replied, shaking his head at the memory and the horrible truth. "They would still be dead."

"True as well," Orrin agreed, the pain evident in his face mirroring that of Kale's. "However, they may have been able to take a few of those scurvy bastards with them before they went if they'd learned to fight." Orrin curled his arm around Kale's shoulder, leaning in so only he could hear his whispered words. "Besides, going to swords with a beautiful woman can be quite...exhilarating."

Kale thought back to moments before, how his blood thrummed through his veins and his muscles hardened at Maura's advances on him. Hell, he still couldn't wrap his brain around it; it was as if there were two separate women residing in one lusciously beautiful body. But which one was the real Maura—the shy, nervous girl or the bold, confident temptress? He'd always favored the former in his trysts with women, choosing the ones that bent to his will, young and innocent. But truthfully, he hoped that Maura was the latter. God help him, he all but prayed for it.

Kale tried desperately to hide the smirk on his face as he looked over at Maura. She was absolutely seething, jaw clenched, nostrils flared, and her succulent mouth pulled tight in the rage that radiated off of her.

"I think she hates me," he said to Orrin.

"Aye, I think they both do." Orrin laughed and poked Kale in the ribs with his elbow. "I'd sleep with one eye open if I were you."

"No, I have a better idea," he said as he pulled his sword free and strode toward Maura.

As the pair began to spar viciously, Aeron sidled up next to Orrin. "Watching your brother and his men, I feel we need to revise our plan of attack on the queen," she said quietly.

"How so?" Orrin asked with a quirk of his brow.

She nodded to men that were battling it out in front of them. "Their skill is near perfect, and they double our numbers. I'm beginning to think we should wait out Her Majesty here on the island."

"Do you, now? I seem to remember hearing that somewhere quite recently," he said, tapping his chin playfully.

"Do not be a smug arse. I haven't decided yet. Darcy," she said as she turned to her first mate, who was standing behind them and taking in the artful melee.

"Yes, Captain?"

"What do you think on the matter?" she asked. "Should we take the fight to the open water or wait it out on the island?"

Darcy blinked at her. "I think," he began, uneasily shifting from one foot to the other, "we should do whatever you think is best, Captain, naturally."

She couldn't blame his uncertainty; she'd never really asked for his or anyone else's input before. Her word had always been law, and that was it. Then Orrin had come along, tilting her world on its ear and forcing her to see things in a new light. *He* had good ideas and thoughts; perhaps Darcy had them as well. If they were going to win this fight, she would have to set her pride aside, at least this time.

"Darcy, you have been with me from the beginning and been at this even before that. I trust you implicitly," she said, laying a hand on his shoulder. "What would *you* do?"

He scrubbed his large, calloused hand over the back of his neck nervously as he looked from Aeron to Orrin and back again. She imagined he'd never been asked such a thing.

"As much as it pains me to say this," he began cautiously, "I think he is right." Darcy nodded toward Orrin. "If we conceal their ship in the cave, the queen's men will never know that Kale and his crew are even here."

Aeron nodded in agreement. "Yes, and if I know Her Majesty, she will be arrogant enough to not waste the entire fleet on taking one ship, but I do believe she will send William, in hopes that we will take care of him out of revenge, I'm sure. Two birds with one stone, as they say."

"Aye, and if we can get to William…" Darcy started, a dark smile curling his lips.

Aeron nodded again with a true pirate's egregious look flashing across her face. "Exactly. If we can get to William, I'm almost certain that we can turn him against her again and use him and his men to our advantage."

"So we wait for them to come to us, just as I said," Orrin chimed in. He smiled, resting his hand casually on the hilt of his sword.

Grabbing the front of Orrin's shirt, Aeron balled it in her fist and used it to pull his face down to her level. "Mind that tongue, sir," she scowled playfully at him. "I've grown quite fond of that tongue and its abilities, and I'd hate to have to cut it out of that pretty mouth of yours."

"God, but I'd love to see you try," he challenged, the pink tip of his tongue flitting out from between his lips.

Their increasingly torrid conversation was interrupted by the sound of Maura's voice echoing across the practice field.

"Do you yield?" she asked, quite loudly, as she knelt on Kale's chest, pinning him to the sand with her sword lying flat across his throat.

"Yes," Kale said.

"I'm sorry, what was that?" Maura asked, tilting her ear toward Kale.

"Yes!" he shouted.

Maura flashed a victorious smile before she slowly rose to her feet and offered Kale her hand. He took it and stood before her, encompassing her petite hand with his as he looked down into her eyes.

"Defeat has never been so sweet, my lady," he said, lifting her fingers to his lips and placing a kiss across her knuckles. Maura blushed profusely, pulling her hand from Kale's grip and handing Aeron her sword.

As Maura trotted off to her duties, Aeron took this opportunity to pull Kale aside and discuss their new plan of attack.

Kale appeared to be listening intently as they laid out the plan, nodding his approval with every passing word, but Aeron could see that his attention was elsewhere. The fact that he continued to steal glances back at Maura, who was arranging some flowers on a nearby table, did not escape her notice. By devil, was he actually chewing the inside of his lip in an effort to hide a smile that just looking at Maura gave him?

"That sounds like an excellent plan. I'm in," Kale said, slapping Orrin on the back dismissively. "Will you excuse me?" he asked, and he wandered off toward the tables and Maura.

"By Christ, he's got it bad," Orrin said as he watched his brother make a quick path to the lovely Maura and do his best to help her arrange flowers.

"So does she." Aeron watched Maura's eyes light up and a bright pink dust her cheeks at the mere sight of Kale heading in her direction.

This made Aeron smile; however, she was also very aware of Kale's reputation with women. "She's not like me, Orrin. Your brother had better mind himself with her, or I swear…"

Orrin slid in behind her and wrapped his arm around her waist, pulling her close to his body. "Don't worry, I will keep an eye on him," he said, dropping open-mouthed kisses on her neck. "So, we should find the priest, don't you think?"

Aeron peeked over his shoulder to see Darcy arch his eyebrow at Orrin's inquiry. "I never said we had a priest on the island," she said as she started to walk away, not wanting anyone else to hear their conversation.

"People marry on this island, do they not?" he asked, following her.

"They have, many times," she answered cryptically. "But I still never said we had priest to marry them. We only have a friar."

"Damn it, woman," Orrin grumbled, stopping as he pinched the bridge of his nose in frustration.

Aeron laughed and circled her arms around his waist. "Wait a moment, now that I think about it, I do seem to recall that *our* friar is also a priest. Come, he should be preparing to bless today's catch on the other side of the island."

She took Orrin's hand and led him away.

Chapter Fourteen

fter their meeting with an exuberant Friar Morgan, Orrin strolled with Aeron along the west shore. As they paused, he found that his eyes naturally shifted to her. He watched her stare longingly out over the water. The setting sun brought out the fire red in her hair as an ocean breeze kicked up and blew wisps around her face. He felt his breath catch in his chest at the mere sight of her. Gliding in behind her, he rested his chin on her shoulder, taking in the distinct scent of her skin tinged with the salty smell of the sea.

"Let's get married here, on this shore, with the setting sun behind us," he said.

"Yes," she agreed, nodding her acquiescence as she turned, coiling her arms around his neck. Against the backdrop of the setting sunlight as it reflected off the water, tiny flecks of gold appeared in her eyes amongst the vivid blues and greens. She was a wonder to behold.

Her hand rose to his cheek, rasping over his few days' worth of whiskers. They were battle-worn hands, covered in rough calluses and scars, but he loved them as other men loved soft and smooth hands on a woman. "I would marry you anywhere, my love. Anywhere." Her breath was warm and moist against his chin as she spoke.

Orrin smiled, and he turned his mouth to her palm to lay a slow kiss in the middle of her hand. He kept his eyes steady, staring a hole right through her as his tongue leisurely slid across the lifeline in her palm.

Her body shivered in his arms. Her sure, strong voice cracked and whimpered his name in a plea as his lips scraped across the pulse-point of her delicate wrist. Yes, he knew exactly what she wanted. Orrin clasped his hand behind her neck and pulled her mouth to his in a heated embrace. He wanted to devour her on the spot, consume her right then and there without a care as to who happened upon them.

However, a strange sense of modesty got the better of him, and he broke the ardent kiss as ferociously as he had taken it. They both stood still, staring at each other and panting with need as water began to rush around their boots.

"We must get back to the village," he said breathlessly, his fingers still clenched at the back of her skull, buried deeply in her hair.

She shook her head, opening her mouth to protest.

Orrin held a long, nimble finger to her lips; he knew if he heard how much she wanted him now, he'd concede. He traced the line of her graceful jaw, leaning in to drop kisses in the path his finger laid. He rose to his full height before her, a positively sinful smirk playing across his lips.

"Tonight, after dinner, you will be my dessert," he crooned smoothly as he tugged her into the jungle and toward the village before she could gather a response.

Aeron was still in a daze at his words when they took up their seats at a table with Darcy and his family. *His dessert.* God's mercy.

As the feast progressed, she surveyed the people before her with great pride—her people. Everyone around them seemed to be having the most wonderful time, laughing with old friends and drinking with new ones. She glanced over and saw Kale pull the chair out next to him and offer it to Maura, who happily accepted.

"You're in good spirits this evening, Captain," Catrin said, tucking in next to Aeron.

"I am." She turned to her friend, her turquoise eyes twinkling like never before. "I truly am."

"Mmhm." Catrin nodded, her eyes flicking to Darcy as she leaned her chin into her hand. "I can't rightly imagine what or *who* could be at the heart of such happiness." Catrin glanced pointedly over at Orrin.

"You have no idea," Aeron said as she stood to gather everyone's attention. She clapped her hands together and called out to the sea of people.

"Everyone, quiet. I have something I'd like to say." Her voice echoed through the square. The boisterous conversations quickly silenced, and every person turned to give Aeron full attention. It was a rare occasion for Aeron to address the entire village like this, so every eye looked to her and every ear listened for this mysterious announcement as she stood before them.

"You all know how much I love each and every one of you. You are my friends, my family. We've seen each other through good times and bad, through battles won and lost. We've buried dear friends and welcomed new." She reached over and took Orrin's hand in hers, pulling him to his feet beside her. "You all know this man, Orrin. He's worked with you in this land of ours and broken bread with you at these very tables. He has brought a new sense of joy to this island and to my heart." Her adoring gaze immediately fell onto the man at her side. "I love him dearly." Her voice caught with emotion, but she continued to speak. "And in three days' time, I wish for you all to join us on the west bank as we make our vows as man and wife."

A shocked silence hung in the square a moment before a round of thunderous cheers erupted.

To Aeron's great surprise, Kale rose to his feet as well, clapping and prompting the entire village to stand in their cheers. Grabbing his cup, Kale leapt up onto the table, teetering ever so slightly. He raised his free hand into the air to quiet the villagers, and when all was quiet, he thrust his tankard of rum into the air and turned to Orrin and Aeron.

"To my brother, Orrin, the greatest man I've known since our father. And to Aeron, who is undeniably his one true match." A strange, heady look shadowed his eyes, like he was having a grand vision. "I believe everyone has one true match in life, and when you find them, you don't ever let them go." He cast a longing glance down to Maura for a moment, and a broad smile spread across his face. "May you have many children, and may you name at least one of them after me," he said as the entire village laughed.

"*Sláinte!*" he shouted — the Gaelic toast — and raised his cup once again. Everyone clanged their metal cups together in a resounding cheer.

The people danced and drank while the night wore on. Even Darcy gave his blessing, after threatening Orrin's life if anything should happen to Aeron in his care.

In amongst all the celebration and well wishes, Aeron managed to lose track of Orrin. Her eyes flittered about the square, scanning every inch until she finally spotted him across the way, filling a pitcher with wine. He smiled over at her as he gathered the pitcher in one hand and a plate of fruit in the other. His gaze never left hers as he sauntered over to her with pure, male confidence.

Aeron had to blink her eyes and steel her nerves as he got closer and closer, the world around her seeming to come unraveled like a spool of thread when he looked at her that way. She drew a lusty sigh as he leaned into her ear, his hot breath washing over her.

"Shall we retire and have our own celebration?" he purred.

"For dessert?" she asked breathlessly, as his scent seemed to linger and swirl around her.

He nodded, a promise of untold pleasure sparking in his eyes.

"I'm famished," she managed to say when her voice came back to her.

Orrin's tongue rolled lazily across his lips as his eyes traveled up and down her body, lingering on the flare of her hips and the swell of her bosom.

"As am I." His voice was low and rich, and the sound of it made her shiver with yearning.

With a kiss on her temple and a saucy wink, Orrin disappeared down the path to the cottage.

Aeron had to take a moment to gather her thoughts and catch her breath before she followed his lead. God, but he made her absolutely insane with want, even when he wasn't being overtly sexual. Watching him simply standing in the square and talking to his brother Kale earlier had made her want to waltz over, throw him onto a nearby table, and devour him in front of God and everyone. With a quick look around, she casually picked up two cups from a nearby table and ducked into the jungle.

Her heart hammered like mad in her chest as she reached the cottage. She easily pushed the door open with her hip and promptly dropped the cups to the floor.

"Is something the matter, my love?" he asked, lounging on her bed wearing the wickedest of smiles and absolutely nothing else.

Orrin's delightfully naked body shimmered with a light sheen of perspiration in the candlelight as he lay on his side, propped up on his elbow. He tilted his head back as he lifted a slice of mango to his lips and proceeded to seductively tongue the delicate flesh and slowly suck it into his mouth. Aeron thought she was going to faint dead away. He licked the sticky juice off his lips as he picked up another slice of fruit and held it out to her in an offering, the sweet nectar spilling over his fingers and down his arm.

Harnessing every ounce of restraint she had, Aeron took her time crawling up onto the bed, slowly leaning forward and plucking the savory mango from his fingers. Looking deep into his cerulean blue eyes, she wrapped her fingers around his wrist and extended his arm out straight as she licked the sweet nectar from the crease of his elbow with a light brush of her tongue, up to the tip of his finger. She slid her free hand down his chest, tracing over the trails of course brown hair surrounding his nipples and spilling down his taut belly. Her finger dipped into his navel as she continued down, but he snatched her hand, rolling with her and trapping her beneath him.

He growled playfully, hovering over her and pinning her arms to the mattress over her head with an iron grip. "Not yet." He bent his head, grasping the ties of her shirt in his teeth and tugging the knots open.

William sat alone in his room, staring blankly at the dagger in his hands and twisting it in the light of the setting sun. Aeron had given him the knife as a gift when he'd become a member of her crew. A knot twisted in his stomach as he remembered his time with her, with the crew, when a knock rattled the door.

"Come in," William said, feeling slightly numb from the three cups of wine he'd consumed.

"Your Highness, the brig *Iona* is no longer in port," a page reported.

Will nodded his acknowledgement of this information. "Did her captain leave word before they sailed?" he asked, filling his cup for the fourth time.

"Yes, Sir, word was that they left to locate the *Mermaid* and her captain. They mean to hold her for you, Sir."

"Thank you," William said, rolling the dagger in his fingers and taking a gulp of wine. "You are dismissed."

"Shall I inform Her Majesty the Queen of this news?"

"No," William answered. "You will say nothing to my mother. No one will. Is that understood?

"Yes, Your Highness." The page bowed as he took his leave.

William looked out at the ships bobbing up and down in the port, digging at the table with his dagger as he waited for the effects of that fourth cup of wine to set in.

The old heavy wooden door of his room flew open and cracked against the wall with a loud bang.

"Why are we still here, William?" Winifred bellowed. "Why are there so many ships in my port?" The queen's voice was growing louder and shriller with each word she spat from her thin lips. "When are we leaving?" she demanded.

"When we are ready," he said, casually filling yet another cup with sweet wine. He refused to look at her, defiantly keeping his eyes on his task.

She crossed the room with the fluidity of vapor and stood menacingly next to his chair. "We are ready now."

"Really, Mother," Will said in a decidedly dismissive tone as he set his dagger down and rolled his eyes at her. "You don't know the first thing about sailing, so what makes *you* think we are ready?"

In a flash of pale skin, the queen grabbed William by the hair and jerked his head back. She snatched the dagger off the table with lightning speed and pressed the steel to his throat. He could feel the sharp edge of the metal as he swallowed hard and grit his teeth against the pain. "You will remember that I am your queen, and you will address me as such. My word is law. Is that understood?"

"Yes," he choked out, wincing as the tip of the blade stung his skin and a trickle of blood rolled down his neck.

"I rule this kingdom, and I say we sail at dawn, understood?" Her voice was so cold and cruel it cut deeper than the dagger at his throat.

"Yes, Your Majesty."

Releasing his hair as if it were a lice-ridden mop, Winifred threw the dagger to the floor. She swept her arm across the table, scattering the items it held and sending the pitcher of wine shattering to the floor below as she stormed from the room without another word.

A sick feeling churned in the pit of Will's stomach at the way his mother had treated him since he'd returned. This was not the way mothers behaved toward their children on Aeron's island, and this was not the way she'd treated him when he was younger.

Yes, when he was a boy he'd heard the whispers in the castle about his mother, the talk of her preference for the company of women, her cool nature and an enjoyment for cruelty that he didn't understand at the time, though for all he was worth he couldn't recall her acting that way toward him. Granted, the memories of his childhood with his mother were horribly blurry in his mind's eye, if there were any memories at all to speak of. But she was his mother, for God's sake; surely she'd harbored some love for him?

He was terribly uncertain of that now.

Reality seeped in, and William wondered what his mother would do to Aeron once she had her, what the woman was really capable of.

Later that evening, as he lay in his bed, William heard cries in the hall outside. They sounded distant, as if they were coming from the floor above: his mother's level. He rose from the bed, crept out of his chambers and down to the stairs. Stalking up the stone steps to the next floor, Will peered around the corner when he reached the top. He had to know the truth, for once and for all, if all the rumors he had heard about his mother were true.

There at the end of the hall, cowering under a table against the wall, was a redheaded servant girl. She looked at William as he slowly walked toward her.

Something flashed in his mind like a bolt of lightning.

A memory from his childhood, one that shook his very core and practically crippled him on the spot.

He remembered being about ten years old and wandering the halls on his way to bed when he had come upon a young Aeron huddled in the hallway, terrified and alone. He remembered she had been sobbing, and there had been blood on her face and dress. He had always been very fond of Aeron as a child; she had made him laugh when all of his mother's other ladies ignored him. He remembered wanting to help her, but he hadn't known what to do, so he did the only thing a child could do: he raced up the stairs and fetched his father for help.

Why haven't I remembered this before now?

Will moved slowly as he gingerly knelt in front of the girl. She pressed herself tighter against the stone wall, a look of complete and utter horror shading her sallow eyes. He spoke softly to her, soothing her, trying to assure her that all would be okay as he helped her out from under the wooden table and to her bloodstained bare feet.

"Step away from her," his mother's voice growled from behind him.

"She's hurt and needs aid. I was only trying to—"

"I said step away!" she shouted, her eyes so piercingly cold he could almost feel her gaze burrowing under his skin.

Seeing his mother like this was like waking up from a dream and realizing that reality was the nightmare, what he'd fled from. William felt a tear slide down his cheek as he whispered an apology to the trembling, sobbing girl and obediently backed away.

"Go back to your room, and you are not to touch my things again unless you want to share the same fate as your father," Winifred snarled.

He couldn't look up from the floor, terror holding him still as he saw his mother's hand shoot out and grab the wrist of the poor girl. The sound of the girl's pleas to be let alone echoed inside his skull as he heard her drag across the floor and the door to his mother's room slam shut.

William jolted at the harsh sound of the bolt locking into place, trapping the poor girl inside with his mother.

He should have beaten down the door. He should have raced back to his room and grabbed up his sword and…

Will swallowed hard, pushing back the thoughts, and slowly walked back to his room, closing the door behind him as the sounds of the girl's screaming flowed through the halls.

With a decidedly numb feeling, Will lay down in his bed and did what he had remembered doing as a child. He tucked himself into a tight ball, pulling the pillow over his head and clamping his hand over his ears. When even that didn't drown out the sound, he took a deep, shuddering breath and hummed himself to sleep like the coward he was.

Chapter Fifteen

eron awoke to a sunbeam spilling through the window. She blinked a few times in the bright light and stretched out underneath the welcomed weight of Orrin's arm. She looked lovingly at him as the sun lit up the contours of his face. He groaned sleepily, and his feet moved underneath the bed sheet, tugging it down and exposing his tantalizingly nude body.

A jolt of lust shook Aeron at the mere sight of this decadent man. His full mouth curled into a smile, as if he could sense her need for him even in his restful state. Carefully reaching up, she traced her fingers through the slightly coarse golden hair that sprinkled across his chest before the temptation got the better of her and she leaned forward to place a gentle kiss near his nipple.

Strong, sure hands gently covered hers, and Aeron could feel the rhythmic beat of his heart accelerating.

"Good morning, my love," he murmured, drawing her attention to his knee-melting, sleepy grin.

Aeron curled her leg around his, rubbing the pad of her foot up the back of his calf. God, he had the most exquisite mouth, and damned if he didn't use it in the best of ways.

"I'd wager that you could tempt a nun out of her vow of chastity with this mouth of yours," she speculated out loud.

"I don't know about that. Hell, once upon a time I couldn't even keep my own wife faithful with it, let alone tempt a woman of God out of her vow."

She looked at him, taking in the full scope of his face. He was so hard to read sometimes. He'd spoken of his wife only once before, sharing the tale one evening as they'd lain together in the dying candlelight. As with then, there was something inside him that was broken, some part left from his former life that she felt only she could repair.

"Orrin, your former wife must have been troubled and innately stupid, for I can honestly say that even if I live a thousand years, plus one, I could never want another man, ever. No other man has touched me the way that you do. No other man has loved me the way that you do. You've crept your way into my heart, into my very soul, and ruined me for anyone else," she said, tracing the line of his brow and down along the sharp edge of his jaw.

"Good," he said, cupping her face and kissing her tenderly. "God, how I love you."

"Mmm," Aeron hummed, soaking up the adoration, feeling the tension that had been in him moments before melt away. His hand started to move down her back, sliding over the curve of her hip, tickling the flesh of her buttock. "Oh no, you don't. You can't start this now. You have got to let me up. I have a session with Maura, and *you* need to check on your brother and his crew and get them sorted." She swatted his hands away and twisted out from under his grip.

After some light protesting and a series of gropes that she almost gave in to, Orrin finally relented and let Aeron leave the cottage.

Aeron stood back in the jungle, watching Maura slash her sword through the air for a moment. Suddenly, Maura closed her eyes. A rosy blush covered her face as she began to smile and absentmindedly toe the sand beneath her feet. Aeron had seen that color in her cheeks and that smile quite often in the last day, almost always in the presence of Orrin's brother, Kale.

"Thinking of anyone in particular?" Aeron asked, startling Maura out of her skin.

"I'm sorry, Captain," Maura said, her blush deepening to scarlet. "Forgive me, I have my focus now." Maura squared her shoulders and rolled her neck as she swung her sword into the ready position. "I'm ready for my training."

"Put your sword away, Maura. We need to talk." Aeron smiled, and she stepped out of the jungle, her thumb hooked around the hilt of her own blade tucked neatly into its scabbard.

A look of panic spread over Maura as her mouth worked to speak, but Aeron put up her hand. "Don't worry, you've done nothing wrong, and you are coming along wonderfully in your training," she said. Maura breathed a sigh of relief as Aeron continued, "As a matter of fact, I want you to come with me."

Maura sheathed her sword and followed Aeron into the jungle.

"You have trained very hard, Maura, and after the way you fought Kale yesterday, you've proven to me that you are finally ready," she said, pushing through the greenery toward her cottage.

As they stepped inside Aeron's cottage, she moved to a trunk inside her wardrobe cabinet. She dug around inside and pulled out a soft, leather belt and sparkling sword. "These are for you," she said and handed the items to a stunned Maura.

Maura gingerly took the gifts, marveling at the wondrous blade and turning the belt in her hands as she gazed at the image carved into the leather scabbard. "A dolphin?"

"Yes." Aeron nodded. "A dolphin looks very docile and unassuming, smiling at the world like an imp, but in truth, they can be quite deadly when provoked. Just like you."

"Captain, I…"

Aeron turned back to her wardrobe and pulled out a bundle of garments. "Here," she said, handing the bundle to Maura, "you'll find it much easier to fight in these."

She watched Maura chew her bottom lip as she admired the pair of trousers and blouse. In all of her training, Aeron had always required that Maura wear a skirt, for she knew better than anyone that if one could effectively fight in a dress, one could fight in anything.

Maura stayed silent, shaking her head as if in disbelief.

"Captain, thank you, this is an honor…"

"But…" Aeron cocked a wary eyebrow.

Maura continued to shake her head as she looked at the clothing and the sword.

"Is something wrong?" Aeron asked, laying a gentle hand on her shoulder.

"No…I don't know," Maura said, finally looking Aeron in the eye. "Captain, can I talk to you? Woman to woman, not crew to captain?"

"Of course you can. You are like a sister to me, Maura. Please, sit." Aeron motioned to the chairs on the other side of the cottage.

Maura set her bundles on the settee and sat in the chair next to her.

"I just don't know what is happening to me," Maura began, wringing her hands in frustration. "I was just fine until he—" She suddenly bound to her feet and began to pace the small room back and forth. "Every time he looks at me, I—" Maura took a deep breath, trying to gather her random thoughts into a single cohesive one. "When he smiles, I just—" Apparently giving up on making any sense, Maura finally flung herself back down into the chair. "Oh, I just don't know what to do!" she wailed.

Aeron smiled widely and tried not to laugh. She knew these feelings very well. "I assume the 'he' you are speaking of is Kale, no?"

"Yes," Maura said, vaulting to her feet again. "Saints, why is it that every time he is near me I feel like I'm about to come out of my own skin?" She took up pacing the room again. "Yesterday, I wanted to strangle him and kiss him all in the space of a breath as we sparred. He infuriates me and makes me feel alive all at the same time," she rambled, twisting her hands in her hair in apparent frustration. "I don't know him from Adam, and he makes me feel like I'm losing my mind."

Maura spun around and faced Aeron squarely. "I never thought I would ever want to be touched the way I want him to touch me," Maura said quietly, uncertainty about her feelings creasing her delicate brow. "After serving in the castle under Her Majesty's reign, I never imagined that I'd ever want to be touched at all, by anyone, let alone a man I barely know." Maura gazed out of the window and hugged herself tightly. "I had all but resigned myself to living a celibate life. I vowed to myself that I would never let another touch me that way again." Maura stared at her hands, her finger threading and unthreading. "But when I look at him, it's all that I want."

Aeron rose and wrapped her arm protectively around Maura as the young woman laid her head on Aeron's shoulder.

"Sweet Maura, please don't let that vile woman spoil what could be something true and good in your life. Orrin taught me that," she said as she stroked Maura's hair and kissed her cheek. "Kale is a good man. I can feel it in the marrow of my bones, and he will be good to you." Aeron took Maura by the face and looked her in the eyes. "Otherwise, I will just have to kill him," she said with a wink, and they both broke into a fit of giddy laughter.

Orrin met Kale in the middle of the village square.

"Kale, what on earth are you doing here? I thought you'd be off following Maura around like a puppy," he said with a wink.

"Yes, well," Kale said as he nervously rubbed the back of his neck, "I need to talk to you. God knows I need to talk to someone, and fast, because I honestly don't know what to do," Kale continued, running a hand through his tousled dark hair.

Orrin closed his eyes, mentally preparing himself for the worst. His little brother was notorious for his uncanny knack of getting into trouble at the least opportune of times. More often than not, said trouble involved women…or their irate fathers or husbands.

"What have you done now?" Orrin asked reluctantly, taking a deep, calming breath. "This trouble of yours couldn't possibly involve a woman this time."

Kale only stared at him and worked his bottom lip between his teeth, a horribly pained and guilty expression on his face.

"Good God, man, please tell me this does not involve Maura. I'm telling you now, do not dally with that one. Aeron is very much aware of your past *indiscretions,* and if your inclinations toward Maura are anything but honorable—"

"Christ Almighty, do I look like an idiot? I haven't laid a single finger on Maura."

"You're damned lucky then, because, so help me, Kale, if you hurt her, Aeron will have your head."

"I half wish she would," Kale said as drew his sword and handed Orrin the hardy blade. "Please, I beg you, as my brother, wallop me good and hard in the skull so I can get these thoughts out of it, for Christ's sake."

"Have you gone completely mad?" Orrin asked, thrusting the weapon back into his brother's hands. On any other day, he'd gladly deliver a sound wallop to Kale's head, but the man wasn't making a lick of sense.

"I honestly think I'm losing my mind because, as much as I try, I cannot get that blasted woman out of my brain." Kale took to pacing. "I can't think, I can't even sleep without seeing her in my dreams, and when she does cross my path in the waking hours, it's all I can do to not rush over and fawn all over her like a blithering fool."

Orrin laughed hard and slapped his thigh. "You're in love, you dumb bastard," he said, giving Kale a swift congratulatory slap on the back.

"God and ghost, how the devil do I make it stop?"

Orrin shook his head with o' grin. "Little brother, you are fighting a losing battle if there ever was one. If you love her, be a man and make her your wife, for you will not find a better woman anywhere on this earth."

"Love just one woman for the rest of my life?" Kale asked with a laugh. "Now who's the barking mad one?"

"Have you tried?"

"Yes, I have," Kale said immediately. Orrin knew this was a knee-jerk reaction; Kale despised admitting he was wrong, which had made their relationship as captain and second-in-command a tumultuous one. "It was…" Kale snapped his fingers. "Christ, what was her name? She was about this tall." Kale held his hand up at his shoulder to indicate the mystery woman's height. "She had blond hair…I think…or was she a redhead…" Kale screwed up his face, evidently trying hard to remember a name, any name.

"Honestly, Kale, *you* can't even keep your women straight, and you expect me to remember one of them that may or may not have blond hair? You can't even pull a single name out of your head. Doesn't that tell you something?"

"Well, there were a *lot* of women," Kale muttered, unapologetically.

"Indeed." Orrin nodded. "And if you can name any one of them that makes you feel even half of what you feel with Maura, you have my blessing to beat my arse stupid."

Kale made a good show of attempting to come up with a name, but Orrin knew his brother well, and in no time, Kale was shaking his head in concession.

"Absolutely none," he sighed, a smile stretching so wide across his mouth there was only one way to describe it: love-struck. "Not a single woman has plagued my thoughts or made me feel like a complete and utter madman the way Maura does."

"Then I believe you've come to a conclusion," Orrin said.

When Kale looked up to dispute his brother's accusations of love, his words gave pause; the very breath he was using to speak had just been snatched from his lungs. He stared across the square at the vision emerging from the jungle.

"What the bloody hell is wrong with you? Have all those blows to the head finally taken hold?" Orrin asked.

Kale's mouth went dry as Maura stepped into the village square; an air of confidence swirled around her like smoke, thickening with each step.

He never dreamed he would find a woman dressed in such a way alluring in the slightest. Gone were the flowing skirts and dainty slippers she wore yesterday. His hungry eyes traveled up the black leather boots that stretched up over her knees, to the fitted black trousers that clung desperately to every mouth-watering curve. She wore a pale pink shirt with a delicate ruffle at her wrists and collar, and her silky brown hair was tied back with a length of shiny black satin ribbon. She looked positively ravishing.

Maura strode confidently over and stood directly in front of him, one hand on her hip and the other one poised on the hilt of the sword. "Do you still believe a woman has no business with a sword?" she asked with a challenging arch of her brow.

"I humbly stand corrected, my lady," Kale said with a sweeping bow. "I honestly have never seen a sword look more beautiful than when it is in the hands of a woman as stunningly radiant as the one before me this very moment." He reached forward, took her hand, and pressed it to his lips.

God save me, this woman is going to be the death of me.

Aeron soaked up the rays of the afternoon sun as she sat in front of Darcy and Catrin's cottage, stitching lavender fins on the collar of a new shirt for Orrin. She'd never thought she would be comfortable caring for a man like this, sewing his clothes and the like, but she loved doing it for him.

He'd been with Kale all morning, and she hadn't seen him since she woke up to his sweet morning kisses and sleepy lovemaking.

The leaf litter behind the cottage rustled with the distinct sound of booted feet gliding along the ground. This could only mean one thing: Orrin was trying to sneak up on her again. Aeron shook her head as a twig quietly popped a few feet behind her.

"Did you try this shirt on to check the fit, like I asked?" she said without turning.

"Christ, woman," Orrin grumbled from behind her. "Can you at least pretend you didn't hear me, just once? I do have a hint of male pride, you know."

Aeron tried not laugh as she stood, carefully setting the shirt and sewing things on the chair. She stepped around it and wrapped her arms around his lean waist, laying her head on his hard chest.

"You are getting better, though," she said in her sweetest voice, trying to ease the sting to his ego. "I didn't hear you until you were right on top of me." She stretched up onto her tiptoes and kissed the square of his jaw.

"On top of you, ay? I *do* like the sound of that." He closed his arms around her and pulled her firmly against his body.

God, he is wicked, and he is all mine, Aeron thought as Orrin smoothed his hand down her back and gripped her buttocks hard.

Just when Orrin bent his mouth to hers, the sound of Darcy clearing his throat stopped them before they could touch lips.

"Captain?"

Aeron groaned at the interruption. "What is it now, Darcy?" She knew that even though Darcy was warming up to Orrin, he still wasn't convinced of where Orrin's allegiances lay. But did he have to interrupt them so often?

"Our crew and the men of the *Iona* have been assembled and are waiting on you both for instruction."

"Noted," Aeron said with a nod. As she turned to kiss Orrin, she noticed that Darcy hadn't moved a single inch and was staring blindly over their heads, trying not to look directly at them. "Is there something else?"

Darcy cleared his throat again, dropping his gaze to the ground as he rubbed the back of his neck and screwed up his face. "Kale appears to be missing. His crew says they haven't seen him all morning or afternoon."

"I was with him all morning, but I left him nearly a half hour ago. I assumed he was going back to his men," Orrin said, looking completely confused and none too happy at what Darcy was implying about his brother. A fight between these two would most assuredly not end well.

"Hmm…" Aeron hummed as she tapped her chin. "He must be here somewhere. Where is Maura? Have you checked with her?" she asked, narrowing her eyes.

"She went to the east shore to practice over an hour ago, as she always does," Darcy answered. "Why do you ask?"

Aeron rolled her eyes and shook her head. Darcy was an incredible pirate, but he was daft when it came to matters of the heart; poor Catrin had had to practically club him over the head to get him to notice she was interested in him.

"Never mind, tell the men that we will be on our way shortly," she ordered before she turned to Orrin. "Come on, I know exactly where your devil of a brother is," she said as she headed for the east shore.

Maura moved with smooth skill across the sand, slicing at the air in front of her with her sword. She let the sound of the waves pounding the shore set her pace. Doing as Aeron instructed, she closed her eyes and let the movements flow, swinging and advancing at her invisible foe. With a quick spin to the right, her eyes popped open with a start as her blade was met with a loud clang. She jumped backward defensively and into a crouching position.

"I must say, I've never seen anyone practice with their eyes closed before," Kale said with a cocky smile as he lowered his sword.

Her heart pounded wildly in her chest just at the sight of him, and she felt her cheeks flush pink. "Aeron taught me that," she explained. "It helps one's focus, which makes for a better warrior."

"Fascinating. I've never thought about that before, but it's understandable." He nodded to her glimmering weapon. "That's an exquisite blade, by the way," he said, taking his stance before her and twisting his own sword into position. "Since I'm here, shall we test it? God knows it could only improve your skill because it couldn't possibly get any worse." Kale grinned with a spark in his eye and egged her on with a flick of his blade.

Maura narrowed her eyes at him as she set her stance, ready for his advance, his words eating away at her focus and calm demeanor. "If you recall, last time I won," she reminded him.

"Indeed." he conceded with a sweeping bow. "However, perhaps I merely let you win."

Grinding her teeth together in frustration and gripping her weapon tighter, Maura took her first swing, intent on removing his damned head.

"You are a…pompous…rotten…ass of a man," she shouted, biting off each word with each strike of her cool blade.

Kale defended himself, blow after blow until their swords crossed above their heads and they stood face to face in the sand. "And you are an amazingly beautiful, sinfully tempting woman," he said, his mouth moving closer and closer to hers.

Her chest heaved, struggling to gain breath as Kale's eyes focused solely on her lips. She wanted to scream in his face and push him away, but she was frozen where she stood, so close to his body that she could feel his heat against her skin.

"You're infuriating," she managed to say in a hoarse whisper.

"You're easy to infuriate, and irresistible when you're angry," he drawled.

His sword lowered behind her back as Kale slowly snaked his free arm around her waist and pulled her into his embrace. Her objection died in her throat when she felt the hard planes of his muscles pressed against her. Her lips began to part unconsciously, inviting him for a kiss.

He didn't move, only stared down at her with the most peculiar expression. "You're shaking."

Maura swallowed a lump of uncertainty in her throat and licked her lips nervously. "I…I've never been kissed before."

Kale immediately dropped his sword to the sand and cradled her face in his hands, sweeping the pad of his thumb across her bottom lip as he looked into her soft brown eyes. "But you are so beautiful. I find it virtually impossible to believe that some man hasn't stolen a single kiss from these perfect lips."

"It's the truth," she admitted as she stared intently at his voluptuous mouth. "Honestly, I've never wanted to be kissed before. There has never been a man so tempting that I would have risked something as intimate, as tender, as a kiss."

"And now?" Kale asked as he swept the back of his fingers across her cheek.

"If you don't kiss me this instant I may go completely mad," she breathed, dropping her sword and tunneling her fingers through his thick hair.

"We can't have that now, can we?" he said before he fastened his lips to hers, pulling her body closer, tighter.

Maura's felt tingles all the way down to the tips of her toes as his tongue slid past her lips and wrapped itself around hers. She gasped at the wondrous sensation and gripped his hair tighter, unconsciously angling her hips into his. He tasted of warm honey and life, and she couldn't seem to get enough of him.

"Ah, you see! I knew if we found one, we'd find the other."

The sound of Aeron's voice wrenched Maura from Kale's grip.

"Captain, I…I was just…" Maura stammered, desperately wiping at her mouth as she looked to Kale and back again in a panic.

"You were what, exactly? Helping Kale find his tongue?" Aeron asked with an arch of her fiery eyebrow.

"We were…practicing," Kale said with a guilty grin as he casually leaned over to pick up Maura's sword and handed it to her.

"Practice," Aeron said slowly, sizing Kale up with a wary eye. "Yes, well, you can pick up your *practice* some other time. We have a fight to plan, and our men await our orders."

Standing on the deck of the Royal Fleet's lead vessel as it bobbed in the water, Will watched his mother stride onto the docks like a harsh, icy wind. Her ornate robes blew about her legs in the salty air as she glided across the plank, eerily graceful.

He remembered watching her as a very small child, how beautiful she was when she would stride through the halls of the castle, so regal and perfect. The way she would gather up her skirts to bend closer to him and kiss his head. He'd been in awe of her, but not afraid, not then. What had happened to that woman?

"How long until we reach them?" She snapped out the question as soon as her gilded slippers hit the deck. No greeting, no royal blessing for the voyage, no words of encouragement to the crew—nothing but demands.

William looked up at the billowing sails and felt the wind blow coolly against his face as he calculated the journey. "A week, possibly five days if the winds are in our favor," he said confidently. That was a fair timeframe for such travels in those waters.

Winifred glared down her nose at him; that was obviously not the answer she was looking for. "You have three days," she said curtly as she walked past William toward the lower decks.

"Three days?" Will stared at her back as she continued across the deck. "There is no possible way to go that far in three days, even with more than favorable weather. Not to mention, if the winds are against us—"

The queen turned her heartless stare on William, stopping any more words from him with a raise of her chin and a cruel twitch of her lip. "If we are not on the shores of that island in three days…" she said calmly, leaving her sentence unfinished. She turned her glare to a man pulling a girl on board. He tossed her roughly to the deck.

Will's spine snapped straight; it was the same redheaded girl he'd seen cowering in the hall the night before. Winifred grasped the girl by the hair and hauled her to her feet before her, grabbing the girl's face in her other hand and twisting it in William's direction.

"If we are not on the shores of that island in three days," the queen repeated, "she will pay. Do I make myself clear?"

The poor girl struggled against the iron grip, holding her face still, tears spilling freely from her exhausted eyes.

"Yes, Your Majesty, three days," William said, casting his gaze to his boots, unable to look the girl in the face any longer.

Coward, his own voice echoed in his head.

"Very good," the queen spat as she discarded the girl to the deck at her feet like a piece of garbage. Turning on her heel without another word, Winifred disappeared below the decks.

"How do you propose we get to that island in three days, Sire?" Jamie, William's first officer, asked as he stepped up behind him.

"I don't know." Will watched one of his mother's servants drag the almost naked young woman after him, who was screaming in terror and kicking her dirty and bloodstained bare feet against the hard wood of the deck. "Just make it happen."

"And if we can't?"

Will thought about his mother's behavior, the young women he'd seen in her company since Aeron. All either had the same red hair or the same startling blue-green eyes. Clearly, she'd gone mad in her want for Aeron and would stop at nothing to get her back.

"Then we have killed that girl," Will said, turning, to the rail as he looked out into the vast ocean. "And God save whoever is next."

Chapter Sixteen

Orrin stood in front of the mirror inside the captain's quarters of the *Iona*, the very place he had called home for the past five years on the seas. Swiping the razor across his face, he removed the last patch of hair that remained on his chin.

He studied himself, turning his head to one side and then the other. How many times had he stood in this very spot, looking into this very mirror, never really sure of who was looking back at him other than an empty man? A man who took pleasure in nothing and no one, a man who woke each morning with a silent prayer that the next thieving pirate, the next bloody battle, would end his miserable shell of a life.

And now?

He saw a man who was happy, who had incredible love for the glorious woman he was about to wed — the woman who had breathed life back into his very soul, who had ignited his body and his mind with temptations and desires he never knew were possible.

A slow smile spread across his face as he closed his eyes and inhaled deeply, the memory of her scent filling his nostrils as if she were standing before him. He could almost feel her lips brushing against his as her sweet, warm breath washed over him, and his skin tingled.

Pulling his shirt from the wardrobe, he slipped it over his head, smiling brightly at the lilac fins Aeron had embroidered on the collar just for him.

In a few short hours, I'm going to make that woman my wife, Orrin thought as he finished dressing.

Maura and Catrin buzzed around Aeron, primping and fussing with the less-than-accommodating bride.

"Quit making that face," Catrin scolded, slapping Aeron lightly on the shoulder. "It won't kill you to look like a lady for a change."

Aeron's face scrunched uncomfortably as Catrin shoved a multitude of pins into her hair to hold it in place. "It just might," she muttered, wincing as another pin poked against her scalp.

"He's not going to believe his eyes," Maura piped up from behind Aeron with a girlish giggle, apparently trying to distract her from the torture she was enduring.

"That's clearly because he's not going to know who the bloody hell I am, for God's sake," Aeron grumbled, fidgeting in her dress and tugging at the overly snug bodice. "Does this have to be so blasted tight?"

"Don't grouse at us," Catrin said. "Your beloved is the one that chose the dress for you."

"I know," Aeron sighed irritably as Catrin pulled on a lock of her hair, tugging and pinning it into place. "And God as my witness, I'm going to kill him for that."

"She is joking, isn't she?" Maura asked Catrin.

"I surely hope so. I'd hate to be scrubbing his blood out of this gown," Catrin replied with a laugh as they fiddled and fluffed.

Aeron lifted her skirts over her knees, bunching it higher around her hips as she twisted this way and that as if she was looking for something she'd misplaced.

"What are you squirming about now? Did you lose something?" Catrin asked while Aeron surveyed herself in the full-length mirror.

"No, I'm just trying to decide where to put my sword."

Catrin fisted her hands on her hips as she stood. "You will put it nowhere," she huffed. "You are not taking that *thing* to your wedding!"

Aeron glared defiantly at her as she grabbed her blade off the dressing table. "The hell I'm not." She flung her skirts up over her hips and propped her leg onto the settee in front of her, tying the thin leather belt low on her hip. "I go nowhere without my sword," she said, lowering the hem of her dress and smoothing out the material to make the weapon invisible beneath the yards of fabric. "Absolutely nowhere."

"God's mercy," Catrin said with a sigh and shook her head in defeat. "Whatever am I going to do with you?"

"To start you can loosen this damned corset before I pass out."

Crystal blue waves lapped at the island's west shore. The low-lying sun's rays glittered against the water as Orrin stood in the sand waiting for his beloved to emerge from the jungle. The hand of God himself could not wipe the smile from his lips or quell the steady beating of his eager heart.

Time crawled by at a snail's pace, and it seemed as if it took five seconds for only one to pass. He needed to bide his time to make it through the next few minutes. A thought occurred to Orrin, and he closed his eyes and thanked God for allowing him live to see this day come to fruition, even after all the times he'd asked otherwise. After a silent amen, Orrin opened his eyes again, and his breath caught at the sight he beheld: Aeron emerging from the jungle's shroud onto the white shores. She was a vision, created by angels and sent straight from the heavens just for him.

Orrin fought every urge in his body to go to her, and everyone else on the beach seemed to melt away into the background. Aeron moved with such grace and confidence, practically floating like a waking dream across the surface of the sand. Her fiery red hair was tamed, intricately woven into plaits and pinned up behind her head, save for a few locks that curled softly around her face. The lavender gown he'd chosen for her clung to her bosom and flowed around her body so delicately, it was as if the fabric had been spun by fairies. Everything was perfect.

The setting sun made for a quick ceremony, and they were both more than thankful for that. The quicker the ceremony, the sooner they could continue on to their own celebration alone. They scarcely took their eyes off of one another for more than a moment.

"You are so beautiful," Orrin whispered to Aeron as Friar Morgan spoke of love and honor. "I have sailed to all the four corners of the world, and I can say that I have never laid eyes on a more beautiful sight than the one standing before me this very moment."

Aeron's cheeks flushed pink, and tears welled in her eyes. "I am so very glad I didn't kill you."

"As am I," Orrin said with a light chuckle. "God, I love you."

"And I you."

"Orrin, you may now kiss your bride," Friar Morgan declared with a sweeping gesture toward Aeron.

Leaning in close, Orrin only hovered, teasing as he brushed against her tender skin. He suggestively ran the tip of his tongue across the seam of her lips, slipping it into her eager mouth for just a moment before he pulled away, leaving her body slack in his arms and her fingers clutching his shoulders desperately for support.

Later in the evening, Orrin and Aeron sat together at their table, practically oblivious to everything going on around them. Glancing down at Aeron's plate, Orrin said, "You've barely eaten a thing," and raised the back of his hand to her cheek in worry. "Are you feeling all right, my wife?"

"I'm fine, husband."

Orrin's heart leapt in his chest at the sentiment that he'd never thought he'd hear again. *Husband.* Yes, he liked the sound of that very much.

Suddenly, she began to squirm and twist uncomfortably in her chair.

"Are you sure you're feeling all right?" he asked again, growing concerned.

"It's just this blasted dress," she said, tugging at the material. "I can hardly breathe in this bloody contraption, much less eat or move properly. I should cut your throat while you sleep for making me wear this monstrosity."

"Perhaps we should bid everyone good evening so I can take you back to our cottage and remove that offending garment of yours," he said, and he slipped his hand under the table. Aeron caught her bottom lip between her teeth as he deftly moved over her skirts. His fingers teased the crease under her knee before he slowly dragged them up. Her legs began to part, just a bit, as he moved along her inner thigh, his touch burning through the fabric. "You are so soft here," he breathed, his lips brushing the shell of her ear as he spoke.

He watched her pulse beat in her neck, and his long slender fingers navigated farther, inching ever closer to her sweet center. But, before he could complete the intimate touch, Darcy stood unexpectedly. Being well into his cups, the large man swayed slightly on his feet as he thrust his hands up into the air to quiet everyone.

Orrin pulled his hand out from under Aeron's skirts with a defeated groan as he turned his attention to Darcy. He held his breath as Darcy stood; the man had never made it a secret that he didn't trust Orrin, so heaven knew what he would say in his altered state.

"Dearest Captain," Darcy said as he looked to Aeron and smiled drunkenly, "dearest friend, I have been with you longer than anyone here. Together we have braved the bad and celebrated the good. On this day, I am honored to witness this good in particular." He hoisted up his cup and turned to Orrin. "To you, for bringing such joy and happiness to my dearest friend's heart. You are one of us now, and I look forward to calling you friend—" he nodded toward the villagers around them "—brother." He raised his mug into the air and faced the people. "To our beloved captain and her mate, may you be half as happy as Catrin and I have been."

Shouts of excitement and revelry rang out throughout the village amongst the thunderous clang of metal cups knocking together.

Orrin sat shocked, and he stared blankly in disbelief for a moment. Everyone stared at him, waiting for a response. He managed to gather his thoughts about him before he stood, raising his own hands to the crowd.

"Thank you, Darcy," he said with a nod. "Thank you all," he continued when all was quiet again. "I am truly blessed to have been welcomed into this most wondrous family." He extended a hand out to Aeron, who happily took it. "And it is with regret that we must bid you all good evening. The food was glorious, the drink was superb, but…" He turned to Aeron.

All the men howled in approval as the women giggled.

Aeron nodded, looking to her crew, her family. "Yes, thank you all for helping us celebrate our union," she said, turning to Orrin with a wink. "I love you all dearly and would like nothing more than to drink with you until the wee hours of the morning. However, you must continue without me. I have a husband to bed."

The entire village erupted with cheers as the wedded couple ducked down into the jungle, laughing excitedly and practically running down the path to their cottage.

Pushing the door open, Aeron and Orrin found the room alight with candles and a table set with a jug of wine, a bowl of freshly cut fruit, and a plate of cheese and bread.

As Aeron took in the state of the room, Orrin slid in behind his bride and wrapped his arms around her waist. His hand rested against something hard and unmistakable hidden beneath the volume of her skirts—her sword.

"What have we here?" he asked as he palmed the weapon through the material.

Aeron covered his hand with hers, closing his fingers around the hilt. "You didn't honestly think I would be without my sword, now did you?"

"Not even for a moment," Orrin said burying his face in her hair, inhaling her alluring scent and kissing the delicate skin behind her ear. "You go nowhere without your sword."

"Nowhere," she murmured as his other hand began to move up her body, skimming her waist and lingering on the curve of her breast before he took her jaw in his hand and tilted her head to the side. Her body molded to his, bent submissively to his will as he lavished the column of her neck with lazy kisses and swipes of his tongue, working his mouth down the back of her neck until he reached the ties of her dress.

Orrin curled a finger around the satin ribbon, tugging the knot open and releasing the constricting nature of the gown, and Aeron sighed with evident relief as the front of the dress loosened on her body. He took advantage of the slack and reached inside, wrapping his hand around her breast and delighting at the way her nipple hardened against his palm through the gossamer undergarments she wore. With a swift tug, he jerked the sleeves off her shoulders, nipping as he continued to push the dress down her body and into a puddle of fabric at their feet.

He gasped in delighted surprise as she reached back and grasped his buttocks, squeezing it and pulling his body closer to hers. As he nudged the lacy strap of her undergarments off her shoulder, he traced along the top of her chemise, slipping just under the edge of the fabric.

"Orrin…" she whimpered as his fingers brushed the top of her breast. Her hand slid down, and she gripped his thigh and pressed her rump against him.

He watched her reflection as they stood before her full-length mirror. Her eyes met his in the glass, appearing to beg him to rip the thin veil of material from her body and take her like a beast. But Orrin was in no hurry this night. He intended to drive her mad with desire, and with one slant of his mouth, one seductive little smirk, he told her just as much.

When Aeron moved to remove her sword, his hand was quick to cover hers and stop her. "No, leave it," he said as he uncurled her fingers from her belt and wrapped them around his thigh again.

His touch moved lightly up and down her arms, fluttering over her skin, barely touching it. He breathed up the back of her neck, his lips but a whisper from her skin. Orrin slid his tongue across the top of her back, from one shoulder to the other as he slipped his hand beneath her undergarments, cupping her full breast in his hand. He felt her body shiver enticingly against his, a throaty moan and a whimper escaping her lips as he rolled his thumb over her nipple.

With that little series of sounds from her, Orrin snapped. He spun her in his arms and proceeded to devour her. His tongue plunged deep, inhaling her breath as he searched and claimed her mouth with newfound hunger.

Aeron sank her hands into his hair, pulling hard as her leg curled around his hips and drew his body tighter to hers.

Orrin grunted and groaned with passion as he hoisted her off the ground. Her legs immediately wrapped around his waist as he turned on his heel and savagely threw her body against the wall with such force that their ravenous kiss was broken.

They stared at each other, panting. Driven by unbridled lust, Orrin ripped the flimsy undergarments from her body as if they were made of paper. He dipped his head to her bare flesh and drew her breast into his mouth. Her heels dug into his back, and the steel of her blade, unyielding against his thigh, pushed against him as she ground her body desperately against his.

The thought, the very idea of taking her like this, wild and rough, with her sword still strapped to her naked hip was all he could take. His fingers tugged frantically at the ties of his trousers as he fought to release himself. The back of his hand bumped against her hot and wet apex, distracting him. Her legs trembled and flexed around him with anticipation as he looked deep into her eyes and taunted her with his fingers. She gasped; she was not expecting another tease. Her eyes widened for a moment before they clouded over with desire.

His tongue curled around his lip as he probed her with one, then two digits. "Mmm, you're so soft," he breathed as he slid his fingers around her jewel, circling it again and again and taking her to the very brink before pulling his hand away.

Pushing his breeches past his hips with one final shove, Orrin swiftly pushed into her, pinning her against the wall. Aeron yelped with pleasure as he drove into her, each thrust harder than the last. He nibbled and licked her neck as he moved deep inside of her, slowly, methodically. She gripped his back as she shuddered, her body shaking almost violently.

Her flesh gripped and released him, and he sucked in a breath as his thrusts became harder and more urgent with need. She cried out again, cried out his name, and Orrin tossed his head back with his mouth open, gasping for breath as he groaned, reaching the pinnacle of his climax.

They struggled to catch their breath, a slick sheen of sweat coating both of their bodies, until their heartbeats returned to a semblance of a normal rhythm.

"No one has ever made me cry out like that," Aeron panted into his ear. "That was the most incredible thing I've experienced in all of my days."

Orrin smiled against her cheek as he juggled her bottom in his hands. "Indeed, and the night has only begun, my wife," he assured her with a sound swat to her naked backside.

Chapter Seventeen

ill looked up at the sails and sighed heavily at the slack canvas. The wind was definitely not in their favor on this voyage. Even with constant rowing, as they approached the end of the third day, there was no sight of the island. Not even a flutter of the top of a palm tree in the distance to signal that they might be upon the hidden paradise.

The girl was going to die tonight, and there would nothing he could do to stop it. It would be on his shoulders, his weight to bear, because he was captaining this campaign and too terrified of his own mother to stand in her way.

A horrid screech permeated the wood, reaching up from below the decks and jolting him back to his boyhood as memory seeped in again.

This was a sound he'd heard before.

He remembered the day Aeron had arrived at the castle. She'd smiled and waved to him when she first saw him, unlike the other ladies. She was the only one of his mother's servants who would even acknowledge his presence; she'd even played endless games of hide and seek with him throughout the day. That was, until the afternoon he had tripped and cut his knee on a stone in the garden. It had been Aeron who rushed to his side to comfort him and cleanse his wound. His mother glared at the two of them, her jaw clenched at what he could only assume now was jealously at Aeron coddling him.

Everything changed that night. Gone were the games he'd played with Aeron, the frivolity with which they'd run about openly. Instead, Aeron made a new game. A game of intrigue that had them meeting in the barn to play quietly, where no one could find them. They had even concocted secret games to play out in the open with hidden messages and sly looks to one another. He had had no idea of the danger she had been putting herself in — for if his mother had known Aeron had been paying any attention to him, even the smallest amount, there would have been hell to pay for both of them.

The evening that Aeron had snuck into his chambers while the castle slept itched at the back of his mind.

"Wake up, William," she'd whispered, gently shaking him awake. When he'd opened his eyes, he'd seen Aeron kneeling at the side of his bed, her fingers smoothing over his hair as she bent to sweetly kiss the end of his nose. "I want you to remember me, Will," she had said, grasping his hands in hers. "Remember your father, and always remember that there is good inside you." She'd gathered him in her arms and hugged him tighter than ever before. "One day, young prince, you will be a great king."

And with that, she was gone.

His mother had been furious the next morning when she'd found Aeron's cot empty. She'd commanded the entire castle to be torn apart and every dark corner and nook searched. Her eyes were wild with rage and fear as she questioned young William, shaking him until his teeth rattled in his head and terrified tears streamed down his face as she insisted he knew more than he was letting on.

But Will had stood fast, drawing strength from Aeron's words, and he'd told his mother nothing about the night before. He'd locked that night away in his mind, so deep and so far, that he'd nearly forgotten it had ever happened.

Then, a year ago, he'd seen Aeron in the village of a neighboring province. She'd looked slightly different, older, wiser, but there had been no denying who she was. He'd known with all his heart that it was her.

When Will had approached her and tried to talk to her, she hadn't acknowledged him other than to claim she'd had no idea who he was and that he must have her mistaken for another woman. She'd insisted her name was Rosaline and that she had never been to the royal village, let alone inside the castle.

Yet Will had been certain of her identity and craved the relationship they'd once had. Desperation had clawed at his chest, and he'd done the only thing he could think of; he had followed her, stowing away on her ship like a rat. When he'd been discovered, the crew had almost thrown him overboard; however, he'd pled with Aeron, praying that their past would soften her heart to let him join her band of pirates. He'd vowed to help them take down his mother and take back his kingdom, and it was only then that Aeron had relented and allowed him to stay.

Never once had he worried about his mother sending word for him to come home while he'd traveled with Aeron and her men. Hell, the woman had probably been happy to finally be rid of him, had most likely hoped he was dead and out of her hair.

As the days turned into weeks, he'd felt himself falling for Aeron the more time he spent in her service. He'd grown to love her, but knew that she had seen him as nothing more than a member of her crew, a friend at most. But he had dreamed of one day winning her over and having her by his side, as his queen, when he took the throne again.

"Your Highness, there is no land of any kind in any direction," Jamie stated as he stood next to him against the railing.

"I know," William said, staring solemnly out into the smooth, calm water.

"And the winds, Sir, they are against us."

"I know, Jamie," Will sighed. "I know."

"Do you think she'll really do it?"

In all these years, as William had sat by and watched his mother rule, one thing he remembered with complete clarity was that he'd never seen her give anyone mercy. Not even a hint of it, ever.

He knew that the kingdom had rightfully belonged to his father, but it had been his mother who ruled it. He was just a boy when his father had been found dead, and by rights the crown should have gone to William. But Winifred would have none of it. She had taken over rule from him as she had from his father, by once again utilizing those power-grabbing lords and ladies in the court. They cared not for what was right, only for what served their purpose to climb the social ladder. They instilled fear in the hearts of the subjects, dispensing of anyone who questioned Her Majesty's authority by immediate death.

Or worse.

William nodded stoically. "Yes, she will."

"What can we do, Sir? We can't let her get away with such—"

"Your Highness," a deck hand interrupted as he came running up with a bow. "Her Majesty the Queen wishes to see you."

With a heavy sigh, Will clapped his hand on Jamie's shoulder before he left. "Stay out of her way, my friend. That is all you *can* do."

The first thing William noticed when he entered the cabin was the redheaded girl half under a table, crying and cowering against the wall. He had to fight every instinct in him that wanted to reach out and help the poor girl out of this hell she was stuck in.

"You wanted to see me, Your Majesty?" Will asked with a bow, not daring to make eye contact with his mother.

Winifred stood at the porthole, looking out of the tiny round window at the open sea. "Why are we still at sea, William?" she asked with an eerie calm that put his teeth on edge and made the hair on the back of his neck stand on end.

Will swallowed hard, knowing it was the end of the third day.

"We have been traveling against the winds, Your Majesty and—"

She slammed her fist against the wooden wall. "I gave you three days, William!" she bellowed so loudly that it rattled his bones. "Three bloody days to get me to that island!"

"As I told you before we left port, Your Majesty, it was going to take at least five days to get to the island if the winds were in our favor, which they are not."

The queen strode across the cabin and hauled the terrified girl to her feet. She gripped the girl's face and turned it, harshly angling it in his direction. "Look at her, William," she said with a curl of her thin lip. "Look at her!"

Will looked into the young woman's hollow eyes, rimmed red and streaming with tears as she choked out her pleas for her life. Winifred pressed her cheek against the girl's and cruelly mocked her fear.

"Help me, please…save me."

The queen laughed evilly. "Can you save her, William?" she asked in her taunting tone. "Is there land on the other side of this infernal vessel?"

"No," he said quietly. He stared at a lamp on the table across the room, unable to look the girl in the eye as cowardice crept up his spine.

"I didn't hear you, William, and I'm most certain that *she* didn't," Winifred said, turning her face in the girl's hair and taking in a deep breath as if she could smell the fear coming off her.

"No," he said as he finally looked at the girl. "We will not see the island for at least three more days." A tear escaped and spilled down his cheek as he saw sheer and utter defeat in the girl's eyes. "I'm sorry."

The queen cackled her same maniacal laugh before her features contorted into pure hatred. She locked eyes with William. "You are your father's child," she spat, her lip twitching with anger as she spoke. "You are a pathetic excuse for what a child born of my blood should be."

Without another word, she dragged the girl by her hair past Will and up the stairs. The girl screamed and kicked her legs for all she was worth, clawing at the floor and the walls, her nails bending and breaking and leaving bloody trails in her wake.

The entire crew stopped whatever they were doing, frozen where they were to watch the queen pull this poor creature across the decks.

When she reached the railing, she hauled the girl up onto her belly without a second thought, without a moment of hesitation. Her face twisted cruelly with effort, and she uttered a very unladylike grunt as she grasped the girl by the ankles and heaved her over the side of the ship.

Half of the crew stood with their mouths agape as they heard that poor girl's gurgling screams while they sailed away. The other half said and did nothing out of what William assumed was fear they would be next.

Winifred turned to the deck hand on her right. "Where are the other girls?"

"Stowed in the cargo hold like you asked, Your Majesty," the young man said with a deep bow.

"Other girls?" William asked, his mouth dropping open; surely he hadn't heard right.

"Of course," she said very matter-of-factly. As they all watched, the lad dragged another girl across the decks and tossed her at the feet of the queen. Her Majesty grabbed the girl by the dingy blond hair and hauled her to her feet. "And if we aren't on the shores of that island by tomorrow, this one will share the same fate."

"No…" William begged, shaking his head incessantly, unable to believe what he was hearing, what he was seeing, what he was allowing to happen. "It is impossible to…"

Queen Winifred's pale hand covered the new girl's sobbing mouth. "Shh, my pet, do you hear that?" she asked.

The girl stopped crying for a moment, halting her stuttering breaths as she listened. Her blue-green eyes widened with fear as the faint sounds of the other girl struggling to stay above water echoed in the distance.

The queen gripped her chin with one hand and squeezed her innocent flesh. "If you do not wish to meet that same fate, little plaything, pray he finds land tomorrow," she said, pointing a bony finger at Will. "And beg *him* for mercy, for you will get none from me."

With that, Winifred dragged the stunned girl below decks. A blood-curdling scream rang into the night as the door to the cabin under Will's feet slammed shut.

Chapter Eighteen

As their wedding night progressed into morning, Aeron and Orrin branded every corner of the cottage and every structure that would bear their weight. Their appetite for each other was insatiable as they flung themselves from one place to the next until they lay utterly spent and panting on the floor.

"Christ, woman, I think you *are* trying to kill me," Orrin panted.

"Indeed, I could say the same to you, husband." The smile on her face widened even more as he reached over to swat her sweaty bottom.

Aeron moved away and started to get up when Orrin grabbed her by the ankle.

"Just where do you think you're going?" he asked as he pulled her back to the floor on top of him.

"Mmm…my darling Orrin," she said, brushing the damp hair off his forehead. She began to slither down his body, dropping sweet kisses on his flesh. "I would love nothing more than to lie here and bathe every inch of you with my tongue…again," she purred as she worked her way down his ripcord-tight stomach. "But if I do not get some food in my belly soon, I'm just going to have to eat you." Aeron opened her mouth wide and bit his right hipbone.

"Damn, you wicked wench, you have quite the mouth on you," he chuckled, deep in his chest, "and you missed."

"I never miss," she assured him with a smile before she parted her lips and took him into her mouth.

"Hold still," Maura giggled. "You're too tall; I can't quite reach the proper angle. You need to be lower."

"If I get any lower, I'll be on the ground," Kale said, trying not to laugh. "Perhaps you should stand on the chair."

"Very funny," Maura said with a scowl, fisting her hands on her slim hips. If Kale didn't know any better, he would swear that she now wished she'd actually clipped his arm with her sword instead of just his shirt when they'd sparred again that morning after the wedding. "Perhaps *you* should stop wiggling about like a fish and sit in the chair?"

"That tiny thing? It couldn't hold half my arse, let alone the whole of it," Kale said, pointing to Maura's near child-sized chair. "Oh, for God's sake, I'll just take off the blasted thing."

Maura's eyes widened as he gathered the bottom of his shirt in his hands, preparing to pull it over his head. Kale hesitated for a breath. Was she going to stop him?

It would have been the proper thing to do, but God help him, he hoped that she was anything but proper. As the fabric of his shirt cleared the top of his head, he saw her gaze fixate on the thick slabs of muscle that banded his torso and the taut ripples of his belly. He knew he was attractive and had struck more than his share of women dumb with his bare body; however, having the effect on Maura made more than his pride swell.

"Are you all right?" Kale asked as her tongue darted out and licked her lips.

She blinked a couple of times as she shook her head and cleared her throat. "Yes," she said. He could tell she was trying to sound annoyed, but she only sounded breathless and sexy as hell. "I'm fine. Why do you ask?"

"Because you're staring, and I can't yet tell if you intend to kill me or kiss me. But might I ask, if you do not mean to kiss me now, please kill me before I go mad," he said, taking a tentative step toward her and holding out the shirt.

The needle and thread fell to the floor as Maura lunged forward into his arms, pressing her lips to his with feverish urgency. She tasted magnificent, sweet, like warm honeyed pears as his tongue slid across hers, rolling and twirling with need.

He hoisted her off the ground, gripping her small body tightly as he held her against the wall. She immediately whipped her legs around his waist, and her nails bit into his naked back as she whimpered into his mouth. He wanted to consume her, and she would probably let him. Truthfully, if she were any other woman, he wouldn't have hesitated in the slightest.

But not her; Maura was different. He loved her.

Even though Orrin had already made that fact clear, the feelings still shocked Kale, and he nearly dropped her on her ass.

Instead, he let the sensation really sink into his bones. He very much wanted to take his time with her, to love her thoroughly, the way a woman like her deserved to be loved.

Summoning all of his will and mental strength, he wrenched his mouth free.

"Is something the matter?" she asked, panting from their kisses and completely confused.

Kale cupped her face in his hands, and it struck him how, together, they were perfectly matched.

"No," he whispered, closing his eyes and leaning his forehead to hers, "everything is exactly right."

"Then why did you stop?" she asked. "Do you not…want me?"

"What?" She actually thought he was rejecting her? "Oh, Maura," he began, "the man I was a week ago would have had you on your back and in a variety of sinful positions without a second thought. But a week ago, I didn't know you…I didn't know this." He smoothed the pad of his thumb across her plump bottom lip.

"Didn't know what?" she asked, her sweet breath washing over his chin as she began to tremble in his arms.

"I didn't know love."

"But, I still don't understand. If you love me, why did you stop?"

Kale smiled as he released her and took a step back. "Because I have to get to my crew; we have a lot of work to do. And the woman *I* love deserves more than a quick tumble the first time I make love to her."

Maura stared blankly at him as he imagined the words were sinking into her mind. She didn't say a word as she bent to pick up the discarded needle and thread. He watched her chew on her lip as she stitched the slice in his shirt.

Kale wished she would say something, anything, even that she didn't love him in return. Anything was better than the silence hanging in the cottage.

When she tied off the thread, Maura stood and walked the shirt over to him. She took his hand in hers and pressed the fabric into his palm, holding it there. Her warm, chocolate brown eyes gazed up at him as she stretched up onto her toes and kissed the curve of his jaw. "I love you," she said.

He could sense the trepidation in her, the way she spoke the words so quietly; these were new feelings for her, all around. He wanted her to say more, but he was certain it had taken everything in her to utter those three little words. He didn't push; there would be more when she was ready.

"Thank you. Until later, my love," Kale said as he kissed the top of her head, then turned for the door with a sweeping bow, waving his shirt around in front of him. He was delighted to hear Maura's giggles at his display, and he left the cottage and tugged the shirt over his head.

He was less than delighted by the wallop to the back of the head that followed shortly after. Kale whirled around to see Orrin scowling at him.

"Ow," Kale howled, rubbing the back of his head. "What in the bloody hell was that for?"

"What was that for? Have you lost your blasted mind?" Orrin asked, gripping Kale by the shirt and hauling him away. "You are damn lucky Aeron wasn't the one to find you here, half-dressed, coming out of Maura's cottage. She'd have your head on a spit before you knew what hit you."

"I've lost *my* mind? You're the one shouting like a raving lunatic," Kale snapped, jerking his arm back. "And mind the shirt. Maura just mended it."

"What?" Orrin asked as Kale pointed to the stitched-up hole.

"Maura and I were sparring earlier on the west bank, and her sword clipped my shirt. It tore, and she offered to sew it." Kale narrowed his eyes at his brother. "You assumed I was bedding her like she was some common whore, didn't you?" he asked as he reached for his blade, intent on defending his sweet Maura's honor.

"Calm yourself, little brother," Orrin warned with a roll of his eyes.

"Fine," Kale said, taking his hand off of the hilt of his sword. "But try alluding to Maura as anything but a respectable woman and I will remove your head," he warned.

"I wasn't alluding to *her* as anything. It was *your* known scandalous behavior I was referring to, you half-wit."

"Oh, shut up." Kale glowered as he stomped away.

Later in the morning, after everyone broke their fast, Kale and Aeron called both crews and every member of the island together in the

square. If they even had a hint of a chance in hell of coming out of this alive, they would all have to be of the same mind in order to achieve it.

Kale's men were then instructed to shadow a member of Aeron's crew and learn everything they could in the short amount of time they had.

"The odds are most definitely not in our favor," Aeron said as she addressed everyone on the island. "I can promise you nothing of the outcome, save that I will fight until my very last breath." With a whoosh of metal leaving leather, she drew her sword and aimed it out toward the people pointedly. "Queen Winifred *will* fall, and we will finally all be free. Even if I have to claw my way back from hell to make it happen, so be it."

The village erupted with cheers, fists raised to the mighty heavens in acclaim.

"It should take Will several days to gather his fleet and head out after us. By my estimation, we have three, maybe four days before the fleet breaks the horizon. Be smart, like I know you all to be. Make the most of that time and train hard," she said to her people.

She then turned to Kale's men. "Be receptive to what my people have to teach you. We have no time for pride. Learn as much of this island as you can from who you can, her strengths as well as the chinks in her armor. And for God's sake, hold who you love dear tonight and the next night because after that, there may very well be nothing left to hold."

Kale reached down and squeezed Maura's hand as everyone made their leave.

It was going to be a long couple of days.

The crews worked diligently throughout the remainder of the morning and afternoon to ready the two mighty vessels and the island for battle.

As the sun sank into the sea and evening fell upon them, Kale and Maura were finally alone on the *Iona* in his private cabin. Kale noticed that she'd been fidgety all day, agitated and strung tight like rope about to snap. Could it be from his declaration of love that morning? She had returned the affirmation, but since taking his hand after breakfast, she'd barely touched or even looked at him.

He, however, made every excuse he could think of to brush against her or look her way. She filled his mind to the brim until there was nothing left but her.

When he suggested he walk her to her cabin, Maura took his hand in hers and asked, "Kale?" Her voice was pitched high, his name sounding strangled in her throat as if it were getting caught. Her chest rose and fell rapidly as her eyes moved to his small bed against the wall, and she licked her lips.

He saw the shroud of lust on her face and could deny his own no longer — especially when faced with the very real fact that they could both be dead in three days, and this might be one of the only chances he would have to hold and make love to her.

Kale kissed her soundly, ravenous at the thought of only having a few moments with her. A soft moan followed her tongue as it dipped into his mouth, and he snapped. He swiftly set to unbuckling his trousers and started backing her up until she fell back against the bed and her hands settled on his chest, suddenly stopping him.

"You're not the first," she said on a breath, casting her eyes away from him. "I wanted you to know before we…before you…" She couldn't look at him as she continued. "I may not be chaste, but…you *are* the first I've wanted to give myself to willingly."

Kale stopped immediately. "What?" he asked with deep concern.

"I'm not a virgin," she explained, taking a deep breath. "When I was in the service of the castle, I was rutted many times by visiting lords, and I am told that I am very good at keeping completely still and quiet, as required in coupling."

Kale had to squeeze his jaw closed to keep it from flopping open; he'd assumed that if she hadn't been kissed, she hadn't been bedded either. He bit his tongue and cringed at the terms she used: *rutted* and *required*. They took a beautiful act and turned it into something repugnant. He'd known men who took women that way, and it churned his gut. If this was how she perceived lovemaking, she was a virgin in his opinion. Maybe not physically, but where it counted.

"Maura, I don't care whether you are chaste or not, and the only thing I require is that you be present, body *and* mind. I want you to have pleasure as well, not just me."

"Yes, but I love you, and I know our lovemaking will be wonderful because of that," she said innocently as she squeezed her eyes shut and grit her jaw tight, opening her legs in preparation to be mounted.

Kale moved off her and began to fasten the buckle on his breeches. He sat down on the small bed next to her as she looked up at him, that same look of rejection on her face that she'd worn that morning when he'd stopped her.

"I want to do something for you," he said, tracing her cheek with the back of his hand and fingertips. "I want to teach you about your body, show you what has been denied you all this time."

She sat up on her elbows and furrowed her brow at him curiously. "But you're dressed. Aren't you supposed to be naked?"

Kale chuckled low in his chest. "I do not need to be naked to give you pleasure, Maura," he said as he leaned over her and began to kiss across her collarbone. "Forget everything you have ever known about *coupling* and just feel the love in my touch and in my kiss." He toyed at the front of her shirt, pushing it open a fraction of an inch and kissing the very top of her bosom. "Let me give you pleasure like you've never known."

"How?" she asked as the flesh of her chest started to bloom with color. "Your…*manhood* is still in your trousers."

"I have many devices, my love," he said, curling the corners of his mouth in a smile. He slipped one finger beneath the fabric of her blouse and skimmed delicately across her nipple.

Maura gasped and sighed and promptly clamped her hand over her mouth in a panic. "I didn't mean to make that sound, I'm sorry. I will remain silent and still, I promise," she said around her fingers.

"While I appreciate your trying remain still, there is no need to be, and you won't be remaining silent if I have anything to say about it." He pushed her shirt open, delighting in the most perfect breasts he'd ever laid eyes on. "God, so beautiful."

He could sense the conflict inside her. There were a good number of *proper* women who believed sex was a service a wife provided for the pleasure of her husband and for breeding, nothing more. He was all but certain Maura had never been informed that she was allowed to enjoy it.

"Talk to me, Maura," he said as he kissed to the right of her nipple, her body tensing unnaturally beneath him. "I want to know that I'm touching you properly, that I'm giving you what you need. Tell me what you want of me."

She shook her head, her mouth pulled in a tight line, sealing it shut.

"Please," he begged, skimming a hand down her taut belly and sliding it over her belt, and the settling it between her legs and over her breeches.

Her body jolted, her thighs trapping his hand. "You…your touch," she panted.

"Where?" His lips brushed against the flushed skin of her breast as he spoke, his hand wiggling temptingly against her.

"Anywhere…everywhere," she breathed.

"Yes." His tongue swirled around her hardened nipple.

"Dear God," she moaned, arching off of the tiny mattress and toward his mouth.

"Ahhh…yes…more," Kale groaned, drawing the tip of her breast into his mouth, suckling the tender flesh.

Maura writhed as Kale moved his hand away from her only to dip into the front of her drawers between cloth and skin. He worked between her legs while he whispered all of the pleasures he wanted to introduce her to, ways in which he would bring her to the very edge of reason and show her the true meaning of pure and utter bliss.

Kale was damn near gleeful as pleasure overtook her and she climaxed with a delectable shudder. He gathered her in his arms and held her close, feeling her heart beat wildly in her chest.

Tomorrow would be on them before they knew it, and after that they would only have another day, if that.

There was one more thing he needed to do.

Kale gathered up all of his courage, swallowing back his pride as he girded himself up. "Maura, there is something I need to ask you."

Lying on her belly in the moonlight in the middle of the bed, Aeron drew lazy circles on Orrin's naked backside with the tip of her finger. She loved his full rump, so firm and delectable.

There was still quite a lot of work to be done around the island, and by rights they could continue to work straight through for the next three days. Aeron knew this. She also knew that if she attempted such, she would be fighting with not only one, but two exhausted crews.

Yes, rest was essential, not to mention time alone with the ones they held dear if they were going to have a fighting chance of making it out of this whole ordeal alive.

She turned over and nestled herself underneath Orrin's arm, pulling her knees in close as she tucked her body into his.

Fear, insecurity, and doubt—all of these feelings she forced down into her gullet. She took the well-being of every person here upon herself. When she was leading her people, she was a fearless warrior, but here, alone in the dark with Orrin, she could relax, expose every part of herself, body and soul, to him and him alone.

The grip she had on him grew tighter as her feelings began to unspool and take over.

Orrin stroked her hair softly while she shook against him. Did he sense that the weight she bore was a heavy one? *Of course he does,* Aeron thought to herself, letting go a little more; Orrin could read her like a map.

"I'm frightened," she whispered. Her voice was so small and quiet she wondered if he had even heard her. It was the hardest thing she'd ever admitted out loud to another person.

"I know," he said, his hold on her tightening. "So am I."

Chapter Nineteen

The next morning, Aeron sat with her husband, taking the morning meal when she saw Maura and Kale step into the village square, hand in hand and heading right for her.

Maura had always been a happy and pleasant person, but there was something that Aeron couldn't put her finger on that had been missing in her, a sense that the girl was waiting for something. That had all changed when Kale set foot on the island. He'd most definitely ignited the spark hidden deeply within Maura and apparently knew how to stoke the flame. Kale was Maura's peace, as Orrin was hers.

"Captain, may we speak with you?" Maura asked, her hand clenched so tightly with Kale's, it was hard to tell where one ended and the other began; each seemed a mere extension of the other.

"Of course, Maura. Please sit." Aeron gestured to the two empty chairs across the table from where she was sitting with Orrin.

Maura smiled at Kale, and he raised her hand to his lips, kissing the back of it—almost reassuringly, Aeron thought—as they sat. She looked down at the table for a moment before she straightened her back and began to speak.

"Kale has asked that I stand with him and fight at his side on the *Iona* when the time comes."

Aeron's body went stiff, her jaw immediately clenched tight, and the only thing keeping her from leaping from her seat to forbid this nonsense was the grip she had on the table. Granted, Maura was her protégé and this is what she'd been training for. However, Maura was so much more to Aeron than just an apprentice; at times, Aeron likened the girl to a child of her own, and while she wanted this for her, she was afraid that it was too much too soon.

Orrin shifted in his chair next to her, and she thought about how comforting it was to have him there by her side even for such a menial, everyday task as a meal. She then realized that she couldn't even fathom going into something as serious as battle without him right there with her.

Fight together, die together was her mindset.

"Absolutely not," Orrin said, shaking his head vehemently before Aeron had a moment to work out her thoughts and speak.

"I don't believe anyone was talking to you," Kale replied, his broad shoulders visibly bristling.

"I don't bloody well care!" Orrin barked, slapping the hard wood table and knocking his chair back as he vaulted to his feet. "I'm barely comfortable letting you lead by yourself, but to take Maura, who has never even been in a battle, on the ship with you is absurd. The two of you are not yet ready for such a task alone, and it's not going to happen. I absolutely forbid it."

Aeron sat back and watched her husband rant and rave. She saw Darcy move to get out of his chair, readying himself to step between the two men if need be, but Aeron shook her head and motioned for him to take his seat again. She knew these two needed to clear the air between them before they even thought about stepping into battle.

Granted, out in the middle of breakfast and in front of the entire village was not the most opportune of moments to get something off one's chest, but time wasn't exactly on their side right now.

"I am not a child anymore, Orrin!" Kale shouted, bounding to his own feet and standing a good inch taller than his older brother as he took a deep breath to calm himself before speaking again. "Look to your wife, the woman that *you* love," he said with a nod to Aeron. "May I remind you that it is *her* side you will be at when the fight begins, drawing strength and courage from your love for each other? May I also remind *you* that you are no longer *my* captain, and I do not require your permission?"

Orrin visibly winced. Kale's words obviously hit hard, and had he been a lesser man, he might have taken them as a direct attack on his manhood. However, Aeron was certain that Orrin knew his brother better than that.

"I've already given Kale my answer," Maura interjected before Orrin could respond, standing next to Kale and taking his hand in hers. They were now a united front. "We came here this morning out of respect and to seek a blessing from the two people we honor the most."

Every eye in the village was on Aeron. Every mouth closed and every ear open, waiting on bated breath for her response.

"Come," Aeron said as she rose to her feet, "I believe we've provided enough entertainment for the morning. Let us walk."

The two couples walked toward the cave where the ships were hidden, moving through the jungle in silence for a good while before Aeron began to speak.

"I'm torn," she said finally, almost as if she was thinking out loud. "On the one hand, I am thrilled beyond belief that your feelings for one another are so strong that you cannot imagine entering into this fight anywhere other than at each other's sides. I do understand that. For if it is my destiny to die in two days, I intend to die fighting next to the man that I love."

Kale and Maura smiled at each other triumphantly.

"However," Aeron continued, "I am also of the mind that this has the potential to end horribly badly. This is Maura's first battle, after all."

When Kale opened his mouth to defend their actions, Aeron held up a hand. "So, I find myself at an impasse as to what to do in this situation. As much as I'd like to protest this decision and outright forbid it," she said, giving Orrin a sideways glance, "I have to consider two things.

"Maura, I trained you myself. I know firsthand, as does Kale, your level of skill and that it is unmatched. However, all the training in the world cannot prepare one for the reaction one would have in an actual battle.

"Kale, I don't know you very well, to be perfectly honest, but I do know my husband." She looked at Orrin. "He is a level-minded man, under normal circumstances, and I trust that he would have never given up his station as captain of the *Iona* to you if he didn't think you were ready for it."

By the time Aeron had almost finished her say in the matter, they were standing on the shore next to Kale's ship. "So, all things considered, I can only speak for myself," she said as she turned to Maura and took her by the shoulders. "As your friend and your *former* captain, I give you my full blessing."

"Thank you," Maura said as she enveloped Aeron in a tight embrace.

"Bollocks," Orrin growled, scowling at the ground and mumbling to himself as he paced in a small circle.

"What is the matter with him?" Maura asked.

"He knows I'm right, and he's highly irritated because he's made a complete arse out of himself in front of the entire village," Aeron said as she watched Orrin have his tantrum.

"I'm damn pissed about it, is what I am," Orrin groused.

"So, am I to gather that we have your blessing as well?" Kale asked anxiously, narrowing his eyes at his brother.

"Yes, damn it," Orrin said, kicking at the ground with the toe of his boot like a child. "But mind you *only* because my wife makes a bloody good argument to support it. *I* still happen to think the entire idea is ridiculously stupid."

Aeron shook her head as she watched Orrin stomp off toward the *Mermaid* while cursing at open air.

He continued to skulk around for the remainder of the day, blatantly refusing to acknowledge Aeron in any way. But she did catch him looking from time to time.

Spiteful bastard of a husband, she thought.

At first, this infantile behavior of his had been amusing, but it had gone on all day, and Aeron had had about enough of his less-than-flattering conduct. As they puttered around their cabin on the *Mermaid,* she sat herself on the bed and quietly removed one of her boots.

She tossed it across the cabin at the wall next to him, trying to gain his attention. Though the noise did make him jump, he didn't turn around.

Aeron narrowed her eyes as she pulled off the second boot and lobbed it straight at his head. *Maybe a sound wallop will knock some sense into his thick skull.*

Unfortunately for her, Orrin was quick and most undoubtedly had come to know what his hot-tempered wife might do next, so had ducked out of the way as soon as the heavy footwear left her hand. Her irritation boiled under her skin, and she was convinced she knew just what would garner his attention.

Aeron yanked her shirt over her head without even untying it. She balled up the material and threw with all her might. It landed with a soft thud against the cabin wall, but Orrin remained where he was across the room, tinkering with God-knew-what.

Fury raging through her, Aeron stripped off her trousers and cursed loudly and most foully when they sailed right through the open porthole window to the right of Orrin's head.

"Are you quite finished throwing things at my head?" Orrin asked without turning around. "I'm assuming you are, since I don't believe you have anything else on your person to remove."

"Yes," Aeron answered with a slight air of annoyance in her voice. "Are *you* quite finished acting like a stubborn, selfish, spoiled rotten child?"

Orrin spun around on his heel and stared at Aeron, laid out on the bed naked.

"Stubborn I'll fully admit to, for I *am* about as stubborn as they come," he said as he walked slowly across the cabin toward the bed, "almost as stubborn as you."

"Indeed." Aeron nodded, her heart beginning to pound from the look in Orrin's eyes alone.

"And spoiled rotten. That is but a matter of opinion, is it not?"

"I suppose," she responded as she deftly crossed and uncrossed her legs.

Orrin gripped the end of his belt and pulled the buckle open with one good, hearty tug. His sword fell to the floor with a clang as he continued to move toward the bed, stripping off his shirt and discarding it over his shoulder. He knelt on the foot of the bed, between her feet. Reaching up, he gripped her just past her knees and dragged her body closer with a sound jerk. He looked deeply into her eyes as he lowered his head and placed a precise, open-mouthed kiss to the inside of her thigh.

"Selfish, on the other hand… I quite take offense to that one." He slid his palms up around her hips, his thumbs skimming over the bone as he bent his lips to her heated flesh, his tongue lingering against the skin while he held her gaze.

"Do you now?" she breathed, a throaty moan bubbling out of her as his mouth worked its way across her body. "We should do something about that."

"Oh, I fully intend to," he stated with a saucy grin, and he shoved his pants out of the way and hitched her leg around his waist.

Night crept over the island like a veil, and the village grew quiet.

Maura's heart fluttered beneath her breast as Kale led her through the jungle to her small cottage on the edge of the square. He smiled down at her, holding her hands in his and kissing the back of each one tenderly as he took a step back. When she saw his mouth open, she could only assume he meant to bid her good eve and head back to his ship. She would not let that happen.

"Please stay," she said quietly, looking up into his eyes; the bits of violet in their blue sparked with the torchlight flickering around them as she clutched his fingers tightly.

Kale closed his eyes and lowered his forehead to hers, swallowing hard before he spoke. "You don't know what you're asking," he said, as if the words pained him. "If I stay tonight, I cannot promise that I will have the restraint I had last night."

Her body trembled with the memory of his hands on her skin, so warm and sure as they navigated her curves, the way his mouth moved over her flesh and brought her to a place she'd never even known existed.

"Please," she breathed as her lips collided with his.

Kale swept her into his arms, kissing her hungrily as he pushed through the door and kicked it closed behind them. His hands fisted in the back of her blouse, and she could hear the delicate fabric beginning to give way under his strength.

Suddenly, he pulled back and set Maura on her feet. She could see all over his face the effort it took for him to slow down.

"I feel as if could devour you, but I can't," he panted.

"Why on earth not?" she asked, breathless with need for his touch.

He smiled down at her. "Truthfully, you frighten me," he began. "I've been with scads of women, in every port from one end of the globe to the other. I'm not trying to brag, or say that it wasn't adequately pleasant, because it was, but there was something deep down inside of me that longed to find the one woman that would satiate me completely. Perhaps that's what I was looking for in them all." He bent to kiss her forehead. "The one woman that consumed me so thoroughly that the mere thought of another female in my bed would be preposterous, and it scares me that I have found that in you." His hands slid up and down her back; the feel of his middle finger dragging along the length of her spine was turning her knees to butter. "And, because you, my love, are not a mug of cheap tavern ale but like a glass of fine French wine, I intend to savor every drop of you."

Maura's passion boiled over as she reached under his shirt, pushed her hands up, and exposed the sprinkling of hair that ran down the center of his belly and disappeared beneath the top of his trousers. She pressed a hot kiss to his sculpted chest as she continued to move the fabric out of her way. His flesh felt perfect under her lips.

"Will you take your shirt off again?" she asked, her tongue darting out to taste his sweet skin. "I quite liked that."

"I'll do anything you like," he breathed as he made short work of the garment, yanking it over his head and letting it fall from his fingers. "Anything at all."

"Then lie with me tonight. Let me feel your naked skin against mine." She reached around, her fingertips sliding over the swell of his mouthwatering bottom. "Let me experience the fullest extent of what love can truly be between a man and woman, at least once before I die."

Maura wanted what she'd seen in Aeron and Orrin, Darcy and Catrin. She believed she deserved to know how beautiful lovemaking could be, with the right person…they both did.

Kale squeezed his eyes closed as if he were contemplating the weight of what she'd just said. Without a word, he hauled her into his arms with one swift, fluid movement and carried her across the small room. He knelt on the floor before her as he sat her on the end of the bed. His gentle, skilled hands skimmed delicately over the surface of her skin as he worked her shirt over her head.

Wrapping his arms around her waist, he settled his warm cheek to her bare breast. She could feel his breath wash over her torso, and she'd never felt so alive, so his. He sweetly kissed the fullest part of her breast before he slowly laved the flat of his tongue over her nipple.

Maura could feel her pulse racing as his fingers moved down her soft belly and pulled on the ties of her trousers, opening them. He easily maneuvered the thick fabric over her hips and pushed the trousers past her feet. Easing back on his haunches, he stared at her. Intense and palpable, she could almost feel it as if it were a touch. She realized her feet dangled a good inch above the floor, and it struck her how large he was.

Dear God, he took up nearly half of the room, and she wondered if he might inadvertently hurt her, crush her with his masculine bulk. But the moment he reached out and slid one finger over the curve of her ankle and up along the inside of her knee, she shivered at his touch and knew he'd take care with her. The moonlight spilling into the cottage lit up their bodies, accentuating how magnificently they complimented each other, his golden, tanned skin against her milky paleness.

"My God, but you *were* created just for me, weren't you?" he said.

"Yes," she answered, leaning forward and urging him to his feet as she began to deftly unfasten his trousers. "Just as you were for me."

As Kale stepped out of his breeches and discarded them, Maura took in the full view of his masculinity. His exquisitely shaped calves paved the way to the smooth muscle covering the length of his powerful thighs and the sharp curve of his hip as it led to his sizable manhood.

In all her services at the castle, she had all but refused to look at the men that required her company. She'd found the whole business of male genitalia repulsive, but not on Kale. He was the most exquisite being she'd ever gazed upon, even in her most wondrous of dreams.

"You are a beautiful creature in every way," she said in wonder as she reached out and traced the line of his abdominal muscle to his navel.

"I am but a reflection of my love for you," he said as he worked his way between her thighs, which spread welcomingly of their own accord.

Her body gave way as he pushed into her, his arms shaking with an apparent effort to keep his movements slow and controlled. Maura could see how he was careful to keep the bulk of his weight on his arms and off of her tiny frame so as not to crush her beneath him.

She winced with the initial bite of pain. It had been years since she'd served in the castle and just as many since she'd been made to lie with a man. It had always been a painful experience. Her small frame had seemed to entice the larger men all the more, and they'd enjoyed forcing their way into her without a single thought as to her comfort.

But Kale moved slowly, allowing her body to accommodate his sizable organ. At the second pass, the searing pain gave way to innate felicity. And by the third, her hips were moving of their own volition, rising up hungrily to meet his as a quiet sigh of pleasure escaped her lips. She was small, but she seemed to fit against him as if her body derived from his.

A carnal smile spread across his face as she began to writhe in ecstasy beneath him. He bent his head to her and drew one of her pert pink nipples into his mouth as his hips flexed with hers. She cried out at the sensation, and her fingers curled in his hair, gripping and pulling with delight. They moved in a slow rhythm, relishing the feeling of each other in this most intimate of embraces. The coil in the pit of Maura's stomach wound into a spring, the tension strung much tighter than it had been the last night. The muscles in her body pulled taut, contracting in anticipation of the impending release.

Maura whimpered in the back of her throat as her breathing became more and more erratic, the sounds of euphoria pouring out of her in audible waves. Kale's eyes widened and his mouth gaped open as her first orgasmic clench gripped him, each thrust ratcheting her pleasure up another salacious notch. His body snapped taut, and he cried out her name as he filled her.

Kale trembled while he enveloped Maura in his embrace, as if he were soaking her into his bones, and he whispered, "I didn't think I would ever find you."

Chapter Twenty

The entire village sat together in the square, breaking their fast before the day's work began. Everyone knew they had little time to ready themselves for the battle that lay ahead, and theyate with great haste.

Morning reverie was broken when young Felix, Lenore's son, burst through the vegetation surrounding the square like Satan himself was chasing after the boy. He skidded to a stop next to Aeron's table, a bright red stripe starting to ooze blood down his cheek—a whip from a vine, no doubt.

"C-Captain," was all he managed to get out before falling to the ground, clutching his side and struggling to catch his breath.

"What the devil…Felix, whatever is wrong?" Aeron asked as she knelt next to her youngest crewmember and tried to calm him.

"Sails," he said, gulping in deep pulls of air as he reached shaky hands out for the cup of water Darcy brought to him.

"Where, lad? Who sent you?" Orrin asked, joining Aeron next to the boy.

"Brendon, on the north shore," Felix replied, in between greedy sips of water.

"Bollocks, how many?" Kale asked as he rose to his feet on the other side of the table.

"Looks to be four brigs, sir," the boy said, his little body finally beginning to breathe normally.

"Dear God." Aeron stood and looked to Orrin. She tried her best to quell the very brief flash of panic in her eyes; however, she doubted she was very successful, especially with her husband.

"We figured on two, planned for three, and they bring four," Orrin said to her. His hand came to rest on her back, firm and sure, lending his strength to her.

"Aye," Kale said, stepping up to Orrin's side, "we're right fucked. We should run while we can, flee the island until we are better prepared for—"

"No," Aeron said without hesitation, a plan coming into fruition inside her mind as she turned to Kale. "You are welcome to take your men and go if you like, but I will not run. If they want a fight, they will bloody well get one."

Aeron knelt once again next to the boy. "Felix, I want you to do something for me. I want you to take the children into the jungle and go into the cave off the south shore. Do you know where it is?"

"Yes," he said and nodded, starting to get up off of the ground, "but I can fight."

"I know you can," Aeron said, placing a reassuring hand on his shoulder. "I've seen you training with Darcy and Brendon, and I know how skilled you are with a sword. This is why I've chosen you for this most important of tasks. Catrin and your mother are going as well, and they will need your protection to guard our most precious cargo."

"We need your help," Catrin reassured him as she juggled the new babe, Owen, in her arms. "We cannot manage all of the children and fight off attackers on our own."

Aeron watched Felix look down at Darcy and Catrin's daughter, Rianna, clutching her father's leg for dear life, and then at his mother on the other side of the square, clutching his baby sister, Sarah, to her breast.

"All right." He nodded, straightening to his full, half-grown height. He turned to Rianna, who was not much younger than he, and presented her with a sweeping bow. "I will keep you safe, my lady," he said, offering the small girl his elbow.

With tearful goodbyes, Catrin, Felix, Lenore, and a few of the other women with new babes disappeared into the jungle.

God be with them, Aeron prayed silently as she watched the last moppet vanish.

When the children were safely away, Aeron felt Orrin's hand engulf hers, gripping it in his and giving it a reassuring squeeze.

"Lead us, my love," he said. "We will follow."

Aeron looked to Kale. He was captain of his own vessel, and she had already given him the option to bow out of this fight. She wouldn't have faulted him for him for doing so, but if he had chosen to stay, he had just as much say as to how this was to play out as she did.

"We will follow," he said surely, nodding in agreement with his brother. "I give you my word as a captain."

She wanted to be surprised at his decision to stay, but on some plane, she knew a man of her husband's blood was anything but a coward. Aeron took a deep breath, closed her eyes, and visualized the plan, letting it solidify in her mind before she spoke it out loud.

"We shall take to the water as originally planned," she began and looked to Kale. "Kale, what I need from you is to position your ship in the cove after we've gone out, block the entrance, and do not let anyone pass," she explained. "It is most vital that they not step foot on this island, do you understand?"

"Aye." He nodded, his back straight and his proud chin thrust forward. "I'll run the *Iona* right through them if I have to. But what of the *Mermaid,* where will she be?"

"We're going to greet our guests, naturally," she replied with a black, sinister veil clouding her eyes and a pure pirate smile curling her lips.

It was the beginning of the sixth day at sea, and William breathed a sigh of relief as an island was spotted off the port side. Her Majesty made her way on deck, demanding to know where she could catch sight of the elusive bit of land.

"There." Will pointed out over the water with a triumphant smile. He'd done it; he'd actually found it.

The faces of the three young women who had perished on this voyage flashed before his eyes, the look of pure terror burned forever into his memory. He would carry the guilt of their deaths until he met his own, and he was happy to do so as his penance for not having the fortitude to put a stop to his own mother. But no innocent girls would die this day.

"I don't see anything. You're lying," Winifred huffed as she glanced half-heartedly over the water before she turned and began to walk away.

"Wait!" William shouted, grabbing her by the arm, stopping her from leaving. "You—you didn't even look." His voice was strained, and there was a subtle bite of anger to it, a tone he'd never used in her presence before now.

She slowly, methodically turned her head, and her eyes narrowed and her nose wrinkled as she glared at his hand. Without a word, she gripped two of his fingers and bent them back with a sound jerk. The bones snapped and the digits contorted unnaturally as William fell to his knees in agony. Blinding pain shot through his hand and up his arm as the queen continued to add pressure, bending the broken extremities back farther still.

"I see no land, therefore, there is no land," she snarled down at him, her lip curling up in rage and her body looming menacingly over him.

Through the agony, Will heard the sound of something drop onto the floor behind his mother. It made a soft thudding sound, but he couldn't see what it was past the massive skirts of her royal gown. When she stepped out of the way, he saw an unconscious, half-naked girl, possibly the smallest he'd seen yet, lying on the damp deck.

"What's this?" the queen asked, shoving the poor girl's limp body with her foot. "Wake her up!"

"We tried, Your Majesty," her page said with a deep bow, the tremor of fear evident in his knees. "This is how we found her in your cabin, passed out cold."

"Useless," she spat. "Get rid of it."

"No!" Will cried, struggling to his feet as he cradled his crippled hand against his chest.

"What did you say?" Winifred asked as she strode over to where he stood, placing herself literally toe to toe with him.

"Leave her be," Will said, trying desperately to gird his spine against his mother. "She's just a child."

The queen clucked her tongue in what sounded like disappointment. "Such chivalry." She looked him up and down as if inspecting him for purchase, and his insides itched with fear at the sheer soullessness of her cold stare. "It really is a pity. You finally gather the balls to stand up to me, and it's too little, too late."

White-hot pain exploded in William's gut as he looked down to see the jeweled hilt of a gilded dagger sticking out of his side. He slumped breathlessly to the ground against the railing and heard his mother give the order to dispose of the girl, but he was helpless to stop her from being cast into the sea like garbage.

"What shall we do with him, Your Majesty?" the page asked.

Will thought he felt the toe of a boot nudge him as he faded in and out of consciousness. He glanced up to see his mother's poisonous glance.

"Leave him, he may be of some use yet."

William could hear his crew shouting the alarm of an approaching vessel while darkness crept up his spine. As his ship pitched on a wave, he caught sight of the familiar sails of a mighty galleon barreling toward them in the distance.

"Aeron," he whispered before everything went black.

Aeron tugged on her leather gloves and slid down the rope, landing on the deck of the *Mermaid* slightly out of breath and flushed from running through the jungle.

"I want every cannon at the ready and every rifle and pistol packed with powder," she called as she moved swiftly from one part of the ship to the other.

Aeron was a natural leader; it showed through the confidence she exuded out of every pore as she commanded her crew and the speed and precision with which they snapped to her order. She bound up the stairs and took her rightful place at the helm, gripping the wooden handles of the wheel. Her heart pumped adrenaline through her body as the *Mermaid* began to float through the cave opening and out into the presently quiet cove. She closed her eyes and took in a deep breath of salty sea air, soaking it into every cell in her body. The pirate in her lived for this moment, the rush of setting out and not knowing if she'd live to see the next day, or even the next hour or minute.

When the ship broke through the calm waters of the cove, the sails unfurled with a resounding whoosh, and the *Mermaid* surged forward into the open sea. Wood smacked against wood, and iron squealed as the cannon doors opened and the heavy weaponry was rolled into place.

"What are your orders?" Orrin asked, taking the place next to Aeron at the helm as they watched three of the vessels break away from the fourth and begin to sail straight for them.

"There," Aeron said, pointing to the last and largest ship. "William will be on that one. That is where we need to be."

She gripped the wheel with determination and turned it a notch. The *Mermaid* immediately picked up speed, sailing faster than ever before toward the royal vessel. Aeron steered her ship as if she could see the invisible flow of the wind, like God himself was handing it right to her.

"Captain, what shall we load into the cannons?" Darcy hollered from the main deck. "Round shot, bundles, or—"

"Chains and grapes," she replied before he could finish. "I want to make sure they are out of commission, not sunk, unless need be."

The men hurried to load the cannons with chain shot, two iron cannon balls joined together with a length of chain. This type of shot wouldn't do much damage to a hull, but, with proper aim, it could take out a mast in a matter of seconds. And grape shot—small iron balls in a cluster—stuffed into the cannon and fired would fan out and shred sails into useless scraps of canvas. Used in tandem, this ammunition would ideally incapacitate the royal ships without destroying them completely.

"We can't take all three," Orrin said as the vessels drew closer.

"I know," Aeron said with a grunt, tweaking the wheel and coaxing even more speed out of the sails. "However, we can disable two and pray that Kale handles the third before it reaches the island."

"Ready the boarding party," Darcy called out, reaching for the rope and grappling hooks.

"Belay that," Aeron countered.

"Captain?" he asked, his eyebrow shooting up in question to her order.

"We need to keep these two from aiding the lead ship, not engage them in a battle," she explained as the *Mermaid* raced mightily with the wind, barreling down on the three vessels like a black cloud.

"Which two are we taking?" Orrin asked as Aeron pointed her bow straight for the ship in the center.

"Gentleman's choice," she said with a wicked grin, holding the wheel steady as she went. "You choose."

"Starboard," Orrin announced without hesitation.

"Starboard it is then," she said with a nod, waiting until the last possible moment before she veered right. Her mighty ship sliced through the ocean between the two smaller vessels, and her voice rang out in command. "Fire on!"

Cannons expelled a deafening boom and iron flew. Fire flashed and smoke curled in the air as the metal spheres hurdled across the water to their destination. The sounds of crunching wood, ripping canvas, and blood-curdling howls echoed around them. Blow after powerful blow met its mark, crippling masts, destroying sails, and maiming sailors in their wake.

Kale easily sailed the *Iona* into position, crossways in the opening of the island cove. If anyone was going to get to land, they were going to have to get through him to do it.

"Drop anchors, bow and stern," he called out to the crew, "I don't want her to budge an inch from this spot, understood?"

When the *Iona* had been brought to, Kale looked out over the water to see Aeron flying across the waves toward the three approaching ships at an ungodly speed.

"Look at her," Maura had said in wonderment as she stood at his side. "Have you ever seen such a sight in all of your days at sea?"

"Truly, I have not. I aspire to be able to sail with such skill."

Kale and Maura pulled up lines, assisting the crew in furling the sails in tight and loading the cannons as a resounding series of booms echoed across the water.

Masts toppled and canvases exploded into shreds in the distance as Aeron maneuvered between two of the lamed crafts and bore down on the lead ship. A third vessel broke away unscathed and pointed its bow right for the cove and the *Iona*.

Kale's skin itched with the urge to haul anchors and run, to let the winds take him where they may and never look back again. He had his darling Maura, and in all honesty, that was all he needed.

He should run.

A smart man would run.

No, he was better than that. His brother needed his help, and the woman he loved needed to be avenged. With a deep breath, he hauled Maura into his arms and kissed her like it was the last time he would ever do so.

"I love you," he whispered into her hair.

The approaching vessel came about, turning right in front of them, its port side exposed, cannon doors open, and weapons rolled into place.

"Hold!" Kale called out to his men, his hand raised in the air and ready to signal the all-fire.

A pop and a zing sounded. Maura's hand flashed up to her left ear, and blood seeped out from between her fingers. Kale hadn't realized that he'd been shot as well until took a breath and his chest seized in pain. The world closed in around him and he fell forward to the floor at her feet.

"Fire!" she shouted, giving the order he could not, and he prayed that his crew would heed the command.

The sound of cannon fire from both vessels was deafening as they both shot everything they had at one another, and Kale prayed it would be enough. Amidst the smoke, flying bits of wood, and his fading consciousness, he heard the sound of boarding hooks grappling onto *Iona's* railing.

They were about to be boarded.

Maura bent, kneeling at his side as she assessed his wound. He saw that he was bleeding fiercely through the hole in his shoulder, but he was more worried about her. Kale tried to get up, but she shoved him back, and tearing the bottom of his shirt off, she tied the fabric around the wound.

Pain wracked his body. "Bloody fucking hell, woman, I'm shot, for Christ's sake," he swore at the pressure being applied. His breathing felt strangled, and he fought like hell to keep from passing out.

"I know that, you daft idiot," she said, as she used all of her strength to tie off the bandage. "I'm trying to keep you from bleeding to death because I can't bloody well marry you when you're dead, now can I?"

Kale watched Maura draw her sword and stake herself squarely in front of his body. Dear God, she meant to defend him, he realized, as thud after thud of footfall smacked against the deck. The wood under him rattled as the offending foe took to *Iona*.

Gritting his teeth and groaning in pain, Kale lumbered to his feet. He palmed his sword in his left hand and stood back to back with Maura, trying his damnedest not to knock her over with his weight.

"If we live through this, I'm going to hold you to that marriage proposal, you know?" he said over his shoulder.

"Right you should. No one else is fool enough to put up with your belligerent arse."

"Your words, my lovely," he said with a grin. "Now let's send some of these bastards to hell, shall we?"

The distinct sounds of carnage echoed on the other side of the dense layer of black powder smoke. The thick squish of metal slicing through flesh reached their ears, but neither Kale nor Maura could see well enough to wage attack on anything; without their sight, they could inadvertently harm a member of their own crew.

A man with a dagger suddenly burst through the haze at Maura, running at her with a scream. Kale watched her swing out her sword with all of her might, relieving the man of his hand and driving her blade between his ribs. Another attacker came at Kale, and he wielded his weapon, engaging his foe just as well with his left hand as he would have with his right.

A third emerged from the left, but his advance was cut short when the tip of a sword popped through the front of his chest. Kale recognized this weapon as a Queen's Navy blade.

The unknown savior pushed the dead sailor off his sword and saluted Kale and Maura with the bloodstained weapon.

"Jamie Gallagher, His Majesty Prince William's second-in-command. Are you the captain of this fine vessel?" he asked Kale.

"Yes," he answered warily, unsure of this man's intentions.

Jamie clicked his heels together and stood at full attention. "In the name of His Majesty, Prince William, I surrender to you and beg your assistance."

"Assistance in what, exactly?" Maura asked, arching an eyebrow at him.

The man turned and pointed to the two disabled royal vessels. "The craft on the right is loaded with explosives. It was to be sailed into the cove, destroying the island and all that inhabit it. It must be sunk. It is the only way to ensure everyone's safety."

Kale weighed his limited options. This could very well be a trap to get him to leave the cove unguarded. However, if it was true, the ship, while obviously dead in the water, was floating right for the island with a hold full of explosives. He looked the man over and went with his instincts.

"I tend to believe him," Kale said to Maura.

Maura nodded in agreement. "Yes, Will has lived with us for over a year. He's determined and stubborn, but he is not cruel enough to kill innocent women and children."

"Then it's settled. Weigh anchors and reload the cannons. We have a ship to sink, gentlemen," he called out with a wink, wincing in pain as he raised the back of Maura's hand to his lips. "And milady."

Chapter Twenty-One

eron crossed herself and said a quick prayer for the injured and the dead. As the *Mermaid* emerged from the cloud of black powder smoke, she set her sights for the ship bearing the royal colors.

The *Mermaid* began to circle the Royal Navy's lead vessel, and Aeron's gut twisted at what she saw. Something wasn't right. There wasn't a single cannon in sight, not one gun aimed at the ready. Hell, there wasn't a soul to be spotted on deck.

"What the bloody hell?" Aeron wondered aloud as her craft made a second pass, sailing closer to the royal ship.

"I don't like this. That ship should be crawling with Her Majesty's Navy," Orrin said with his hand gripping at the hilt of his sword.

"Captain," Darcy said, looking through a brass scope. "There is someone lying on the decks…Dear God, it's Will."

She snatched the scope from Darcy to peer through to the other ship and saw Will sitting slumped against the railing, blood soaking his shirt. "Get in closer and get me a line," she barked as one of her men took her place at the helm.

"Aeron, wait," Orrin said, trying to grab her arm. "Do not forget all the lies he told Kale and that *he* is here to hunt *you!*"

"You don't know him like I do," she snapped, jerking her arm free and taking the line Darcy offered her.

Orrin closed his hand over hers in an attempt to still her. "I still don't like the feel of this, if you would just take a moment to —"

"He doesn't have a moment, Orrin. He's injured!" she shouted, gripping the rope tightly as she swung over to the other ship. The moment

Aeron's boots had touched down on the royal vessel she ran across the deck, sliding onto her knees at William's side.

"Will!" she cried, cradling his face in her palms and feeling the pulse in his neck still beating. "William, can you hear me?"

"Aeron…" he said quietly, his eyes fluttering open. "Is that really you?"

"Yes, Your Highness," she answered, working her arm around his waist to help him up. "We need to get you on your feet. I'm going to take you back to the *Mermaid.*"

"No, go back to your ship." He struggled to pull away from her as he clenched his stomach.

"We must get you back to the island and get you to Catrin immediately. She can fix that hole in you in no time."

"Damn it, Aeron." He grunted, trying to get to his feet, pushing at her with bloody hands. "You have to—"

The sound of loud, slow clapping pulled Aeron's attention away from Will, and as she turned, her worst nightmare floated over the deck like an apparition.

"Well isn't this a touching reunion." The voice she'd hoped never to hear again purred as it slunk closer.

Aeron froze. The world as she knew it came to a screeching halt and twisted sickeningly on its axis, churning up nausea in her gut.

"Look how lovely you are, my pet, just as I remembered you."

"It's not possible. You can't be here," Aeron muttered, trying to scurry backward. Her hand had reached blindly for her sword, but her shaking fingers wouldn't function properly to close around the hilt.

Aeron had dreamed of this exact moment so many times over the years—one moment, one opportunity to come face-to-face with Queen Winifred. She'd played over in her mind, time and again, the ways she would use her blade to dispose of, piece by sickening piece, the woman who'd stolen her life.

But here now, in this moment, staring into the eyes of the devil herself, the old fear crept into Aeron's mind. She craved to take her sword in hand and cleave the woman in half, but she couldn't will her body to do so.

"You know," Winifred mused, walking ever so slowly toward Aeron, "after you ran away, I had your parents brought to the castle. They hadn't heard from you, of course. You were too smart for that." She knelt down to Aeron as if she was approaching a terrified child. "Your father was belligerent, as men will be, vapid creatures that they are," she said with a murdering glare at William. "But your mother, she was so very much like you, the same beautiful hair and nearly the same eyes, that I couldn't resist the enjoyment of her company in my chambers for a time."

Her icy hands moved over Aeron's cheek, soft and loving, and Aeron instinctively shrank back as far as she could against the ship's unforgiving railing.

"She was delicious in her own right," the queen said, "but she broke far too easily, couldn't withstand my methods of…enlightenment."

"Stop," William said, his voice sounding like an echo in the back of a cave inside Aeron's head, and she was vaguely aware that he was struggling to his knees next to her. "Haven't you hurt her enough already?"

The queen nodded briskly to her page, and with a swift boot to the jaw, the man knocked William back, unconscious, and Her Majesty continued to speak as if she'd never been interrupted.

"That was what I so adored about you, my love, don't you see? Try as I might, you were never fully broken. You always had a certain spark, a real fire that hasn't been matched since. Even when I freed you from the burden of that ridiculous child that you seemed to care so much for, you still fought me." Winifred reached out and caught a lock of Aeron's silky, auburn hair and curled it around her finger, taking a long, luxurious whiff of it. "Ahhh, just as I remember."

Aeron scrambled out of her grasp only to be shackled by two of Her Majesty's guards, massive fellows who Aeron found to be ridiculously loyal to such unrighteous rule. The queen rose to her feet, brushing off her gown as she reached behind her back, pulled the silver-tipped cat-o'-nine-tails out of her belt, and tapped it once against the flat of her palm.

"No!" Aeron screamed, her eyes growing wide with terror at the sight of the torturous tool. The scars across her back began to itch and ache. She shook her head violently, pulling at her arms and kicking her feet as she struggled against the iron grip of the guards.

Aeron barely registered the sound of a thunderous boom as it rattled the deck. Darcy landed squarely next to one of the guards holding her. With a swift thrust, he ran the man straight through the belly before the guard even knew what hit him.

Unfortunately, Queen Winifred's weasely page sounded an alert by blowing the wooden whistle around his neck. Twenty men or more filed up from below, swords at the ready as they bore down on Darcy.

A telltale crack echoed from across the water, and the page's head snapped back. Blood began to trickle from the perfectly round hole between his beady eyes as his scrawny body slumped to the ground.

"Kill them all!" the queen shouted, ordering her men to battle.

The wondrous thrum of Aeron's crew boarding the vessel gave her hope, until she glanced around and could find Orrin nowhere in sight. Had he been struck down already? She looked up at Darcy, lunging and parrying with three men at once, but he could only return her gaze with a shake of his head and a sorrowfully mouthed "I'm sorry."

Her vision began to tunnel, and the atmosphere around her went black. The one thing that might have brought her back from this hell was gone. Orrin was dead, and she had nothing in the world left to live for.

Aeron's body went slack, defeated, broken, and the guard on her right arm released her to attempt to remove Darcy's head. She sank dejectedly to her knees, her hands resting lifeless in her lap as a blank stare fell over her face. No spark. No fight. No soul. She didn't even feel the touch of the leather as Her Majesty drew the handle of the cat along Aeron's jaw, forcing her face up and positioning it just right before rearing the device back. The intended destination of the whip was more than clear in the queen's eyes, but Aeron couldn't find it in herself to care.

"Get me a line!" Orrin shouted as he whirled around and ran across the deck to swipe an offered bit of rope. A rogue wave rolled under the ship and pitched it back, moving away from the other craft.

"Orrin, wait," Darcy said, placing himself in front of Orrin to effectively block his way. "We're too far. We have to come about again."

Gripping the rope uneasily, Orrin watched as Aeron landed safely and began to approach the fallen William. His eyes scanned the decks of the vessel for any signs of suspicious behavior.

All seemed to be quiet from what he could see, until the *Mermaid* came around the starboard bow. Orrin's breath caught in his throat, and his heart seized in his chest when he saw the doors leading to the lower cabins open and Queen Winifred herself step out onto the deck.

He felt as if all the air had been sucked out of his body, suffocating with helplessness as he watched Aeron turn around and fall to her knees in paralyzing fear.

"No…" he began to chant, terrified.

Aeron crawled backward against the ship's railing, trying in vain to escape the waking horror.

"No…"

The *Mermaid* rounded closer, but still not quite close enough.

"No…"

Orrin saw the sun glint off something tucked into Her Majesty's belt. It was hidden behind her back—the silver tips of the God awful cat-o'-nine-tails.

"NO!" He swung out over the water as far as he could before anyone could stop him, released the line when it reached its end, and dropped into the sea, just short of the royal ship's deck.

Dripping wet and determined as hell, Orrin hurled himself over the railing and lunged, stretching his arm out in front of Aeron to protect her face from the cat's blow. The strips of leather wrapped completely around his forearm, the barbs biting into his flesh and the hooks piercing his skin, locking in place. Orrin knew he only had one shot at taking control of this situation. Gritting his teeth against the pain, he jerked against the torturous device with all his might, pulling the queen off balance enough that she stumbled and fell to the deck in front of Aeron.

He expected to see Aeron leap to her feet, draw her sword, and end the vicious excuse for a human being. But Aeron sat perfectly still, petrified and inert, clearly unable to move even an inch.

"Aeron!" he called, trying to snap her into the present and fight as he detached the cat from his torn flesh, but she appeared to be very well beyond the point of response.

Moving far quicker than Orrin had expected, Winifred leapt to her feet and hooked Aeron under her arm. Her long, bony fingers gripped Aeron's throat in a vice just as Orrin drew his sword and aimed it at her.

"I will snap her delicate little neck if you move one inch closer. I will share her with no one; do you understand?" Winifred snarled, her fingers pinching and squeezing against Aeron's throat.

Orrin froze, blade poised as he searched Aeron's eyes and looked for something, anything that hinted that she was still in there. He had to do whatever it took to reach the woman he knew: the fighter, the captain, the pirate.

"Please," Aeron mouthed as she began to squirm against Winifred's hold.

Processing his options at breakneck speed, Orrin held firm, the tip of his sword at the ready, blood from the torn flesh of his arm dripping down and off his elbow as he considered what move to make. Did he risk injuring or losing Aeron to rid the world of this demon of a woman and her rule? Or did he pull back and surrender to save Aeron's life, sacrificing her sanity in the process? No, the answer was clear.

"Orrin…please," Aeron begged, her voice small and shaking with fear.

He felt the world close in around him as he knew what he must do.

As Orrin took a deep breath and steeled his spine for the impending thrust, he saw Aeron's eyes flick down and to the left, trying to draw his attention to her body position. By God, in her struggling against Her Majesty's hold in what Orrin thought was desperation, Aeron had managed to contort herself to the right, thus leaving him the narrowest of paths in which to drive his blade and take out Winifred once and for all. Saying a silent prayer, Orrin exhaled and plunged his blade into the queen's chest, just under the pit of Aeron's arm.

Aeron cried out in pain as the tip of his sword sliced through and grazed her flesh when it passed into Winifred.

Orrin saw his wife's consciousness falter as Her Majesty's grip tightened around her throat. He pushed his weight against Aeron, trying to keep her upright as he saw her fighting the fog of oblivion that threatened to cloud her eyes.

"That was for my sister Iona," Orrin said as he eased the blade in deeper still. "And this is for my wife." He twisted the blade, hearing Winifred's bones crunch and feeling the side of his sword inevitably scrape against one of Aeron's ribs, likely cracking it as well.

The queen's mouth hung open in a silent scream as she gasped for breath, and her hand released its grip on Aeron. Her Majesty slowly sank to her knees, the hilt of Orrin's sword jutting out of her body.

Orrin heard grunting to his left and saw Prince William wincing in agony as he gripped the railing in an attempt to get to his feet, a hand pressing over the gaping wound in his gut. Orrin next saw Darcy slay the last of the queen's men and rush over to aid the injured young man.

"Your Highness, let me help you," Darcy said, carefully heaving William to his full height.

"To my mother, please," Will said, his face contorting with pain and the effort to stand.

The dying Winifred sputtered, blood oozing out from around the sword buried in her ribcage as Orrin rushed to aid Darcy in moving Prince William across the deck and holding him up in front of his mother.

"You are hereby charged with treason and the murder of King Richard the Sixth, my father. Your sentence, dear mother, is death, to be carried out forthwith." While William struggled to breathe, his voice had managed to grow stronger and more regal with every word.

Winifred began to cackle maniacally, blood spitting from her lips and staining her teeth, and her mouth twisted into a sadistic smile. "You don't have the balls to kill me," she snarled.

"I do," Aeron said as she stood, wrapping her hands around the hilt of Orrin's sword, gripping it with all of her might, and jerking it from Winifred's body.

The once glossy sheen of Winifred's obsidian eyes turned to a flat, dull black as she slunk forward, her life's blood flowing out of her and onto the deck. The deafening silence of the moment was shattered as Orrin's blade fell to the ground with a clatter and Aeron crumpled into his arms, sobbing.

"Shhh," he whispered to her, stroking her hair as he kissed her temple. "It's all right. She's gone. It's over."

"May the devil show you the mercy you could never give to others, Mother," Will uttered sadly as he collapsed against Darcy. For all her wicked behavior and cruel nature, he chose to remember the kind creature he'd glimpsed as a child and clung to that memory.

"Hold on," Darcy said. "Your ship is fast, Sire. We're going to get you to Catrin in no time, and she will fix you right up. You've done well, Your Majesty," Darcy said with a bow, smiling down at the new young king as he passed out cold.

Chapter Twenty-Two

s William was to learn later, Kale's craft had made short work of the royal bomb ship and sent the vessel into the murky deep of Davy Jones' locker. They had hooked a line to the disabled ship and towed it back to the island for scrap, while Jamie directed the remaining royal vessel into the cove.

The crews had made haste in spiriting His Majesty off of the ship and directly to Darcy's wife, Catrin. She treated him first and foremost, not because of his station as the new king, but because he had been among the most severely injured. Passed out cold from the pain and loss of blood, they'd carefully maneuvered him into the small bed inside the cottage.

Catrin had then utilized his unconscious state to set the bones in his hand. She had just begun to dress and care for his abdominal wound when he roused.

"You're very fortunate, Your Majesty," she said as she began to cleanse around the hole. "The queen managed to miss any of your vital organs. Otherwise you'd most likely be dead already, best I can tell."

"Thank you," he said weakly, hissing as Catrin brushed the cloth over the surface of his wound. "And please, call me Will, as before."

Catrin smiled softly down at him as she continued. "Branna was kind enough to offer her home for your recovery, seeing as mine is full of children at the moment. She is also my apprentice and can care for you after I'm done mending you."

"Where is she? I wish to thank her for the use of her home," he said, glancing around the small room the best that he could from his place in the bed.

"Tending to the others," Catrin said solemnly as she rubbed a cool healing lotion on him that he recognized the scent of egg yolk, rose oil, and turpentine. He'd fetched ingredients for the tincture on many an occasion for Catrin when he was new to the island.

"Others?" he asked, feeling an immense sense of guilt. If only he'd confronted his mother sooner and put a stop to this crusade for Aeron before it had ever begun, the outcome would have been far less dire.

"Yes." She nodded, tears welling up in her eyes as she covered his wound with a folded cloth.

William felt nausea roil in his belly, not from the searing pain of a cloth pressed against his body, but at the sight of the grim expression on Catrin's sweet face. He swallowed back the bile rising in his throat.

"Lost?" he asked, even though he was certain of the answer.

Catrin nodded curtly, a tear rolling down her cheek.

"How many?"

She shook her head. "I don't know how many royal sailors were lost, Sire."

He placed a gentle hand over hers to still her.

"No, I meant us, the people of the island." He held her hand to his chest, over his heart. "I may be the ruler of an entire country, but this island, these people, will always be my home and my family as long as I draw breath."

"Hold him still," Branna instructed Darcy as he leaned the majority of his weight atop a squirming and highly irate Kale. "Maura, hand me that other tool, the long one. We have to get the bullet out of his shoulder or it's going to fester."

Reaching over, Maura plucked a pair of long metal pincers off the table and handed them to Branna. With device in hand, Branna shoved it deep into the wound and probed incessantly.

"For the love of Christ!" Kale shouted, trying to wrench his arm from Darcy's iron grip. The man was solid muscle, and in Kale's weakened state he didn't stand a chance of escape. He had tried to dull the pain with three tankards of rum before Branna set to rooting around inside his shoulder; however, the effects had all but disappeared when she began to prod.

Branna ferreted around in the open wound, twisting the tool this way and that, thrusting and retreating as she sought out the bullet.

"Got it!" she declared, clamping the metal ball and extracting it from his body with the precision of a surgeon. "There, now you can mend properly."

"Let me see it," Kale grunted. He desperately needed to lay eyes on the infernal thing, but when he tried to sit up, he found he was still anchored to the table by Darcy.

Branna leaned over him and showed him the small, round lead bit—still clenched in the jaws of the bloody instrument—that had caused him so much trouble.

With the shaky fingers of his uninjured arm, he took the ball and wiped it clean on his shirt. "Maura…" he said, his voice straining.

"Yes, my darling, I'm right here," she said, immediately at his side. She stroked his hair and kissed his sweaty temple.

"Are you still fool enough to marry a belligerent arse, such as myself?"

"A thousand times over," she answered with a laugh.

"I only require the once." Kale took her hand in his. "I do not have a ring, or any riches to speak of, save for my ship, and since I can't put *that* on your finger, I hope this will do." He smiled, setting the tiny ball of lead into her palm.

The touching moment of love was shattered as Orrin burst through the door. He was in a near panicked state as if the devil himself was breathing down the back of his neck.

"Is Aeron in here? Has anyone seen her? We were helping all the wounded into the village, and she disappeared."

"West bank," Maura, Branna, and Darcy all said in unison, knowing full well where their captain would go if she was troubled in any way.

"Of course." Orrin nodded and was gone from their company as fast as he had come upon it.

"Oh, and I'm fine, by the way," Kale shouted after him before hissing as Branna poured stinging liquid over his open wound. "Thank you for asking, *brother!* God's blessed arse, what the hell is in that potion? It burns like fire!"

"You are worse than an infant. It was only water," Branna chastised, rolling her eyes as she put down the pitcher and picked up a pot of salve and a bottle of rum. "However, *this* will hurt," she warned before she splashed the wound with spirits and applied the emollient. Kale wailed and clutched at Darcy's arm for dear life until he passed out from the pain.

Orrin stepped onto the white sands of the west beach and watched Aeron's hair blow in the salty sea air, licking at her face like flames; her knees were tucked up under her chin.

"I spoke with the king," she said without turning. "He intends to pardon us all, and anyone who wishes to may return and stay in the castle for as long as they desire." She looked down at her open palms. "He also bade our assistance when he is well enough to travel back to the mainland. He will need help restoring his kingdom to what it was before his mother stepped foot in it."

Orrin took a seat on the sand next to his wife and placed a hand on her knee. He could practically see the tension and despair rolling off of her in waves, and he wished he knew how to fix that.

Aeron took a slow, deep breath and looked out over the ocean.

"I know she is dead. I watched her life's blood drain out onto my boots," she said as she dug the toe of her boot into the sand, the white grains sticking to the dried blood. "But that woman, she haunts me still. That place, the castle, she's inside the walls, etched into the stone." Aeron visibly trembled as she shook her head. "I want to help William, I honestly do. But I can't go back there, not yet."

Orrin slung his arm around her shoulders and pulled her body close to his.

"I know this is madness," she continued, "but there is a small part of me that half expects her to come walking up out of the ocean, like an immortal demon." Aeron twisted in his embrace and buried her head in his chest. "I couldn't move, Orrin," she cried, clutching his shirt. "I saw her there in front of me, and I was that frightened girl chained to a table all over again." She tilted her face to his. "And when I thought you were dead, I had naught to live for anymore. But then you were there, like an avenging angel sent from the heavens to save me. I saw you and your strength, heard your voice, and it brought me back, you…"

He saw her suddenly spy his arm, the shredded fabric of his shirt and the deep gashes left by Winifred's wicked cat. Aeron cradled his injured forearm in her lap and inspected the vicious wounds.

"These need to be tended to," she said, quiet concern etching her features.

"I'll be fine," Orrin said dismissively, hissing as she poked at the torn flesh and attempted to gauge the depth of the wounds. "I'm not as bad off as some of the others. How are *you?*" He lightly touched the spot along her ribs with his free hand and felt the ridges of a bandage under her clean shirt.

"That's not of consequence. Catrin stitched everything up in no time. I've had far worse," she said, standing up and dusting the sand off her backside. "But we need to get your arm cleansed immediately. The smallest of scratches can cause great illness if not treated properly, especially in the jungle. Now get off of your arse and let us get you taken care of so that you can help me with the others, all right?"

"Yes, Wife," Orrin answered with a smile as he ambled to his feet, caught her around the waist, and kissed her soundly before they made their way back to the village.

Back in the square where the wounded men lay about on the tables and benches, Aeron tended to Orrin's arm, cleansing the gashes thoroughly and applying a healthy amount of Catrin's healing ointment before bandaging him up.

The two of them worked side by side for the remainder of the day and well into the night, stitching up slashes and treating every last injured soul. After all was done, Orrin watched proudly as Aeron stood on her table, commanding the attention of everyone present.

"I want to commend you all," she began. "This was not an easy battle to fight. We were out-gunned, out-manned, and we lost some dear friends in the process." Her voice started to break, and she paused for a moment before continuing. "Their sacrifices will never be forgotten by anyone here. As you all well know, we honor our dead greatly. However, in their loss, we have gained a new king and a newfound freedom for us and our children."

"Hear, hear!" Darcy called, juggling baby Owen and Rianna in his big arms.

"Our new king has been kind enough to promise a pardon to us all for the act of piracy and wishes to extend his home to anyone who desires to return to their families on the mainland. His word is true and just, and I trust that he will rule with a gentle and fair hand as his father before him. He is a good and honorable man, and it is my honor and privilege to call myself his subject."

"Long live King William," one lone, familiar voice echoed in the crowd. Orrin looked up to see Kale, pale as a ghost. He was either half-drunk or hal-dead, maybe a little of both, but he grinned wide and proud as the entire village responded in kind.

Aeron raised her cup high in the air in offering to the fallen. "To our brothers who gave their lives, and to our new king. May his rule be long and just."

Orrin looked at his wife as he saw the living members of the Royal Navy bow their heads in respect to her. He knew that time would heal the wounds of their men as well as the scars Aeron carried on her heart, buried deep where no one could see. It would take a lot of work on his part, but he would help her tend to those invisible bruises, support her in her efforts to lock them away with her retched past in the only place it belonged, behind her.

Chapter Twenty-Three

As the weeks passed, Aeron's mind settled more each day with the reassurance that Winifred was really gone and she was finally free.

The people of the island had returned to a sense of normalcy as the wounded mended, and they'd stripped apart the salvaged ship, using its parts to repair old cottages and build new ones.

His Majesty, King William, had healed well under Branna's watchful eye. It warmed Aeron's heart to see affection blossom between the two of them, and she was not surprised in the least to see Branna among those choosing to return to the mainland. She'd noticed the way William had begun to look at the bright young healer with obvious favor. Branna was a strong woman who would keep him on his toes and serve as a reminder of his promises to stay true to his soul.

Kale and Maura were married, under the blessing of King William, the day before they were to sail back to the mainland. The *Iona* would accompany the *Mermaid* in escorting the King and his vessel home and would assist in restoring the land to the respectable kingdom they all knew it could, and would, be.

Aeron ran her finger over the railing of the *Mermaid* as she walked along the deck, whispering to herself.

"Talking to your ship again?" Orrin asked as he sidled up behind her, wrapping his arms around her waist and nuzzling the back of her neck. "I do adore that about you, the way you talk to her." He pushed her braid over her shoulder and skimmed his nose over her flesh. "You have yet to pack for our trip to the mainland, my wife. Perhaps you intend to be naked the entire journey." He hummed appreciatively as he kissed the spot behind her ear. "Not that I would complain, mind you, but the crew might worry if their captain never leaves her quarters," he murmured as he slid his hand up over her breast.

Aeron smiled to herself as she intertwined her fingers with his and his hand began to roam her body freely. She did love the way he touched her like this; she was going to miss it greatly.

"I was telling her to take care of you, to keep you out of any storms and to return you to me posthaste."

"What on earth are you blathering about?" he asked, as he continued to kiss her.

"I'm not going with you, Orrin," she said, leaning her head to the side as his mouth moved over the column of her neck. "You are going to captain this voyage in my stead."

Orrin pulled back from her slightly, settling his hands on her hips and his chin on her shoulder as he spoke. "My darling, you have got to make your peace with that castle if you are going to ever be rid of that woman's hold on you. I will be there with you the entire time to help you. You know that."

"I understand, silly man, but that is not why I'm staying here."

"Why then?"

"Catrin suggested that in my current condition I should stay put on dry land and not be tossed about on a ship, for the sake of our child."

Orrin froze behind her, and Aeron could feel his throat working, most assuredly trying to process the words. "Our child?" he asked, his voice breaking.

Aeron took his trembling hand and settled it low on her belly.

"Yes, our child," she said, smiling proudly as she kissed the underside of his scruffy jaw.

"Then I'm staying as well. Darcy can take lead, and—"

"Don't be ridiculous," Aeron laughed, "Will is going to need *your* help getting settled. Darcy is a good man, yes, but he's more likely to frighten His Majesty's subjects into submission than anything else, which is what we are trying to overcome, yes? Besides, I'm far from alone. Catrin will be here to help me along, and she's had far more experience in this type of thing than you."

"But it could take months to get everything in place," he argued.

"And by the time you return, I will be so enormous and round you will most likely mistake me for a whale." Orrin opened his mouth, obviously intent on arguing the point further, but Aeron placed a single finger over his lips. "I want this baby born here, on our island," she said firmly. "If we are going to be away from each other for months, are you truly going to spend our last few moments arguing with me, you hard-headed bastard?"

With a conceding smile, Orrin kissed her finger and knelt before her, carefully maneuvering her shirt up over her belly.

"What on earth are you doing?" Aeron giggled as his lips moved along her flesh.

"Asking our girl to look after you until I return," he murmured against her skin.

Aeron's heart swelled as tears of joy pricked the back of her eyes. Sniffing back the emotion, she smiled down at her husband.

"Fancy yourself a girl, do you?" she teased.

"Mmm," he hummed as he nodded, "I can see her already." He turned his face and pressed his cheek to her stomach, his hands stroking up and down her back. "Auburn curls and a smile just like her mother's."

"With her father's mischievous blue eyes and undeniable charm," she mused as she ran her fingers through his golden brown hair. "But what if *she* is *he?*"

"It doesn't matter either way," he said, rubbing his hand over her stomach. "Our child will be perfect, because he *or* she is part of you."

Orrin was grateful that the voyage to the mainland was more than uneventful. He sailed the *Mermaid* with a skill only matched by her true captain. Darcy grudgingly took up as his second-in-command, but by the second day at sea he couldn't find a bad word to speak about Orrin's abilities to captain a ship. Darcy offered a new sense of respect, something the large man did not give out easily, and Orrin was honored to finally have it.

As they made land, Orrin and Kale moored their ships in port and accompanied His Majesty to the castle. Once inside, the king wasted no time ordering every trace of his mother removed and systematically burned in the courtyard. The entire palace was stripped and scrubbed free of the woman who had tortured for sport, every hidden room and secret corner gutted or sealed off for the rest of eternity.

His Majesty appointed Orrin to his court and offered Kale and his ship a place in the Royal Navy, granting them both land and homes of their own if they chose to make a place in his kingdom proper. And in their gratitude, the Walsh brothers took to the outer-lying villages, delivering the news to the people of Winifred's demise and the announcement of a new, promising king.

All went well in their travels on the mainland, and at the end of seven months in the king's stead, Orrin and Kale headed home, both aboard the *Mermaid* while the *Iona* stayed behind to be painted with her new royal colors.

The night sea air blew across Orrin's face as he leaned against the railing, listening to the water rush past the hull of the mighty galleon. He closed his eyes as he ran his hand along the smooth pine; he could practically feel Aeron's presence in the wood.

"Take me home, girl," he whispered, and the sails fluttered to life as if the *Mermaid* had heard his request and was just as eager to return to her rightful port.

"Brother, you must sleep," Kale said, coming up on deck. This was the very statement Kale had said to him almost a year ago when they had sat on the *Iona*, ready to take Aeron and her island.

Orrin smiled to himself, knowing his answer would be quite different this time. "I'll sleep when I'm finally home with my wife in my arms."

A sense of calm and completeness fell over Orrin as the sun broke over the horizon, and he made out the tops of the island palm trees swaying, waving him in.

As the crew guided the *Mermaid* into the cave and settled her inside her hidden cove, Orrin couldn't wait any longer. He leapt onto the dock, taking off in a run and slipping into the jungle. He couldn't explain how he knew where Aeron would be at this moment; he just did. Something in his bones, inside his soul, tugged him in the right direction. He pushed his way through the now familiar terrain, moving large green fronds and vines aside as he glided silently over the ground.

He could hear Aeron's voice humming a tune in amongst the sounds of a gentle waterfall as he neared the very bush he'd crouched behind when he'd first come upon the island and spied a very naked, very beautiful Aeron enjoying her bath. Parting the shrubbery surrounding the lagoon, he laid eyes on his glorious wife, floating atop the water in the same manner she had been when he'd happened on her twelve months ago. Bands of sunlight peeked through the vegetation and lit up her flesh, stretching across her swollen belly.

Orrin was certain there was never a more glorious creature in all the world.

"Honestly, I hope our child inherits *my* ability to move through the jungle undetected, because you, Husband, are hopeless. You sound like a herd of wild rhinoceros tromping through the trees."

Grinning wide, Orrin leapt out of the brush and into the water, clothes, boots, and all, and trudged through the water toward his radiant wife.

"Orrin…your clothes…" she said, trying to stop him, but she gave up in a fit of laughter as he continued along without a care.

Aeron squealed when he hoisted her up into his strong arms. He sighed happily, pressing his forehead to hers as he ran a thumb over her bottom lip and a hand over the swell of her belly.

"God, how I have missed you," he said, bending to kiss her and humming with contentment at the feeling of her mouth under his and the sweet taste of her tongue moving over his. Her fingers curled into his hair and held him tightly.

"You are impossible; do you know that?" Aeron asked as they parted.

"Indeed, would you really have me any other way?" he asked her, delighting in the feeling of his child moving inside of his wife's belly.

"I would not," she sighed, lying back in his arms as tiny blossoms rained down from the trees above and the sun bathed them in its warm light.

Epilogue

Aeron ascended from her quarters on the *Mermaid* to the upper deck. The crisp sea air filled her nostrils as her eyes held transfixed on the site before her.

A chubby little hand clenched against the back of Orrin's shirt as the other pointed out over the water amidst the sound of excited squeals and ramblings of gibberish that only Orrin seemed to understand. A single auburn curl escaped the confines of a white bonnet and danced against an alabaster forehead in the breeze as crystal blue eyes lit up with joy.

"Yes, my sweet," he said, nodding to the gulls hovering over the water. "Those are birds. Bir-d." He enunciated the last word, making it easier for her to understand.

"Burburbur!" the girl chattered, her tiny brow creased in concentration as her cupid's-bow lips pursed with the effort to make the sound precisely as he had.

"Very good, Iona," he said, cuddling their daughter closer to his chest and kissing the top of her head. "Do you know what that means? It means we are almost to our destination." Orrin tucked his head into Iona's fleshy neck and blew against her skin, making a rude sound that most assuredly tickled and made her giggle incessantly.

Aeron closed her eyes and reveled in the most glorious sound in the world, the sound of her daughter's laughter at the hands of her husband.

The *Mermaid* sailed into King William's port with ease, and Aeron and her family were promptly greeted by His Majesty's own royal carriage to escort them to the castle.

As the countryside passed by Aeron's window, she tried to focus on Iona, who clapped and squealed with glee at her first carriage ride.

However, it was growing increasingly hard for Aeron to remain calm as the coach bounced down the road toward the palace. She was beginning to wonder if this trip was a good idea for her.

Aeron clenched her eyes shut and twisted her hands in her lap, trying her best to keep a handle on her quaking body as she heard the iron and oak portcullis rattle up. The last time she'd heard that sound was when she had run away from this place, huddled under a carriage as it left. The slow grind of the pulley wheel and clank of the heavy metal chain as the counterweight raised the gate echoed in her memory, and she braced herself for the dark, sinister courtyard looming in her memory. Steeling her will and drawing strength from her husband and her child, Aeron opened her eyes and glanced out of the coach window.

In the years that had passed, the dismal foreboding that had hung in the air around the castle had given way to a bright, open, and welcoming aura. The gnarled, blood red rose bushes that once ran rampant in a thorny, tangled mass had been replaced with rows and circles of brightly colored flowers of purple, yellow, and pink. The thick covering of ivy that had once clung to the stone like a shroud had been scraped away to reveal the beauty of the limestone underneath.

When the ornate wooden door flew open, King William emerged to greet them. He looked older than Aeron had remembered, more mature and regal, just like his father. Emotions she hadn't realized she still possessed for King Richard bubbled up as tears welled in her eyes.

"Are you all right?" Orrin asked as he ran over to pluck Iona out of a flowerbed, her pudgy fist full of brightly colored blooms.

"Yes, I'm absolutely perfect," Aeron answered honestly, swiping the tears away before they could fall as she leaned over and kissed their daughter on the nose. "What have you there, little one?"

"Ma-ma," Iona said in her choppy child-speak, and she thrust the mangled flowers at her mother.

"Thank you, my love." Aeron gently extracted the crushed petals from Iona's grip and tucked them carefully into her pocket.

As they entered the foyer of the castle, the sound of chatter, children, and laughter filled the air, whereas before there had been barely a hushed word out of fear of raising Her Majesty's ire. Dozens upon dozens of candles had been added to the decor to bathe everything in a warm light; no more dark and ominous shadows hovered along every wall and surface.

The hell from Aeron's memories had been transformed into a welcoming home.

His Majesty prattled on about the changes made in the palace as Aeron carried Iona in her arms while they made their way up the enormous staircase to the room they would be staying in for their visit. Counting the floors in her mind as they ascended, Aeron paused and gazed up the stairwell when Orrin and William broke off onto the third floor and continued down the hall there.

Aeron clutched Iona to her side as she made her way up the next two flights, stopping at the top and peering down the treacherous hall. The table she'd hidden under in an effort to escape Winifred's tirade had been removed; however, in her mind, Aeron could still see it there against the wall, mocking her. Gathering all of her courage, she took a deep breath and slowly walked down the hallway, one unsure foot in front of the other, to the door that had once been Her Majesty's chambers.

"Give me strength, little one," she bade Iona as she clutched her daughter to her breast, turned the handle, and pushed the door open.

The dark wooden bed that had been covered in thick, heavy fabric had been replaced with one made of birch and draped with colorful linen. Recently lain brick covered the entrance to a hidden room against the back wall of the chambers. Everything she'd remembered, every ounce of despair that had hung in the very air of that room, was gone save for the heartache that was etched in her soul.

"Burburburbur," Iona babbled, kicking her feet excitedly as she pointed to the window.

Aeron turned and saw a white dove perched in the window that Winifred had utilized to discard Aeron's first child, moments after she was born. Iona twisted in her arms, trying desperately to get at the contents of Aeron's pocket, the flowers. Aeron reached in and pulled out the small handful of blooms, noticing that all but two were crushed beyond oblivion before she placed them into Iona's waiting palm.

Walking to the window on shaky legs, almost as if she were in a trance, the knot in Aeron's stomach twisted tighter with every step she took. As they reached the opening, the dove cooed at them once, tilted its white head at them, as if acknowledging them, and flapped away into the clear blue sky. Iona gasped in wonderment as she shoved her little hand out of the window and opened her fist. The cool sea breeze swept the petals from her hand and out across the horizon.

"Bye-bye," Iona said, and Aeron could have sworn she'd detected a hint of sadness in her daughter's voice.

Tears burned the back of her eyes, and sorrow clenched at her chest as Aeron gazed on Iona's perfect features. What would her elder daughter have looked like today? Part of her wanted to leap out of the window herself, to finally join the child she'd never been allowed to know. The impulse only lasted a moment; the rational part of her mind warned her of what that would do to Orrin and little Iona. No, she couldn't leave them with the heartache that had gnawed at her all these years from having lost Richard and the baby. Angelica, her little angel. She would always love them both, but it was time to let them go.

"Yes, goodbye." Aeron nodded as she watched the two flowers float along on the breeze.

Iona curled her arms around Aeron's neck, squeezing tight, and a true calm settled over Aeron for the first time. The weight she had borne—of never having said goodbye to her firstborn and her inability to have prevented the happenings in this room—finally lifted.

"Are you all right, my love?" Orrin asked from the doorway, startling Aeron.

"God in heaven, Orrin, you have positively scared me out of my skin," she said, swiping the tears off her face.

"Did I, now?" he asked, grinning triumphantly as he sauntered through the door to his wife and daughter. "The thundering hooves of a thousand angry rhinoceros didn't give away my whereabouts?"

Aeron rolled her eyes and shook her head as Orrin wrapped his arms around them both.

"Oh, shut up and kiss me," she said, leaning into his embrace.

"Gladly." He plucked their daughter from her hands and balanced her in one arm as he swept Aeron back slightly in the other. "My saucy little pirate," he said with a smile as he pressed his lips to hers.

In that moment, a new light sparked in Aeron's soul, one that burned with the promise of a new future with her family so bright it would outshine a thousand suns.

ACKNOWLEDGMENTS

I would like to thank Omnific Publishing for giving me the opportunity to share my words. To my amazing editors, Colleen Keough Wagner and Katherine Teel, thank you for making my words the best they could be. To Traci Olsen, you are a fabulous marketing agent and great friend, thank you for all you do. To Micha Stone for creating a beautiful cover. To Victoria Michaels, my own personal Yoda, thank you for taking me under your wing, my friend; I adore you. To Kimmy, Mindy, Lecia, and Caryn, thank you so much for being the best friends… no, sisters. I love you all so much. And last, but definitely not least, my readers, I do this for you as much as I do it for me—you all rock hard!

ABOUT THE AUTHOR

Patricia Leever is a wife, stay-at-home mom of four, and owner of one dog and one really old cat. On the average school day she runs about town like a lunatic picking up and dropping off kids and trying to find a moment of quiet to write down a word or two. She's a sci-fi geek that loves to dress up like a zombie and participate in the local zombie march down Main St. and laugh as much as possible; laughter frees the mind and heals the soul.

Live. Breathe. Write.

PatriciaLeever.wordpress.com

<h1 style="text-align:center">check out these titles from
OMNIFIC PUBLISHING</h1>

Contemporary Romance

Boycotts & Barflies by Victoria Michaels
Passion Fish by Alison Oburia and Jessica McQuinn
Three Daves by Nicki Elson
Stitches and Scars by Elizabeth A. Vincent
Trust in Advertising by Victoria Michaels
Take the Cake by Sandra Wright
Indivisible by Jessica McQuinn
Pieces of Us by Hannah Downing
Gabriel's Inferno by Sylvain Reynard
The Way That You Play It by BJ Thornton
The Redhead Series: The Unidentified Redhead and *The Redhead Revealed*
by Alice Clayton

Romantic Suspense

Whirlwind by Robin DeJarnett
The CONduct Series: With Good Behavior and *Bad Behavior* by Jennifer Lane

Paranormal Romance

The Light Series: Seers of Light and *Whisper of Light* by Jennifer DeLucy
The Hanaford Park Series: Eve of Samhain and *Pleasures Untold* by Lisa Sanchez
Immortal Awakening by KC Randall
Crushed Seraphim by Debra Anastasia

↞——↠Young Adult↞——↠

Shades of Atlantis and *Ember* by Carol Oates
Breaking Point by Jess Bowen
Life, Liberty, and Pursuit by Susan Kaye Quinn

↞——↠Anthologies↞——↠

A Valentine Anthology including short stories by Alice Clayton, Jennifer DeLucy, Nicki Elson, Jessica McQuinn, Victoria Michaels, and Alison Oburia

Summer Lovin' Anthology: Summer Breeze including short stories by Hannah Downing, Nicki Elson, Sarah M. Glover, Jennifer Lane, Killian McRae, Carol Oates, and Susan Kaye Quinn

Summer Lovin' Anthology: Heat Wave including short stories by Kasi Alexander, Debra Anastasia, Robin DeJarnett, Jessica McQuinn, Lisa Sanchez, and BJ Thornton

↞——↠Alternative Romance↞——↠

Becoming sage by Kasi Alexander

coming soon from
OMNIFIC PUBLISHING

The Guardian's Wildchild by Feather Stone
Grave Refrain by Sarah M. Glover
Small Town Girl by Linda Cunningham
Poughkeepsie by Debra Anastasia
The Crystal Pendulum by Trisha Wolfe
Embrace by Cherie Colyer

And more from Sylvain Reynard, Jennifer DeLucy, Alice Clayton, and
Hannah Fielding